CAPE CORSE

Paul Weston

www.paulwestonauthor.com

Copyright © 2023 Paul Weston

www.paulwestonauthor.com

The rights of the author to be identified as the Author of this Work have been asserted in accordance with the Copyright, Designs and Patent Act 1988.

This novel is entirely a work of fiction. The names, characters and incidents portrayed in this book are the work of the Author's imagination.

No part of this book may be reproduced, or stored in a retrieval system, or transmitted in any form or by any means, electronic, mechanical, photocopying, recording, or otherwise, without express written permission of the Author.

Cover picture is a detail from:
'Night Clear and Pleasant'
by
Mark Myers

Note - Glossary at end for readers unacquainted with antiquated nautical words and phrases

For Julie Musk

CONTENTS

Title Page
Copyright
Dedication
Prologue — 1
Chapter 1 – Bermuda — 6
Chapter 2 – Blonde — 8
Chapter 3 – Escape — 12
Chapter 4 – Pump or Drown — 16
Chapter 5 – Trevennec — 20
Chapter 6 – Julia — 26
Chapter 7 – Devonport — 32
Chapter 8 – The Lawyer — 40
Chapter 9 – Mortgage — 45
Chapter 10 – Fortuneswell — 52
Chapter 11 – The Downs — 56
Chapter 12 – The Island — 59
Chapter 13 – Deptford — 62
Chapter 14 – A Secret — 66
Chapter 15 – The Patent Log — 70
Chapter 16 – The Scheme — 74
Chapter 17 – Trials — 78

Chapter 18 – Coasting	82
Chapter 19 – Sea Reach	84
Chapter 20 – Paoli	86
Chapter 21 – Planning	92
Chapter 22 – Their Lordships' Pleasure	97
Chapter 23 – Passengers	103
Chapter 24 – The Rifle	108
Chapter 25 – Corsairs	110
Chapter 26 – Leghorn	119
Chapter 27 – Macinaghju	124
Chapter 28 – Landing	127
Chapter 29 – Betrayal	130
Chapter 30 – The Traitor	133
Chapter 31 – Giotto Luciani	137
Chapter 32 – Cape Corse	141
Chapter 33 – Recruiting	145
Chapter 34 – Calvi	150
Chapter 35 – Malta	153
Chapter 36 – Fever	158
Chapter 37 – Merchant Ships	161
Chapter 38 – Ambush	167
Chapter 39 – North	172
Chapter 40 – Rendezvous	175
Chapter 41 – The Hill	182
Chapter 42 – The Warning	187
Chapter 43 – The Sound of Guns	190
Chapter 44 – Oleander's Return	193
Chapter 45 – Coast Road	195

Chapter 46 – Surrender	202
Chapter 47 – Kennedy	207
Chapter 48 – Fortification	210
Chapter 49 – Rondine	213
Chapter 50 – A Nice Bit of Work	216
Chapter 51 – Siege	222
Chapter 52 – Aground!	227
Chapter 53 – Barricades	229
Chapter 54 – Departure	232
Chapter 55 – Torra di Santa Maria	236
Chapter 56 – Rescue	241
Chapter 57 – The Poet	245
Chapter 58 – Hyères	252
Chapter 59 – Rade de Toulon	257
Chapter 60 – The Château d'If	262
Chapter 61 – Gibraltar	269
Epilogue	271
Historical and Geographical Notes	273
Glossary	275
About The Author	285
Books In This Series	287

PROLOGUE

Waterwitch at St Peter's, September 10th 1803

Dear Mr Stone

Recently, we were engaged in a military operation in Brittany, a good distance from the sea. In an action to destroy some of the enemy's materiel, your son was wounded. I was not a witness to that part of the event, but I am reliably informed by one who was that you son's injuries were not very serious. However, being sorely pressed by the French, we were obliged to retreat, and it is very likely Jack has become their prisoner.

I have no doubt he will be treated well by the French in accordance with the usages of war, and I am hopeful that he will in due course be exchanged for a French officer.

It is with great fondness that I recall my stay with you and your wife in Portland, and I hope before long Jack will be able to return to his home.

Your obedient servant.

Percy Snowden

Waterwitch at St Peter's, December 1ˢᵗ, 1803

Dear Mr Stone

Today I heard from Captain Wain of the Marines, who was captured at the same time as Jack in the action in Brittany. Wain has been exchanged and is presently in England.

    Wain has told me that Jack was indeed captured by the French. His wound was grievous, but it was treated with great skill by a French surgeon, and Jack was making excellent progress towards recovery. However, I have to tell you that after some time in the French hospital, Jack was taken by the French authorities and, Wain believes, has been conveyed to Paris.

    Wain does not know the reason for this, but from his conversations with the French, he believes Jack is accused of theft, because, during his previous actions in France, he took a fishing boat to escape back to England with intelligence of the French scheme to capture His Majesty. At the time of this act, Jack was a civilian, and I understand there are some in the French government who wish to punish Jack for his brave acts.

    Please be of good heart. I am sure the French nation will refuse to countenance any ill usage of an honourable enemy and that soon we will hear of Jack's release.

    Your obedient servant.

    Percy Snowden

Waterwitch at St Peter's, December 15th 1803

Dear Mr Stone

Today I have received orders for Bermuda, but before I depart I would like to inform you of what little news I have concerning Jack.

I have had an interview with Admiral Sausmarez, of the Channel Islands Station, and discussed Jack's predicament with him. Sausmarez has a high opinion of Jack. He was already aware of the situation, and has informed the Admiralty of it. He has also written to Lord Whitworth, lately our ambassador in Paris, to ask whether the good offices of some neutral country might be employed to determine Jack's situation.

I must depart imminently, but *Waterwitch*'s commander, Captain Wilkinson, has agreed he will inform you directly he receives any intelligence of Jack's situation.

My regards to Mrs Stone.

I remain your obedient servant.

Percy Snowden

Waterwitch at St Peter's, January 15th 1804

Dear Mr Stone

Before his departure to Bermuda, Lieutenant Snowden charged me with advising you of any intelligence concerning Midshipman Stone. I have today been informed that the Admiralty is in receipt of a letter from Midshipman Stone, apparently dispatched from France, to the effect that he has resigned from the Navy.

I do not fully understand the import of this news, but I would like to inform you of the great regard I and my colleagues have for the brave actions of Midshipman Stone, and I am sure he has done nothing to dishonour the service.

Your obedient servant.

Harold Wilkinson, Captain RN

Brandywine, May 15th 1804

Dear Father and Mother

This letter is brief as a man is waiting by the door to take it to the packet which is awaiting the tide. I am well and I hope you are also. I have recently arrived in the United States of America, safe and well. I am married to Dominique, a Frenchwoman, who I am sure you will love, as I do, when you meet. We stay with her mother's relatives, who are industrious and prosperous. I will explain all that has happened to me in my next letter, but I received a wound in France from which I have fully recovered. I was a prisoner of the French for some time. I have resigned from the Navy, as I have found that I abhor conflict, and hope to make my way in the United States in some peaceful and useful profession. I would like you to convey this news to Percy Snowden, who may still be at Guernsey.

    I will write more soon.

    Your loving son, Jack

CHAPTER 1 – BERMUDA

In the cedar-scented drawing room, Snowden stood, knocking over his chair in the violence of his movement. He looked again at the letter in his hand:

"… Mr Stone's father has written to inform me that his son is alive and well in America. He is recovered from his wound, and is married, to a respectable Frenchwoman …"

Your etc

Harold Wilkinson

Snowden felt as though a great weight had been lifted from him. Jack was alive. Alive, and not in some French prison, but in America, and married. The praise that had been heaped upon Snowden following his return from France had felt hollow, overshadowed by the guilt he felt because he had instigated the reckless action that had, in his worst imagining, led to Jack's imprisonment and death.

He looked out of the window, where the ship, his ship, lay at the wharf, trim and lean, with her enormous raked masts and long bowsprit. She was a beauty, and she'd sailed like a dream last week during the trials. Not a frigate, he thought, but that would come in time. Beyond the ship, the sea shone, bright blue, ruffled by small waves.

Men from the yard worked on board, putting the finishing touches to the ship before she was formally commissioned into the Navy as *Oleander*. Bermuda's social structure was complex, opaque to an outsider like Snowden, but he knew that many of the yard's workmen, including some of the most skilled ones, were slaves.

Snowden heard a knock at the door and looked up to see the Master Shipwright, a tall, competent-looking man dressed in culottes and a rough shirt.

"Come in."

"Thank you, Sir." He glanced at the fallen chair and the letter in Snowden's hand. "Not bad news, I hope?"

"No, anything but." Snowden picked up the chair and took a bottle and glasses from the sideboard. "Very good news – in fact, exceptional. You'll join me in a glass?"

"I will, Sir. Would you care to enlighten me?"

"You may remember that I was involved in a raid in France, just before I came here."

"Indeed I do, a famous operation. Put Boney's nose properly out of joint."

"Well, I suppose it did, but my friend, Midshipman Stone …"

"I've heard of him, hero of Weymouth and all that. I heard the Froggies had him."

"Yes, that's the one. He was wounded as well, and he has enemies in high places in France. I have been dreadful worried about him, but I have just had word he's well, that he's escaped and is in America."

Snowden raised his glass. "To Jack Stone, and confound Boney!"

CHAPTER 2 – BLONDE

Snowden, lying half asleep in his cabin, snapped awake when he heard the hail from the lookout at the foretop. "On deck there. Sail, a point on the starboard bow."

Feet padded on the deck above his head as he got to his feet, resisting the urge to go on deck immediately. The Master, Kennedy, was the same age as Snowden, and Snowden was determined not to cause unnecessary resentment by rushing on deck at every minor incident.

There was a knock on the door.

"Come in." The door opened to reveal a red-coated soldier standing outside. A young seaman entered the cabin. "Yes, Pirera?"

"Mr Kennedy's compliments, Your Honour. Lookout's sighted a sail and Mr Kennedy requests your presence on deck."

"Thank you, Pirera, I will be there directly."

Snowden emerged onto the deck, into the bright sunlight. He looked aloft at the sails, bellying in the fresh north-westerly breeze. The sea was blue, the deep indigo blue of the Gulf Stream, the waves topped with white crests, sprinkled with patches of bladder weed. He tipped his hat to the Master. "A fine breeze, Mr Kennedy."

"Aye, Sir, tramping along nicely she is. A sail, Sir …"

He was interrupted by a shout from the foretop. "On deck there! She's a three-master. Just the topsails on her."

Snowden looked at the Master. "I'll have a look, Mr

Kennedy." He thought he saw a slight frown of disapproval on Kennedy's face, but damn it, he wasn't going to stand on his dignity. He went forward and climbed rapidly to the foretop, nodding towards the young lookout, undoubtedly chosen for the duty because of the sharpness of his eyes, which helped him remember the man's name, Kenny Iris.

"Good morning, Iris. Where away?"

Iris pointed. "There, Your Honour."

Snowden saw the ship, closer than he had expected. He steadied himself against the mast, raised his glass to his eye, and as he focused it the ship ahead swam into view. She was quite a large three-master, running slowly before the wind under easy canvas. Headed in the general direction of Spain, but wasting a fair wind, Snowden thought. Despite her slow speed, on her present course, *Oleander* would pass well astern of her.

A neutral merchant ship would take advantage of the breeze, and British merchantmen would probably be in convoy. The French Navy was largely bottled up in port, and a French blockade runner would be crowding on sail, not loitering like the ship ahead. A blockade runner would be keeping as sharp a lookout as *Oleander* and would immediately turn away as soon as another sail was sighted. Snowden's suspicions hardened in his mind. He handed the glass to Iris, who studied the ship.

"Man o' war do you think, Iris?"

"Umm, I reckon she might be, Sir," replied Iris, in his pleasant Bermudian drawl.

Snowden thought quickly, made his mind up, and climbed down, joining Kennedy near the wheel.

"What do you think, Sir?"

"I think, Mr Kennedy, we may have a fight on our hands."

"Man o' war, Sir?"

"Frenchie Privateer, I believe."

Kennedy glanced at the other ship, which was now visible from the deck. "Frightful big for a privateer."

"I've heard there's one or two like that. Malouine, but based in Corunna."

"We're by no means worked up, Sir."

Bloody pessimist, thought Snowden, but bit back a sarcastic reply. "I know that, Kennedy, we'll have to do the best we can. *Oleander*'s pretty fast." He pointed towards the other ship. "Let us determine that fellow's intentions. Wear the ship and steer south by west. Watch those …"

He stopped himself. Kennedy did not need to be reminded of the danger of failing to control the enormous booms during a gybe.

"Aye, Sir, wear ship, south by west."

He turned to the midshipman, Poore, who was standing slightly apart. "Mr Poore, hoist 'enemy in sight', and the battle ensign."

"But Sir …"

"Mr Poore, I am very well aware that none of our ships will see the signal, but the Frenchman, if that is what he is, will."

Poore smiled in sudden understanding and moved towards the signal halyards.

Snowden, to his slight discomfiture, found himself relishing the prospect of action, as he would in anticipation of a night at the card table. He had come to realise that the odds of success in battle, as at cards, were considerably improved by careful playing of one's own hand, and by understanding, as far as possible, the other players' cards and their motivations and characters.

Men tallied on the sheets as the ship gybed and the great booms swung above the decks. As *Oleander* steadied on her new course, Snowden studied the other ship. After a few minutes he saw her alter to starboard, her courses and topgallants loosed from their yards and sheeted home, and the wave at her bow increase until its crest was almost level with her deck.

He's after us, he thought, and that means he's almost certainly a Frenchman. A cool character as well, to ignore our signal hoist. Either he doesn't believe there are any other ships for us to signal to or he is counting on his ability to escape if British men o' war are really just over his horizon.

Snowden turned to the Master. "Have the hands fed, if you please, Mr Kennedy. This could be a long job."

Snowden now knew the other ship was hostile and that it was larger than *Oleander*. If it was indeed a St Malo privateer, the ship would be heavily armed, well worked up and manned by a large, skilled crew. *Oleander* would stand no chance, no chance at all, in a straight fight.

"The ship is yours, Mr Kennedy. I am retiring to my cabin briefly."

Kennedy looked surprised. "Very well, Sir."

In his cabin, Snowden sat at the table thinking, while Cox, his servant, put food before him. Due to her size, the French ship would be faster than *Oleander* when sailing directly downwind, but the Bermudian schooner would sail closer to the wind than the square rigger, and would be much more manoeuvrable. Running downwind and attempting to escape under cover of darkness was a forlorn hope. The summer weather was clear, the days were long, and the chase would end before sunset, and in any case, there was a nearly full moon. On the other hand, it would be nice to erode some of the Frenchman's weather gauge.

Decided, Snowden turned in his seat and addressed his servant. "Cox, if you please, my compliments to Mr Kennedy, and ask him and his colleagues to come to the cabin directly."

CHAPTER 3 – ESCAPE

"So that is the plan, gentlemen. *Oleander* can get away from the Frenchman if he has to chase us to windward, but we cannot put our ship hard on the wind while he has the weather gauge. The trick will be to get *Oleander* past the Frog when he has lost most of his weather advantage. We cannot expect the scheme to work exactly, but I have no doubt you will be able to improvise as necessary. Are there any questions?"

Snowden looked at the men seated round the table. They murmured their assent, stood up as far as the limited headroom allowed, and made their way from the cabin. Good men, he thought, and their confidence in him and the ship would increase if they were successful in the next few hours. He did not dwell on the consequences of failure. He wished he knew his ship better.

Back on deck, Snowden could see the larger French ship was gaining on them, though it would be several hours before she came up with *Oleander.* He called to the Master, "Kennedy, please send one division below, we may as well have a rested crew when we come to action."

"Very well, Sir."

The men at the wheel changed, the outgoing pair giving a muttered explanation of the course and set of the sails to the men who were relieving them, and the ship sailed on as before.

The sun was in the west when the Frenchman opened fire with his bow chasers. The shot fell some distance astern, but it was a foretaste of things to come.

Snowden called for the Gunner, Trott, a young but energetic Bermudian who had been very effective when they had been commissioning the ship in Bermuda. "Trott, could you get one of the long nines on the quarterdeck so the Frenchman won't have things all his own way?"

"I believe I could, Sir."

"Then do it, quick as you like. Tell the armourer to get the forge up as well."

"Aye aye, Sir."

In another half hour, the enemy's shots had become more accurate, but the cannon hastily moved to *Oleander's* quarterdeck had started to reply, firing red-hot shot heated in the forge.

A ball smashed into *Oleander's* stern. "Felt that, I did," said the helmsman, "through the wheel", and there were an anxious few minutes before the carpenter reported the rudder was undamaged.

The gunner tugged at Snowden's sleeve and pointed to the enemy ship. "Look at that, Sir." Snowden turned and saw a thin column of smoke was rising from somewhere in the forepart of the French ship. He felt a surge of elation. That was more like it! "Dropped down a hatch, I reckon," said the gunner with a grin. "Devil of a job to put it out."

"Sail room perhaps. Guns, well done, see if you can get the next one into the powder locker."

"I'll certainly try, Sir. Come on lads, is there another one cooked and ready to serve to our French guests?"

The men, including the ones nominally resting below but who had made their way back on deck, cheered as the gun fired again. Now's the time, thought Snowden, and turned to the Master, he hoped betraying none of the excitement he felt. "Hands to quarters, Mr Kennedy."

To the beating of the drum, the men went to their quarters. Slowly, over the next fifteen minutes, *Oleander* edged round to starboard, closer to the wind, the French ship, very near, shadowing them astern and to windward as the British ship turned. The wind, now blowing vigorously across the French ship's deck, seemed to increase the quantity of smoke coming from her. One or two of the most forward of the French ship's port battery could now be brought to bear, and she fired, accurately and quickly. Snowden felt several balls strike his ship, and a carpenter's mate approached him.

"Begging your pardon, Your Honour. Carpenter sent me to tell you she's holed just below the waterline, smashed a frame as well, quite bad. Making water she is. Carpenter says can we have more men for the pumps, Sir?"

"Compliments to Mr Trimingham. Please tell him to do what he can, but presently we need the men to fight the ship."

The man moved away, to be replaced by Butterfield, the Surgeon's Mate, who Snowden knew would not be bearing good news. Two men were injured, one with a smashed leg which would have to be amputated. Snowden knew the punishment would only increase as the French ship overhauled *Oleander*. It was now or never.

"Put her hard on the wind, Mr Kennedy," he said, and *Oleander* heeled as the wind came forward and the sheets on the great booms were tightened, the wake hissing and surging along the lee gunwales. "Ready, Guns," he shouted, all pretence of calmness gone, overcome by the lust of battle, the pitting of his wits against the enemy. "As you bear, starboard battery ... Luff her, Mr Kennedy, NOW."

Oleander came upright as she headed into the wind, her great sails roaring as they shook in the wind. He saw the Frenchman turning to answer *Oleander's* manoeuvre, but she was less handy than the British ship, and she was heeled so much that her port battery was on the waterline, almost useless.

Oleander's starboard battery fired together, sending an aimed cloud of canister shot into the French ship. Snowden saw men fall. He gripped the taffrail and turned to the Master. "Take her round, Mr Kennedy, if she'll answer."

"Aye aye, Sir, don't you worry, she will."

The staysails were backed, and the ship tacked, agonisingly slowly, but surely, through the eye of the wind, the breeze now quite strong, coming round onto the port side. The staysails were sheeted home, and suddenly *Oleander* was sliding past the stern of the French ship. He saw her name, *Blonde*, picked out in gold, as the port battery fired its chainshot at her rigging, each gun aimed unhurriedly by Trott, who sighted along the barrels, giving instructions to the gun crew who moved the guns with handspikes and wedges.

He watched, spellbound, as the French ship's mizzen mast, with tricolour and St Malo flags flying, crashed slowly into her deck. *Oleander* clawed her way into the wind, overcanvassed, water sluicing along her lee deck, but Snowden knew, as he watched men working with axes on *Blonde's* deck to cut away the wreckage, that they had escaped. He supported himself on the binnacle railing, suddenly drained of energy, surprised by Kennedy's voice. "Shall I reef her down, Sir?"

"Indeed you shall, Mr Kennedy, and well done, pass my thanks to all hands. When she's reefed send the starboard division down, and splice the mainbrace."

He walked to the ladder. There were wounded to visit and damage to inspect.

CHAPTER 4 – PUMP OR DROWN

The Western Approaches to the Channel were wide, but the ship, forging slowly ahead under her topsails, was enclosed by a blanket of white fog. Snowden looked over the side of the ship, checking the sails which had been rigged to cover the outside of the leaks were still in place. Despite their best efforts to stem the flow, the pumps had had to work almost continuously since their encounter with *Blonde*, and the crew were in a state of near exhaustion.

Although the ship was equipped with chronometers, they had not had sight of the sun for several days. Kennedy approached Snowden as he paced the quarterdeck, alert to any cry from the masthead.

"Thick weather, Sir. Hard on the men when we're close to the land."

"I know, Mr Kennedy, but if it is a choice between another day's pumping and running her up on the Scillies …"

"I know, Sir." Kennedy nodded towards Midshipman Poore, who was at the rail, looking intently towards where the sun should be, sextant in his hand, his younger colleague Pascoe at his side ready with watch and slate. "I don't think there's much chance."

"Probably not, Mr Kennedy, but they may as well try."

"The lead, Sir?"

"Yes, bring her to."

Sails were backed, the ship slowed, and Snowden and Kennedy walked over to watch the deep sea lead cast.

"That's the bottom, Sir," said the Bosun, Rubert, but known to the crew as 'Spanish Bob', feeling the line which seemed to have some slack in it. He looked at the markings on the line. "Sixty two fathoms, Sir." Deep, thought Snowden as the lead was retrieved.

As it came aboard, men, glad to have been released briefly from pumping duties, clustered around it to inspect the sample of the seabed which the tallow in the base of the lead had captured. Kennedy looked closely at it and rubbed a sample between his fingers. "Fine sand, Sir." He gave some to Snowden.

"Get her under way, Mr Kennedy, if you please, and join me in the cabin."

From the cabin, Snowden briefly heard the sound of canvas flogging as the sails were set and felt the ship heel and then right herself as she gathered way and was settled on her course. Snowden was intent on the chart as Kennedy entered. "Well, Mr Kennedy, I believe sixty two fathoms shows we are some distance from land."

"I believe so too, Sir, though 'tis fairly steep to on the Ushant side."

Snowden looked closely at the chart. The soundings marked on it were sparse, but he could see what Kennedy meant. "We can't be that far south!"

"No, Sir, I don't believe we are. We must have some faith in our reckoning ..."

The cabin door banged open and Midshipman Poore entered, sextant in hand. Kennedy looked up from the chart. "Upon my word, Poore, you would do well to remember this is the captain's cabin."

"Sorry, Sir, but I thought you should know directly. We had a glimpse of the sun and I think the horizon wasn't too bad. Pascoe has the sight on his slate."

Kennedy looked at Snowden, who nodded. "Come in Mr Pascoe. Let's see what you have."

Snowden waited until both midshipmen were at the table, then held his hand out for the slate and looked at it critically. "Barely legible, Mr Pascoe, but we shall see how it falls out. What time was it?"

"Wanted a few minutes of noon, Sir."

"And what does that mean?"

Pascoe looked at Poore before replying. "Sun's almost due south, Sir. The sight will give us more or less our latitude."

"Indeed it will. Gather round and we'll work it up."

Snowden worked at the figures, occasionally explaining what he was doing to the midshipmen. When he had finished, he looked at Poore. "Lay this off on the chart, Mr Poore, if you please."

Poore leant eagerly over the chart and carefully drew a position line, his face falling when he saw where his sight put the ship.

"Mr Poore, either you are mistaken in your sight, we have worked it up wrong, or unbeknownst to us the ship is presently in the north part of Cornwall."

"Sorry, Sir, I was sure I had it."

"Let us work it up again. Mr Kennedy, perhaps you would care to lead this time." He turned round to Kennedy, who was standing with the sextant in his hand, carefully examining the scale. He held the instrument out. "Mr Poore, you locked the instrument when you took the sight, did you not?"

"I did, Sir."

"I suggest you look at the reading and compare it with the figure Mr Pascoe noted down."

Poore looked at the scale and then at the slate, his face suddenly registering comprehension. "Oh, Sir, indeed I'm sorry, I believe I have called out the wrong figure to Mr Pascoe. I am out by a degree."

They reworked the calculation, marked it on the chart and laid off a course. Snowden turned to the midshipmen. "That's more like it, lads, well done, your perseverance paid off. Mistakes like that are easily made, and usually we find them out, as they disagree with some other fact. I think we can congratulate ourselves, Mr Kennedy. Our reckoning seems to agree with the sight. I think North by East should be about right. Let's get a bit more sail on her."

The fog cleared in the night, and before long the Eddystone light came into view. By the time *Oleander* came under Rame Head, the sun was shining brightly and the green of the fields looked astonishingly vivid after weeks of blues and greys.

"Looks awful pretty," said Kennedy to Snowden.

"Yes, it does. I never thought I'd be quite so pleased to see Plymouth," said Snowden.

There was a shout from the lookout. "Fort's signalling."

Pascoe picked up his glass, trained it on the flags and looked at the signal book. "If you please, Sir, we are to proceed directly to the dockyard."

"Thank goodness for that, Kennedy, though I don't know if I'll be able to sleep without the sound of the pumps."

CHAPTER 5 – TREVENNEC

Snowden reined in his horse, and looked down at his home, Trevennec. Even from that distance, he could sense the air of decay. The fields and hedges were unkempt and the parkland around the house unmown. He sighed and made his way into the valley.

That evening, after dinner, he was sitting in the small parlour, unexpectedly feeling very cheerful, chiefly due to the presence of the woman who sat across the fire from him. She was, Snowden thought, in her late forties, her piercing eyes carefully set off by a necklace bright with stones of almost the same shade of green, glittering in the firelight. They were discussing Snowden's trip to Paris during the brief Peace of Amiens.

"I don't mind telling you, Mrs White, that Fouché frightened me."

"I am not surprised, Mr Snowden ... or should it be Lieutenant Snowden?"

"Percy would suit very well, Mrs White."

"Very well, Percy it shall be, and I am Julia. The Revolution brought the worst out in some men, and women too, but Fouché is truly evil, one of the worst. At Toulon ... I believe Napoleon himself is frightened of him." She frowned. "Your friend Stone was very lucky to escape. Perhaps he has friends in high places."

"Perhaps he has. He said in his letter he had married a 'respectable Frenchwoman'. I hope for more news when my letters catch up with me. There was none at the dockyard, as we had orders for the Downs."

"The Downs?"

"The anchorage near Dover. Ships often wait there for favourable winds."

"I see. And when will your ship be repaired?"

"In a few weeks, they say, and then we are to proceed to Deptford, on the Thames near London."

"Why there?"

"The Admiralty is interested in the ship. It is the first sizable vessel they have built in Bermuda, and they wish to examine her before they order more."

"And is the ship a good one?"

"She is a very good ship, and I think the Navy would do well to buy more like her. As you know, we had an encounter with a Frenchman, and I believe, having had more experience with the ship, that we could have avoided fighting by hauling our wind and outrunning him – perhaps not directly downwind, against a big square rigger, but I am coming to the conclusion there's not a ship to touch her on any other point of sailing."

"Where will you go after Deptford?"

"The people in the Dockyard, who generally know about these things, say we are to go to the Mediterranean, but I do not know where."

Snowden noticed she sat forward at this, paying close attention. "I believe you have some experience of that part of the world, Julia."

"Yes, I have spent much time abroad, and hardly any in England. As you know, I am related on your mother's side, and to Whitworth."

"I know, our man in Paris, or at least he was, and we met him there."

"Whitworth was under no illusions the Peace would last, and in fact was grossly insulted by Buonaparte ..." She pronounced the name in a way that Snowden had not heard before. "I was in Paris, and Whitworth advised me to leave, and I did, as soon as I could. This was the only place in England I knew of. I had visited when I was a girl, and your parents very kindly took me in, after Whitworth wrote to them."

"Were you long in France, Julia?"

"Not very long. Like you, I went there during the Peace. I have spent most of my time in Italy and in Corsica."

"Corsica – I have been there, on my first ship. I was at the Siege of Calvi ..."

"You must have been very young, and so far from home."

"I was, twelve, but really, the Navy is my home, whichever ship I am in." He gestured around the room. "Not this place. Since I joined the Navy, I have spent little time here."

"That is sad. Your parents ..."

"... I think had my best interests at heart, but they scarcely had the means to pay for a proper education, and the Navy relieved them of that necessity."

"It was an exciting time for us, in Corsica. We thought our dream of freedom was to come true, and it did, briefly."

"I found it very exciting as well, in *Agamemnon*, Nelson's ship. I spent most of my time in the boats. We landed soldiers and guns, and the ship was in action against forts on the shore on several occasions, strange round buildings, but I must say I did not know much about the reasons for our fighting there. Any enemies of the French are our friends, I suppose. It all came to nothing in the end, I believe. We were a long way from home, and a good number of our men were sick. You said 'us' – are you

Corsican?"

Julia looked at him, her face sombre. "My father was Corsican and my mother English. I grew up in Leghorn, where my father was a merchant, trading with Corsica, importing honey and wine from the northern part. My mother strove to make our house in Leghorn a little piece of England, but we often entertained Corsicans, exiles who had made their home there. I expect you have been to Leghorn, Percy. The English Navy called there often."

"Indeed I have. We were a little wild in those days perhaps, but I have some pleasant memories of the place. I remember Cape Corse as well, especially those forts, and the scent of the bushes, we could smell the land miles off. You said you were recently in France. May I ask what you were doing there?"

"Yes, you may. My husband is Corsican, a ship owner who traded with my father. He is a true Corsican patriot, but he was taken by the French, and I was in Paris, agitating for his release."

At that moment, Lord and Lady Penzance entered the room, and Snowden realised with displeasure that neither were entirely sober, and that their conversation was harsh and unpleasant, sprinkled with derogatory remarks about their neighbours, to Julia's obvious discomfort. After a short time, she went to her room.

Snowden turned to his father. "Why do you and mother have to speak so? It seems you have good words for nobody, and it makes it most disagreeable for myself and your guest."

"Guest? She was more or less forced upon us by your mother's relation, Whitworth, and it transpires she has almost no money, or at least her money is abroad where it is of no use."

"She seems to be a most charming woman."

Snowden's mother interjected, "Most likely takes after her mother, who was no better than she should have been."

Snowden bristled. "I shall go up directly, and I hope you are both in a better temper tomorrow."

Snowden was sitting at the desk in his room when there was a knock on the door, and his mother entered and chose to sit on a chair near him.

"I am very sorry, Percy, that you find your father and I such bad company. It is just that we are presently very hard pressed by our creditors, and there seems to be little hope of rectifying the situation."

"What happened to Mr Halstock? I thought he was beginning to make his mark." Halstock was the steward who his father had hired, on Snowden's insistence, to take charge of the running of the estate, after the departure of the previous man. Snowden had met him and thought him experienced and competent.

"He was, but your father sent him away. Your father went to the estate office and knocked over some things on Halstock's desk. Mr Halstock forgot himself and said some harsh words to your father, accusing him of being drunk, and in return your father charged him with feathering his own nest and told him to leave. Later, your father went to find him, to apologise, but he had gone. He left a note saying it was a shame that your father was unable to distinguish between those who did their duty and those who took advantage of him. I hear he has a very good position now in Devon."

"That was most unfortunate."

"It was more than unfortunate, it was a disaster. Your father has tried to run the place himself since Halstock left, but …"

"The drink," said Snowden glumly.

She nodded. "Yes, the drink, a terrible thing. I know I indulge myself, but your father is so far gone …"

"You have some money yourself, Mother." He couldn't help himself and instantly regretted it. He knew very well her money had vanished at the gaming tables. Her eyes filled with tears and she dropped her head.

CHAPTER 6 – JULIA

Early next morning he was on the clifftop with Julia White, looking out over the sea, sparkling in the sunshine. He turned in his saddle.

"Clear weather and a steady south westerly. We could have done with that a few days ago when we were feeling our way in the fog."

"It must be anxious work, bringing a ship up the Channel in the fog. When do you leave, Percy?"

"Tomorrow morning. Mr Kennedy, the Master, is exceptionally capable, and I wish to signal my confidence in him by not attending closely while the ship is in repair. However, I must show myself now. And you?"

"I intend to travel to London soon. There are people there who I must look up."

"You know people in London?"

"I do, and Whitworth has given me some introductions. I will let you know where I am staying, and perhaps you will call on me when your ship is in Deptford."

Snowden felt strangely cheered by this, but the afternoon was marred by an unpleasant interview with his father. Snowden went to the estate office, where his father was seated at a desk covered in disorganised heaps of papers.

"Good afternoon, Father. How's the estate business progressing?"

His father shook his head briefly, but did not reply.

"Are you seeking Mr Halstock's replacement, Father?" he said mildly.

"No, I am damned well not. Fellow was robbing us blind, they're all like that."

"Are you sure? He seemed a steady fellow to me."

"Insolent man as well. I should not be insulted in my own office."

"I think you need someone. I have some coin, probably enough to pay for his first year's wages."

"And how did you get that?"

"Some prize money, and at the tables."

"At the tables, eh? Take after you mother I suppose."

"The difference is, Father, I win."

His father grimaced, his breath smelling of alcohol despite the early hour. Snowden felt something turn in his mind, and, almost against his will, said, more harshly than he intended, "I have not said this before, but you cause me great injury. When I return to Trevennec, you do not welcome me, and though I offer you prize money, you do not ask how I came by it. I have been in the Navy near twelve year, and you have not once asked about my service. I used to tell you, at first, but you took no notice. It is very hard for a son to do without the approbation of his father, or at least some display of affection or interest."

His father looked into the distance, unspeaking. Snowden, enraged, banged on the desk. "Although you do not ask, I will tell you about my service. I was at the Siege of Calvi, in Nelson's ship. I was at the Nile, still in *Agamemnon*, in the thick of the action, and I saw *L'Orient* blow up. Off Ushant, I took my boarders through the stern gallery of a French frigate, forced her to strike, and took her safe into port. I destroyed Napoleon's invasion barges fifteen leagues inland from the coast – you must have read or heard of that – and I have just brought my own ship back from Bermuda, across the Western Ocean, fighting off a French privateer, the famous *Blonde*, on the way."

He thumped his fist on the desk again, making his father jump back. Snowden realised his father looked old, frightened, and that tears ran down his cheeks. Suddenly, his rage abated. His father looked at him.

"I know I have done you great wrong, Percy. I have been ashamed and I do not know how to tell you of it. I have allowed the estate to go to wrack, and I have let your mother gamble away her inheritance."

"Yes, Father."

"I was away at the wars when I was a young man."

"I know you were."

"Terrible things happened to me there, before and after Minden. No, that is not true. It was I who did terrible things, deliberately. My mind became deranged, and I did horrid things that I cannot tell you of. The regiment was disgusted with me. I lost my friends."

He shuddered. "I bought myself out, before I was cashiered, and went home. Your grandfather was very harsh with me, but I made a good match, your mother with her inheritance. But I suppose I was embittered, and I began to drink. Your mother and I, well, there were other women, and she could not stop herself gambling. I was deep in melancholy, and I knew you could not stay at home. The Navy was the only choice I could make. When you came home, and the depths of our degradation were plain for you to see, I could hardly bear to talk to you. I am truly sorry, Percy. And now I have driven Halstock out, I do not know what I was thinking of."

He paused for a moment. "That is not true, I shall be honest. I was damnably drunk and I gravely insulted him. He was a prickly man, no doubt, but no man with any self-respect could have accepted what I said, and he was quite right to leave.

He was immediately snapped up, and now has a good place in Devon. What a fool I was."

He gestured to the litter of papers on the desk, in abject despair. Snowden found himself reaching out and putting his hand on his father's shoulder, deeply moved.

"I know war does things to men, Father, I have seen it with my own eyes, and I feel it myself. I know I should not love battle, but I do. In a fight, I become beside myself, I scarce know what I am doing. I also could do terrible things, but in the Navy there are people nearby who can moderate one. When I boarded that ship, I would have killed her captain if a Marine had not stopped me, a private soldier. The Frenchman was wounded and had surrendered, but I would have killed him where he stood, though he was proffering his sword. He was probably a man much like me."

He gripped his father's shoulder. "Our nation's hero, Nelson, is another. In Corsica, I saw the light of battle in his eyes. He was injured there, but he did not have to be ashore, at the front of the guns. The Lord knows what he would be capable of if he were not constrained by the customs of the British Navy. He would be a Barbarossa."

Snowden sat down, reached across the table and took his father's hands in his own. "Come, Father, it is not so bad. I have some money, and we can hire a competent man. Let us go and see Mother and plan what we should do."

After dinner Snowden again sat in the parlour with Julia White.

"You have been busy this afternoon, Percy?"

"I have, Julia, we've been working on the estate accounts."

"Is it very bad?"

"It is not good, but I believe that with care and with proper management there may be some hope for the future. The tenants are generally good people, but no money has been spent on improvement or indeed maintenance for many years."

"Since I have been here, I have thought your parents very depressed in spirit, but today I believe I have noticed some improvement. Your father drank nothing at dinner."

"Long may that continue. We have had a discussion, and I believe we have agreed what should be done. I will go back to my ship as planned tomorrow, but I will endeavour to come away here as often as I can while she is in the dockyard. We will have to try and find a steward for the estate, but it may be a long process, and in the meantime, the accounts are in a terrible state. We are pressed hard by one creditor in particular. I consider he scents blood, and believe the estate may fall into his hands at a knockdown price. I have some money, but it is difficult for me as I know nothing of accounts or business."

Julia looked at him. "I grew up in the house of a Leghorn merchant, and my husband is a ship owner. He is frequently away and I run the business, which is a substantial affair. Accounts and business matters are no mystery to me, and, if you would like, I can assist with the estate until I leave for London, when perhaps you may have found a suitable factor."

"But I thought you were shortly going to London."

"I can put it off. I was going because, well, because I have some business there, but it is not urgent."

Snowden felt a glimmer of hope.

The conference took place at ten in the morning, in the estate office. Snowden glanced at his parents, who looked as though they had not slept, and then at Julia White.

"Mrs White, here, is the daughter of a merchant, and her husband is in business in a fairly big way, a ship owner. In Italy, they like to keep the business in the family, apparently their mansion in Leghorn is part warehouse, and she knows very well how to keep accounts. I propose, until we find a replacement for Mr Halstock, that Mrs White reviews the accounts and puts them in order. Father, I suggest you work alongside of her while she does it."

His parents looked startled, but, Snowden thought, beat down sufficiently to grab at any passing straw.

"If you agree, I will leave her some coin to, as we say in the Navy, 'work the ship' for the time being."

In the early afternoon, Snowden went to the office to say his goodbyes. His father and Julia White were sitting side by side at the desk. The mess of papers had been transformed into several neat piles.

"Father, Mrs White, I am off to my ship. I hope to be back in a few days. Do you make progress?"

"I believe we do," said his father. "We have opened all the letters I have been afraid to open, and we are starting on the accounts."

Absorbed in their task, they plainly felt they had little time for conversation, and after a few minutes Snowden bid them goodbye and set his horse's head to the east, along the coast, his heart considerably lighter than when he had arrived.

CHAPTER 7 – DEVONPORT

The dockyard was a noisy hive of activity. *Oleander* was dwarfed by the other ship in the dry dock, a seventy-four. He went with Kennedy and the carpenter to the dock bottom to inspect the work.

"Six frames were broken, Sir," said the carpenter.

"And about sixty feet of planking sprung, and the copper hanging off. No wonder the fothering didn't work," added Kennedy. "Damned lucky to have made it. Would have been a long row back." In his mind, Snowden heard the clanking of the pumps. Pump or drown, he thought.

He spent the next week in a haze of activity, often remonstrating with the dockyard officials about the speed of the repair, but he quickly realised the dry dock would only be flooded and *Oleander* floated out when work on the seventy-four behind his ship was complete.

It was an overcast Monday morning when he returned home. To his surprise, there were men in the parkland near the house with scythes, mowing. A wagon was standing outside the estate office, and when he entered he found Mrs White and his father standing in discussion with a man who was presumably its driver. They saw Snowden enter, greeted him briefly, but continued their discussion, which seemed to involve the rate for carrying straw from field to barn. The business concluded and the man left, touching his forelock to Snowden as he passed.

"Drives a hard bargain, does he not?" said Snowden's father to Mrs White.

"He does, but until our own wagons are repaired, he is in a strong position. Now we have settled the wheelwright's account, I believe we will not have to use him for long."

Snowden thought how pleasant her voice was, with its slight foreign accent.

After dinner, Snowden sat again in the small parlour with Julia White.

"Dinner was a much more agreeable affair, was it not, Julia?"

"I am glad you thought so."

"And the house seems cleaner."

"We had some people in to clean. We do not have many staff of our own."

"And no drink at dinner. I suspect your hand in that."

"Not really, Percy. It was your parents' decision. We have even spoken to Tanner." Tanner was the butler, a long-standing employee. "And he agreed he would resist attempts by your father to call for drink."

"That could put him in a delicate position."

"I know, but I probably exceeded my authority and told him you would guarantee his position here. He knows, anyway, that if things continued as they were, his future would by no means be secure."

"I will speak to him and reinforce what you said. Thank you. And the management of the estate?"

"I think it is improving. I have got to grips with the accounts, and the situation is not hopeless, but we have a difficult issue with Mr Miller."

"I think I recall the name, but nothing else."

"He is the lawyer in Fowey. He advanced your father money, in return for a mortgage. Your father was advised by the previous factor, Jenkins."

"I remember Jenkins." Jenkins had worked at the estate since Snowden was a child.

"He left, abruptly, but before he went he advised your father that he should borrow money from Miller."

"Much money?"

"Yes, there is a mortgage and we are in arrears."

Snowden noticed the 'we'. "By how much?"

"It is not something that would be a major obstacle if you were prepared to clear it with your own money, but there is a problem."

With a sinking feeling Snowden asked, "What is the problem?"

"A clause in the document states that if there is a default for two consecutive quarters, the lender may take possession, at his discretion. Miller visited last month and told your father of his intent to take possession."

"My God, did he?"

"Yes, just before your first visit."

"No wonder Father and Mother were unhappy. What is to be done about this?"

"I do not know. I only know what we would do in Corsica." To Snowden's astonishment she looked at him and drew her hand slowly across her throat. "That is how we would deal with men like him."

Snowden, shocked, could only say, "My word, Mrs White, I don't believe we can do that here."

The next day, Snowden was shown into Mr Miller's musty, book-lined office in Fowey. Miller, a slight man with an ingratiating and, to Snowden, irritating smile, rose from his chair, holding out his hand. "Good morning, Sir."

"Good morning, Mr Miller."

"I believe you are here on the business of your father's estate."

"My Father's now, but in the future, mine."

"Well, Sir, we know there is a problem with that."

"Please explain, Mr Miller."

"Well, Sir, some time ago your father was in dire straits, *in extremis* you might say, and he came to me on the recommendation of his steward, Mr Jenkins, a most respectable man, one I have known since we were boys together." He paused, licking his lips.

"Pray continue, Mr Miller."

"Well, Sir, I was prepared to lend your father the money, at a very reasonable rate, but, you will understand, Sir, I required security, and drew up documents ..."

"A mortgage, you mean?"

"Yes, Sir, a mortgage." Miller's voice was hoarse and he stood up, went over to a sideboard, poured water into a glass and drank it. "Excuse me, Sir."

"Of course, pray continue."

"A standard document, legally binding in every way. I had to have it, you see, as I was risking a deal of money."

"There is a clause, I believe ..."

"Yes, Sir, I think you refer to the foreclosure clause. I discussed it with your father a few weeks ago."

"You did."

"As I pointed out to him, I have no option but to exercise

that clause as he is seriously in arrears, and I can see no prospect of repayment in future."

"I believe you can, Mr Miller. We are in funds and can make the payments."

Miller poured himself another glass of water and gulped it down. He looked at the area around Snowden's feet and mumbled, "Alas, the procedure has started."

"Speak up, man. I said I can pay you."

The lawyer gathered himself and looked up. "The procedure has started, and I will not back down."

Snowden recognised the anger rising in him, stood up and jammed his hat on his head. The lawyer shrank back. "Good day, Mr Miller."

He went out of the office and into the narrow street, and walked to the quay, which was lined with coasters, some with sails drying in the breeze. The sight of the ships calmed him and he felt his anger subside. It was after midday and he realised he was hungry. There was an inn just off the quay, which he entered and sat at a table, deep in thought. After a few minutes he became aware of someone standing near him, and he looked up.

"Good afternoon, Your Honour."

The man seemed familiar. "Good afternoon – I say, have we met before?"

"We have, Sir, but you were much littler then."

Recognition dawned on Snowden. "Good heavens, Rawlinson. I remember all right. The old *Agamemnon*. It was you who pulled me out of the water at Calvi, was it not? Bosun's Mate then, I believe."

"That's right, Sir. Like a drowned rat you were, if you don't mind me saying so."

"Yes, I was a little premature jumping over the side of the longboat when we came to the shore. I haven't forgotten that lesson. And what happened to you?"

"Got the fever in Calvi …"

"A number of men did, unhealthy place."

"Then I joined *Billy Ruffian*, got made up to Bosun, and stayed in her until a couple of years ago, when I came ashore for good. We bought this place and sometimes I do a little rigging on the ships at the quay. Like toys, they are, after *Billy Ruffian*."

"I expect they are. Are you a local man?"

"No, Sir, from Polperro, I am. You, Sir?"

"I've just brought a new schooner back from Bermuda. Damaged by a French privateer, so she's in Devonport dry dock. She can't leave until the seventy-four she's sharing the dock with is finished."

"And what brings you to this part of the world, Sir, if you don't mind me asking?"

"My family place is here."

Comprehension dawned on Rawlinson. "Of course, Sir, I didn't realise. The name, Snowden."

The door opened and a group of seamen came in, steady looking men, probably Masters from the merchant ships. There was a call from the bar.

"Excuse me, Sir, I'm needed elsewhere. I'll send the barmaid over to attend to you directly." Rawlinson walked off and a girl came and took Snowden's order. As he ate, he thought of the day when *Agamemnon* had been in Calvi, the sound of the guns, the smoke blowing over the blue water, the snow-capped mountains, and Nelson being helped over the side, his face heavily bandaged. He looked up from his reverie and noticed Rawlinson was talking to another familiar looking man at the bar. The man seemed rather the worse for wear, and when he eventually left, Snowden realised it was Jenkins, his father's former steward.

When Snowden finished his meal, Rawlinson came over to clear the table. "Everything to your satisfaction, Sir?"

"Indeed, yes. Very good. I feel more like myself now. I was thinking of that time in Calvi. That was the day Nelson lost his eye, was it not?"

"It was, Your Honour. A lesser man wouldn't have been ashore with the guns after dragging them all that way along those accursed paths."

"I saw you speaking to Jenkins. He used to be my father's factor."

"Him? Of course. In his cups, as usual." Rawlinson looked at Snowden, his face concerned.

"Sir, he is often in here, a good customer. But I've just put two and two together, and I think, well, it's not really my place, but we ..." He hesitated. "Well, as I say, he's often in here, half-drunk like as not. I hear tell, Sir, he plays regular at cards, up at the 'Anchor'. They've quite a school going there, and I believe he loses, heavily, Sir. He has been saying for months now that he has a big payday coming. I don't listen real close, but it is something to do with an estate."

Snowden leaned forward, recognising the man's awkwardness. "Well, Rawlinson, I have to thank you for saving my life already, so you may as well put me further in your debt!"

"Yes, Sir. Jenkins says he has something going with that lawyer, Miller – you know, the one just up the street." He gestured vaguely in that direction. "And, I don't know the details, but it seems they have some scheme to get hold of an estate, which must be your father's, Sir, by some underhand means. As I said, I have never paid much heed to his talk and I don't know the details, but I think ..."

He gathered himself. "I think that your Mr Jenkins has misrepresented the condition of the estate and persuaded someone, presumably your father, to sign some document which will bring about his downfall. Your father's that is, not Jenkins or the lawyer. I've wondered how Jenkins comes by his stake."

Snowden grinned broadly. "My word, Rawlinson, I think you may indeed have put me further in your debt!"

CHAPTER 8 – THE LAWYER

Snowden was on the quarterdeck of *Oleander*, still in dry dock, talking to Kennedy. They had just returned from an inspection of the ship's hull.

"Well, Sir, it looks like we are watertight."

"They've done a good job, Kennedy."

Kennedy gestured to the seventy-four behind them. "Seems they're making progress."

"They are, Kennedy. I was ashore last night with Robinson." Robinson was the captain of the seventy-four. "And he told me his hull was watertight, and coppered. He believes there is not more than a week's work to be done on his ship."

There was a hail from the side of the dock.

"My family, I believe, Mr Kennedy. I will be gone a couple of hours, some business in town. I'd be grateful if you would join us later in the cabin, and perhaps bring the midshipmen as well. There'll be a cold collation."

"I'd be very pleased to, Sir. I hope things go well ashore."

Snowden glanced at him quizzically, realising he would not be surprised if rumours of events at the estate had reached the ship.

In the office of the lawyer Snowden had engaged to help him, the meeting was drawing to a close. Snowden looked around the room, which was much bigger than the one in Fowey, with large windows, almost ceiling to floor, giving a splendid view of Plymouth harbour. Anderson, the senior partner, Dobney, a young lawyer from the firm's branch in Fowey, and a clerk sat around a polished table with Snowden, his parents and Mrs White.

Anderson waited for the scratching of the clerk's pen to stop, looked across the table and said in his cultured voice, "To summarise. Payments due on a mortgage on the estate are in arrears. The money was lent by one Miller, a lawyer in Fowey, who has given notice that he has invoked the foreclosure clause in the mortgage. This is quite straightforward."

Snowden's father started to speak, but his wife put her hand on his arm. He subsided into his chair and the lawyer continued.

"What is less straightforward and unusual is that offers to pay off the arrears have been refused. The mortgage includes the normal foreclosure provisions, to allow Miller to realise his security by taking ownership and possession of the estate, but you as the debtor have the equity of redemption if you pay off the debt. As a lawyer, Miller must be aware of this."

Snowden's father stood, his face a mask of despair. "Damnit, Anderson, I've been played for a fool. The arrears were mounting, and last month Miller came to see me. He proposed that I could remain on the estate for life if I signed a collateral document which I understood gave the estate to him in exchange for a lifetime tenancy, with Miller taking possession on my death. This is a copy of that document."

He pulled a paper from his pocket and held it out to Anderson. The room was silent as the lawyer scanned the document at length and then looked up.

"I can see what Miller was attempting. His view of the situation may have been coloured by the perception that your son" – he nodded towards Snowden – "has been many years absent at sea and appears to have no interest in the estate."

"On the face of it, the law does not allow foreclosure when the debt can be paid off, but the position is complicated by this second document. The situation is uncertain, but I believe it would be possible to make things difficult for Miller, to the extent that he may abandon his attempt to take over the estate. However, if it went to court, defending it would be time consuming and expensive. It also seems to me that the actions of your former steward …"

He looked at the clerk.

"Jenkins, Sir."

"Thank you. Jenkins, the former steward, apparently misrepresented the state of the accounts to your Lordship, so much so that you were convinced a mortgage on unfavourable terms was the only course of action left to you. It is believed that Halstock, the recently departed steward, had realised this when …"

"When I forced him to leave. What a fool I was."

"As I was saying, it is possible to argue that the mortgage and the collateral agreement were obtained by false pretences and are therefore not valid. How well this would stand up, and how long that will take, is unknown. Nevertheless, our object is not to ultimately win at a trial but rather to make the outcome sufficiently uncertain in Miller's mind that he will accept a settlement. Is this understood?"

There were nods around the table.

Snowden asked, "It seems to me this will be a drawn out procedure. I would not care to go back to sea with the position unresolved."

"Unfortunately, it could be a lengthy process. We must first examine the accounts very carefully, to try to determine whether the taking out of the mortgage on such terms was justified. I understand, Mrs White, you have made considerable progress in this area."

"I have, Sir. I looked at the figures Mr Halstock had written up, and I believe that the estate, while I think you would call it stagnating, had no need to borrow to that extent. It was not a particularly large sum, but even so it does not appear to have benefited the estate. Mr Winn, the banker, is visiting tomorrow."

The lawyer continued, looking at the junior lawyer, "I suggest Mr Dobney here returns to Fowey and approaches Mr Rawlinson with the aim of securing a statement from him about his conversations with Jenkins. It is hearsay, but nevertheless it is unlikely to do our cause harm."

Snowden spoke up. "If Mr Dobney has no objection, I will accompany him when he sees Rawlinson. We are old shipmates and that may ease the process."

The lawyer continued, "Very well. Meanwhile, I will compose a letter to be sent to Miller. It will offer to pay the arrears in return for the abandonment of the foreclosure process. It will point out the difficulties, uncertainties and expense Miller will be exposed to in pursuing the foreclosure process." He paused. "I do not like to be unduly mercenary." Snowden inwardly guffawed. "But I would like to have some payment on account before we put this scheme into operation." He looked at Snowden.

"Of course. I will discuss it with you in private."

The gangway to the ship, from the side of the dry dock, was rather narrow, but Snowden's guests tackled it seemingly without qualms. Kennedy, forewarned, had done his best, and Snowden felt a surge of pride as he was piped aboard his own ship, in front of his family and Mrs White, and the salute of the marine at his cabin door, very smartly turned out with musket and gleaming fixed bayonet, was absurdly gratifying.

The cabin, which seemed rather crowded with Snowden's visitors and the ship's officers, still smelled sweetly of the Bermuda cedar from which the ship was built. The sideboard was covered in a white cloth and the table was set. Admittedly the places were rather close together, but Snowden felt the effect was pleasing.

Later, he took his father on a tour of the ship, including a trip to the bottom of the dock to show him the repaired damage.

"The damage was all along here, where the copper is new. We were very lucky not to lose her. The *Blonde* has an evil reputation, and she was full of men. If it had come to boarding it would have been all up with us. As it was, we had to pump her all the way home."

He realised with pleasure that his father was looking at him with respect.

"You have done very well, Percy. I am proud of you."

CHAPTER 9 – MORTGAGE

On the following evening, in Fowey, Snowden went into the Anchor, a public house on the narrow main street, and spoke to the woman at the bar.

"I understand you have a private room."

She looked at him, appraisingly. "We do, Sir, at the back. If you would like to follow me, I will show you." She led Snowden into a room with a table set up at its centre. Several men sat at cards round the table, and others lounged on chairs or stood overlooking the players, one of whom was Jenkins. He looked up, recognised Snowden, and then bowed his head over his cards. When the hand was finished, one of the players asked Snowden if he cared to join them.

"No, thank you, I will stand and watch for now."

The man nodded and they went back to their game. Snowden studied the men at the table, judging what he inwardly called the rhythm of the game, and considering what he would do if he were playing. He thought the men were middling players, not taking great risks, except for one well-dressed, calm man at the end who might be a worthy opponent. Jenkins, he realised, was drunk, and this affected his playing. He was losing, quite heavily, and was clearly a worried man.

After a while, Jenkins slapped his cards down and stood up, swaying a little.

"Going so soon, Jenkins? We'll be sorry to see you go," said the well-dressed man.

"I am sure you will, but my money is spent."

"Will the landlord not lend you more? You'll win it back, I have no doubt."

Snowden saw uncertainty on Jenkins' face. "No, I cannot borrow any more from that scoundrel. I bid you goodnight."

He left the room. The men around the table exchanged glances and recommenced their play. Snowden slipped through the door and went out onto the street. He saw Jenkins walking slowly ahead of him and caught up with him at the entrance to an alley.

"Mr Jenkins, a word if you please."

Jenkins turned, saw who had spoken and started to walk on. Snowden quickly overtook and stood in his way.

"If you please, Mr Jenkins, this way." He pointed to the alley.

"I have no business with you, Your Honour."

"I believe you do." Snowden moved his coat to one side, and Jenkin's gaze fixed on the pistol in Snowden's belt. "Do not be alarmed, Mr Jenkins, I am sure I have no need of any weapon." He gestured again and Jenkins walked before him into the alley.

"I watched you at cards this evening. I have had some experience of playing, and I marked you out as a frequent loser." He observed Jenkins closely as he spoke. "Is that correct?"

Jenkins looked round for an escape route. Snowden moved a step closer. "Mr Jenkins?"

"It is true sometimes the cards are not as kind to me as they are to other men."

"Is that so?" He moved another step closer. "Can you tell me how this losing at cards is funded?"

Jenkins did not reply.

"Come, Mr Jenkins, we have known each other for a long time. I think you can be honest with me." Snowden, seemingly carelessly, touched the butt of his pistol and remarked, musingly, "A reliable piece, work of art really, a Beretta, my constant companion since I was a midshipman. Seen off many a Frenchman, I can tell you. I remember once, at Bastia …"

Jenkins took a step back, so that he was pressed against the wall. As Snowden advanced, Jenkins gave him a despairing look.

"Theft, Mr Jenkins, is a serious crime. I think you should know the accounts of the estate are under examination, and I am sure it is unnecessary to bring to your attention the conclusions that might be drawn if irregularities are discovered."

"Your Honour, I served your family faithfully for many years, though your father was a difficult Master. I was weak, and I became a devil for the cards, like your own mother, in fact. Some of the paper I issued ended up in the hands of Miller, the lawyer. He told me that either I did as he said or it would be the debtor's prison. I had no choice, Sir."

"Perhaps you did not, Mr Jenkins, perhaps you did not, but there is a path to at least some redemption."

"What is that, Sir?"

"An affidavit, sworn before a duly authorised person, giving account of your actions. I expect to see you at the offices of Mr Dobney at nine tomorrow morning."

Jenkins looked distraught, and Snowden felt a pang of pity. "Mr Jenkins, I am sorry it has come to this. As you say, you served my family faithfully for many years, and if anyone knows of the depredations of the gaming table, I do – my mother, as you said. I promise I will do all in my power to ensure things are as easy for you as they can be."

At nine the next day, Snowden sat in Dobney's office, awaiting Jenkins' arrival. After what seemed like a very long period of silence, Dobney pulled out his watch.

"Half past the hour, I think he has had second thoughts."

"I do not believe it, he had no alternative," said Snowden, and then reconsidered. Jenkins could have run, could even have taken a coaster leaving on the early morning tide.

"Mr Dobney, would you come with me to Mr Jenkins' house? Perhaps we should make sure he has not had second thoughts, or overslept."

Dobney asked the clerks in the outer office for Jenkins' address and they set off along the narrow streets. When they reached the rather mean cottage, the door was open and a knot of idlers stood on the street outside. With a sinking heart, Snowden realised what must have happened.

"He's killed himself, the poor devil."

Snowden and Dobney pushed their way into the cottage. Several men and women were gathered round a figure lying on the floor – Jenkins. Snowden saw the end of a rope hanging over a beam near the fireplace.

"No, he hasn't," said Dobney, as a rasping breath came from Jenkins, followed by another.

"What happened?" the lawyer asked of a woman wearing an apron.

"I came in just before nine, like I always do, to make his breakfast, and there he was, hanging, but his feet were just on the floor. He was struggling hard. I went to the kitchen, got a knife and cut the rope. He fell down, knocked his head on the fireplace pretty bad and just laid there."

She stifled a sob. "Left a note, he did." She pointed to a piece of paper on a desk in the corner and turned back to the drama surrounding the fallen man. Snowden motioned to Dobney, who went over to the desk, glanced at the paper and unobtrusively folded it into his pocket.

Snowden did not feel that they could do any good at Jenkins' house and so they left, shortly finding themselves on the quay. Dobney pulled the note from his pocket and handed it to Snowden. "It is addressed to you, Sir."

Snowden sat on a bollard and read. When he had finished, he returned the note to Dobney, who read it and looked up. "What do you make of that?"

"Well, Sir, it seems to be an admission of criminal behaviour on the part of Jenkins, and in all likelihood a conspiracy instigated by Mr Miller."

"It seems like that to me as well."

"You have the affidavit from Rawlinson with you?"

"Yes," he patted his coat, "I have it here."

"Do you have any advice? Let me know what you think, quickly. I'll not hold you to it."

"It seems to me that Jenkins was the ball in Mr Miller's musket. It would perhaps be difficult to make a watertight criminal case, but the civil matter is different, and I think probably foreclosure is now unlikely, though if Miller fights, and I believe he is an able lawyer, it is possible that he could drag the matter out."

Snowden realised that Dobney was becoming caught up in the excitement of the morning and said "Let us visit Mr Miller and see what he has to say for himself. Will you accompany me?"

"Do you have your pistol?"

"No."

"Then I'll come with you."

"Let's be on our way."

They entered Miller's office, Snowden pushing past Miller's protesting clerk. The lawyer looked up as they entered and, when he saw that Snowden was the reason for the commotion, retreated behind his desk. Snowden felt his anger rise. He pulled out a bag and let golden coins rattle onto the desk. Miller's eyes followed the stream of gold.

"Three quarters' payment, Miller. You will take it and sign a document confirming …" He looked at Dobney, who, picking up the cue, said smoothly, "Confirming that there are no arrears, that you have no intention of proceeding with foreclosure, and that you accept the instalment for the next quarter. The document will also confirm there will be an indefinite holiday on payments of capital and interest." Good man, thought Snowden. Thinks on his feet.

Miller croaked something inaudible. Snowden moved to the sideboard and poured him a glass of water. The lawyer drank and found his voice.

"I can do no such thing. The mortgage is entirely proper and I …"

There was a loud knocking on the office door and Miller's clerk opened it. "A word, Mr Miller. Great importance." Miller left the room. Snowden looked at Dobney, who smiled briefly. Miller returned, looking shaken. Snowden's anger became a tangible thing.

"Not good news, by the look of you – Mr Jenkins, perhaps? We have just come from his cottage."

Miller nodded. Snowden walked to the desk and started to pick the coins up, slowly, returning them one by one to the bag. He looked at Miller. "And what do you think we happened to see on his desk?"

Snowden held out his hand and Dobney passed him the note. "A note, Mr Miller, addressed to me. Shall I read it to you?"

Miller stared at Snowden, his eyes wide. Fear, thought

Snowden. Miller shook his head." There's no need."

"Shall Mr Dobney draw up the document?"

Miller nodded.

CHAPTER 10 – FORTUNESWELL

They had left Plymouth early in the morning, and now, at noon, were a couple of miles off the Devon coast.

"A fine south-easterly, Sir," said Kennedy.

"It is," replied Snowden, making up his mind. "Mr Kennedy, if you please, I've a mind to go ashore briefly tomorrow at Portland." Kennedy looked surprised, but remained silent. "If this south-easterly holds and there is little surf running, I shall go ashore in the bay on the west side of the Bill. I think there will be no need to anchor, we can heave her to. An hour or so is all I need."

Kennedy did not dissent. "Very well, Sir."

They moved to the chart on the table.

As dawn broke, the familiar outline of Portland became visible against the lightening sky. Kennedy shivered. Like any English seaman, he knew of Portland's evil reputation. "I don't like this place, Sir. Any west in the wind, it's a death trap. Very steep to as well, the beach. A man can't get out of the water for the undertow."

"You are quite right, Kennedy, but I believe we shall have no difficulties today. There is hardly any surf on the beach, and the local fishermen have launched their boats."

The ship glided closer in under the forbidding cliffs.

There was a cry from the leadsman at the chains. "By the mark, nine."

"If you please, Sir, I won't take her too far inshore, in case we lose the wind. I think she's close enough now."

"Very well, bring her to and we'll launch the gig. Mr Kennedy, the ship is yours. If the wind comes westerly, please signal the boat to return and take her round to the east side of the island. Take heed of the Shambles and keep her well clear of the Bill. Remember the south-going current."

"I will, Sir."

As the gig's keel crunched on the stones, Snowden leapt ashore and the rowers backwatered, taking the boat away from the beach. He struggled up the steep slope of pebbles and was immediately in the little town of Fortuneswell. In a few minutes he was banging on the door of Jack Stone's parents' cottage. The door opened and Jack's mother appeared, looking at Snowden in surprise.

"Don't you recognise me, Mrs Stone?"

"Good heavens, Percy. Please come in."

The cottage was warm and tidy, with newly whitewashed walls. Jack's father, who had been sitting at the table, rose to greet him. Snowden held out his hand, and Mr Stone took it, looking at his uniform.

"Lieutenant Snowden, it would appear, now. Well done. Please sit down."

"I was passing."

Mr and Mrs Stone looked at him quizzically, and Mrs Stone said, "Passing? Portland is off the usual road."

"Passing, in my ship. She's hove to in West Bay."

Jack's father nodded. "She'll be safe enough there with this wind."

"The reason for my visit – I had a letter from Jack when I was in Bermuda. It must have been written some time ago and I have heard nothing since. I wondered if you had any more recent news."

Mrs Stone smiled. "We do, we have had two letters."

"And is he well, Mrs Stone?"

"He is, Percy, very well. Do you wish to read them?"

"I would like that very much, if you don't mind."

As he read, a glass was put on the table near him. He nodded his thanks and drank. He looked up briefly. "My word, Mr Stone, this is good stuff. Where did you get it?" He realised his mistake as Stone's face broke into a grin. "Sorry, sometimes I don't think before I speak."

He finished reading the letters. "Well, here's a turn of events. He seems to have landed on his feet, and in America as well. I don't blame him for leaving the Navy, he was a great asset, but his heart wasn't in it."

Mrs Stone took one of the letters. "And married, to a Frenchwoman. What do you think of that?"

"I am astonished at the way events have occurred. He seems to have been under the protection of Captain Morlaix of the French Navy and married his daughter. I have come across Captain Morlaix twice, and if his daughter takes after him I think you need have no apprehension for Jack's future. And now, I must get back to my ship."

Jack's father looked at him keenly. "I think it best if I accompany you. The Navy is not always popular here – the press, you understand."

Mrs Stone interjected, "I'll come as well."

They walked quickly to the shore, cresting the pebble slope. Mr Stone halted when he saw *Oleander* hove to a mile or so offshore.

"Well, I'm damned, Percy. That is a fine-looking ship. New, is she? Those great masts, and at such a rake. Fast, I'll be bound, but you'd have to take care when gybing her. You must be well proud."

"She is all of those things, Mr Stone, and we do take care. I was with her when she was built in Bermuda, and brought her back across the Western Ocean. We've been in Devonport as a French privateer gave us a mauling. *Blonde*, you may have heard of her."

The gig was lying a hundred yards or so off the land, the men resting on their oars. Poore at the helm saw Snowden and the boat pulled into the beach. Snowden made his goodbyes, boarded the gig, and within ten minutes *Oleander* was underway, tacking out of the bay in the freshening breeze. Snowden watched Portland fading astern.

"Good run ashore, Sir?" asked Kennedy.

"Very successful, thank you, Mr Kennedy. I may as well tell you I went to visit the parents of Midshipman, or should I say former Midshipman Jack Stone."

"Jack Stone, Sir. I mark the name very well. He was prominent in the affair at Weymouth, and he was with you in Brittany, was he not?"

"Indeed he was, but he was captured by the French. Wounded, and he had a hard time of it. Now, he is in America with a French wife."

He slapped the taffrail. "The daughter of Captain Morlaix of the Republican Navy, Boney's especial friend. Did you ever hear of anything like it?"

CHAPTER 11 – THE DOWNS

The evening breeze was cold, still from the south-east. *Oleander* pitched, occasionally sending spray across the deck. The movement of the ship beneath his feet felt wonderful to Snowden after so long ashore, dealing with unpleasant business.

"South Foreland abeam, Sir."

"Yes, so I see, Kennedy. Time to bear away I believe."

Kennedy gave an order and the ship turned to port, the men running to trim the sails as the wind came aft. "Moving along nicely," said Kennedy, as he watched the shore slide past, the outlines and riding lights of ships in the Downs coming into view.

"Any convenient spot, Mr Kennedy."

"Aye, Sir, I'll slow her down, get the lead going."

In the early hours of the morning, Snowden was awakened by the wind howling in the rigging, and went immediately on deck, in the dark almost running into Kennedy.

"Came up dreadful quick, Sir. I'll call all hands."

Snowden went along the deck, his eyes adjusting to the gloom. A man, just turned out of his hammock, bumped into him. He went forward and felt the anchor cable. It was taut, but there was no vibration from the anchor sliding along the bottom and he went back to the quarterdeck.

"I don't believe she's dragging, Mr Kennedy, but we should get some men forward with axes, just in case."

There was a shout, and Kennedy said conversationally, "We may not be dragging, Sir, but *she* certainly is." A ship, quite a large merchantman, was bearing down on them, travelling at perhaps three knots.

"She'll be on us in a trice. Mr Kennedy, cut the cable."

Kennedy ran forward and Snowden heard the sound of axes striking the cable and then a whistle, followed by a cry, audible above the wind screaming in the rigging, "Cable's gone." Freed from her anchor, *Oleander's* head started to swing. Snowden turned to Kennedy, shouting to make himself heard. "Ken, get the staysails on her. If we port the helm, I believe she'll fall off onto the starboard tack. I'll con her. You go forward and look after the sails."

"Aye, Sir."

The merchant ship dragging her anchor was frighteningly close. Snowden turned to the men at the wheel as he heard the sound of sails flogging forward. "Port your helm, hard over."

He shouted into the darkness, "Back staysails." The sound of flogging sails abated. He looked at the other ship and saw men aloft on her yards. She was very close, but *Oleander's* head was swinging quickly under the influence of the backed staysails and the rudder as the ship started to make sternway. Now, he thought. He shouted, "Sheet home, let draw."

There was a brief cracking of canvas as the staysails were sheeted and began to pull the ship forward. He turned to the helm: "Midships." And as he felt the ship gather way: "Starboard your helm." For an agonising moment Snowden was sure the other ship would collide with *Oleander's* starboard bow, but, slowly, *Oleander's* head veered to port and she swung clear. "North by East when she answers."

Kennedy returned to the quarterdeck, his clothes dripping seawater. "Damned close. I could have leaned over the taffrail and touched her."

"It was, but we'll be ashore if we don't get some sail on her. Reefed mains'l."

There was a shout from the foredeck. "Ship dead ahead, Sir."

For an hour *Oleander* worked her way northward through the Downs, avoiding ships and keeping in the channel between the shore and the offlying sandbanks. At dawn they were hove to off the North Foreland, and by the evening the ship had been safely warped into a basin at Deptford Dockyard.

CHAPTER 12 – THE ISLAND

Snowden's parents sat with Mrs White in the small parlour after dinner. Lord Penzance was dressed in the clothes he had worn during his day in the saddle. He was quiet and soon began to snore gently.

"The harvest, Mrs White?" inquired Lady Penzance.

"I think it will be satisfactory. After Corsica, it seems astonishingly bountiful."

"Corsica is rather a barren place, is it not?"

"It is – mostly mountains. There are some plains, but they are best avoided on account of the fever. There are almost no fields, as you have here. Olives, honey and some wine."

"Is it a large place?"

"Well, it is a large island, perhaps a hundred miles long. Sardinia, another large island, is just south of it."

"I have no clear idea of the geography of that area. Perhaps if we went to the library you would be good enough to show me on a map. We have not had the maps down for a long time." There was a snore from the chair. "I don't believe Horace will miss us."

In the library, which was rather dusty, they stood over a large map laid out on the table. Mrs White pointed with her finger. "This is Corsica. You can see it is quite close to Italy, and to France as well. These are the mountains, most of it in fact.

Sometimes there is snow on the highest peaks all year round. Around the coast there are towns, which are fortresses as well. Here is Calvi, this is Bastia and this Ajaccio."

"Are there many people on the island?"

"According to Boswell, there are about two hundred thousand."

"I remember his book about Corsica – something of a sensation at the time. Two hundred thousand, a large number."

"Yes, but sometimes we are our own worst enemy."

"How so?"

"The vendetta. It is not so bad as it formerly was, but there are feuds between families which pass down through generations and often involve other branches of the clan. It is a curse, there are many murders, and it divides us amongst ourselves."

"You consider yourself Corsican?"

"Yes. I was born in Leghorn, but my husband is Corsican, as was my father."

"And what were we doing in Corsica, us English, I mean? I know the Army and Navy were both involved."

"Why were the English there? Really, I suppose to annoy the French, but as with everything in Corsica, it is complicated. For hundreds of years, we were ruled by the Genoese, or rather the Bank of St George. We Corsicans are famously fractious, but we united and rebelled against the Genoese. We bottled them up in their citadels, and eventually they paid the French to aid them. When the French left again, we beat the Genoese, but they gave us to the French in repayment of their debts. We were sold by our oppressors. The French are now our masters, but for a few years we had our own republic, with a constitution. Now the French have almost extinguished our resistance, and their Revolution was not kind to us. The English have helped us from time to time, but we are a long way from England, and we are only a small pawn in the game."

CHAPTER 13 – DEPTFORD

When he returned to *Oleander*, after a visit to the Dockyard offices, Snowden sought out Kennedy. He found him inspecting the new anchor cable, which was flaked down on the deck.

"My cabin, if you please, Mr Kennedy."

When they went into the cabin, Snowden noticed a pile of letters and packages on his table, and his mood brightened. "It seems the mail's arrived at last."

"Yes, Sir."

"I've just returned from the offices, Mr Kennedy, and I had an interview with the Master Shipwright. It seems they will be on board later to inspect the ship. The Shipwright thinks this will take several days as they wish to do a thorough job."

"Very well, Sir. Is there anything in particular we should do to prepare?"

"I think not, except to make sure everything is in good order."

"Of course."

"There is more. The Controller wishes to compare *Oleander's* performance against other ships, and so I think we will spend considerable time here at Deptford, and probably also anchored at the Nore."

"Very well, Sir. Do you think we'll be able to hold on to the crew, with London so close and other ships working up?"

"We may have a few runners, perhaps, but the ship seems happy enough to me at present."

"She is a happy ship, Sir."

"And the Bermudians are probably likely to prefer to stick together. In any event, I think the dockyard is very interested in *Oleander*, and I expect they will make sure we are fully manned for the trials."

Kennedy left and Snowden turned to his letters, finding two addressed in Jack Stone's untidy and barely legible writing. He had just finished the first letter when he became aware of an insistent knocking at the cabin door. Snowden looked up from the letter, still deep in thought – Jack, my boy, he thought to himself, you've outdone yourself this time. The knock came again, accompanied by Midshipman Poore's voice.

"Excuse me, Sir, but the Master Shipwright and some other people have come aboard. I've been here some time knocking."

"Thank you, Mr Poore, I was reading and didn't hear you. Please show them in."

The Master Shipwright, a tall rangy man who radiated energy, entered, accompanied by two men equipped with measuring tools and notebooks. Kennedy trailed behind, looking harassed.

"Welcome aboard, Mr Parrett."

"Thank you, Lieutenant Snowden, this is the first Bermuda-built ship ..." He stopped in mid-sentence and walked over to a frame which had caught his attention, feeling at the end of a trenail and speaking to his assistants. "Nice work." He turned to one. "Sketch this, if you please." The assistant opened his notebook.

The Master Shipwright looked closely at the timber.

"Close grained, this cedar." He addressed Snowden and Kennedy. "Is there much of this timber on the island?"

Kennedy answered, "A good amount, in my opinion, Sir. 'Tis said it grows very rapid."

"And what were your impressions of the yard?"

Snowden's mind was still preoccupied by the world described in Jack Stone's letter, taken back to the vision of that brightly lit room in Paris and Stone with Dominique Morlaix in her tricolour sash.

"Lieutenant Snowden?" The Master Shipwright's tone was sharp.

"Sorry, Mr Parrett, I have just had some extraordinary news …"

"Yes, very well, but we have a deal of work to get through and your full attention to the matter at hand would be much appreciated."

Snowden glanced at Kennedy, who was making very little effort to conceal a grin. The next few weeks with this martinet would be difficult, thought Snowden.

It was late before he finished Jack Stone's second letter. He sat back, the litter of his solitary dinner on the table before him, and re-read the final paragraph:

I hope you understand, Percy, that I cannot go back to the Navy, and to war. I have seen the tyranny of the French state at first hand. It is something new in the world, and I know it must be stopped. In order to stop the state, however, we must kill individuals, French men and women, sink their ships and lay waste to their country. Even at the risk of disgrace, this is something that I must leave to others. I have found useful employment here with Mr du Pont and intend to stay in the United States with my wife. Perhaps one day you will find yourself in this country, and I hope that if you do, we can meet.

If you have the opportunity, please visit my parents at Portland.

Yours, with great affection.

Jack

Well, Jack, thought Snowden, for a man who despises warfare, you have an exceptional talent for it, and the Navy's loss will undoubtedly be Mr du Pont's gain. He picked up his hat and went ashore to seek entertainment.

CHAPTER 14 – A SECRET

It had become the habit of Lady Penzance and Julia to spend their evenings in the library, which housed an extensive but rather dusty collection.

"Here it is," said Lady Penzance, climbing off a stepladder, holding a book in her hand.

Julia looked round. "What is it?"

"Boswell's book – *An Account of Corsica, and Memoirs of Pascal Paoli*. I knew we had it."

Julia said vehemently, "It is a very good book."

Lady Penzance sat in a chair and opened it. "We've had it in the library for years. I have never read it, but I'll start immediately."

Several days later, they were again in the library.

"I have finished Boswell's book, Mrs White."

"And what did you think of it?"

"I thought it most interesting, but I believe I would find Corsica rather forbidding. Perhaps we could get the large map down again and have a good look at the place."

They stood over the map on the table. Lady Penzance looked at it closely. "Could you point out Corti to me, my dear?"

Julia indicated, "It is here, in the mountains – an

astonishing place, with *such* a citadel!"

"The whole island seems to be fortified."

"It is. There are round towers all around the coast, to watch out for corsairs, the Moors. They were a horrid scourge, and they took many people as slaves."

"I suppose the French will keep them away now."

"Yes, they are afraid of the French, but despite being ruled by a Corsican, the French are not our friends."

"Are they better than the Genoese?"

"I suppose they are, but while they may intend to be more beneficial, they are at the same time more effective, and it is difficult to escape their rule. There are many in Corsica who would fight them if they could."

Later that week, the two women again sat in the library, reading.

"I say, Mrs White, that Mr Paoli (I think that is how you pronounce his name) sounds like a splendid chap, although I rather suspect Mr Boswell is prone to hagiography if he admires his subject."

Julia's face coloured. "Paoli is indeed a very good man."

Lady Penzance looked at her quizzically. "Have you met him?"

"I have, and I know Boswell is right."

"Forgive me, my dear, I have been bursting to ask you for some time, in fact since we have been discussing Corsica, about your family and your connection with Corsica. I understand about your husband, but perhaps you would explain a little more."

Julia did not answer for some time, but stared out of the window. Eventually, she looked at Lady Penzance. "If you wish, I will tell you, but before I do, you must promise to keep what I will say a secret, even from your husband."

"A secret from Horace?" She smiled. "My dear, I have never kept anything from him! You may speak freely. On my honour I will not repeat what you tell me."

"Very well. My grandparents, on my mother's side, were English. My grandfather was charged by our government with some mission to Ferdinand, the King of Naples, and they stayed in Naples for some time. Their daughter, my mother, accompanied them. She was about eighteen years old, very beautiful. At that time there were many Corsican exiles in Naples, and my mother fell in love with one of these, an older man. The relationship was clandestine, and eventually my mother became pregnant. It was clear to my mother that marriage to this Corsican rebel, although he was a cultured man, would be a tumultuous and uncertain business. She was concerned for her child, and her love for the man cooled. There was a Leghorn merchant, Corsican, but a prosperous and stable man, who had fallen for my mother. He agreed to treat the unborn child as his own, and they were married. The marriage was long and happy. He was as good as his word, and I could not have wished for a better father."

"I have heard of such things before, Mrs White, but it is still an extraordinary tale. Do you know who the Corsican was, your natural father?"

"I do. It was Pasquale Paoli."

"My word, how extraordinary. You, the daughter of Paoli. Please continue."

"Many Corsicans came to our house when I was young, and I met and married one of them. He was a ship owner, prosperous, and I thought a reliable man, but shortly after I married him, he placed the business in my father's hands and he became a rebel, and we went to Corsica. It was a heady time, turbulent, my husband fought with the rebellion, and I did as well, sometimes bearing arms like a man."

"And what became of your husband, Mrs White?" said Lady Penzance, fearing the answer she would receive.

"He was captured by the French, betrayed by his countrymen in a vendetta. He was taken to France, to the Château d'If."

"I believe I have heard that name …"

Julia spoke vehemently, with tears in her eyes. "It is a castle on an island near Marseille. It has dreadful dungeons and terrible things happen there." She wiped her eyes. "I went to France, to Paris, to see if I could intercede for him, but I was warned by Lord Whitworth, who had just been insulted by Napoleon, to leave. Whitworth believed there would be war again, and I might be thought of as English. I had to abandon my husband."

"I am sure you did not abandon him. You had no choice."

Julia's face hardened. "I despise the French, and I envy Percy's opportunity to strike at them. Would that I could do the same."

CHAPTER 15 – THE PATENT LOG

The Master Shipwright's inspection was complete, and *Oleander* lay against the wharf in the wet dock at Deptford. In the cabin, Snowden was speaking to the ship's senior people.

"The Surveyor of the Navy has entrusted the Master Shipwright to measure *Oleander's* sailing abilities and, when that is complete, to compare *Oleander's* performance with other ships. This is a great honour, gentlemen, although a deal of hard work will be involved. We will proceed to the Nore, and from that anchorage carry out a series of experiments under the supervision of this dockyard's Deputy Master Shipwright, Mr Briggs. Captain Ackworth, who is an expert in navigation, will accompany Mr Briggs and will be in charge of measuring the ship's performance. Are there any questions? … Mr Poore?"

"Sir, what's in those boxes?" Poore gestured at the polished wooden boxes lashed to the frames at the side of the cabin.

"Instruments, Poore. Captain Ackworth has devised instruments for measuring the performance of the ship, and there is also equipment which may be of benefit to the fleet and which he wishes to assess. I expect you to give him every assistance."

"I will, Sir."

Later that day, *Oleander* slipped down the river with the tide and for two days lay anchored at the Nore, a few cables from the old First Rate moored there as guardship.

They were joined on the third day by Mr Briggs and Captain Ackworth, who had made the guardship their base for the trials, and a pilot, who had an expert knowledge of the London River and Estuary. Under the direction of Mr Briggs, they sailed the ship up and down the channel, Sea Reach, while Captain Ackworth, with the enthusiastic assistance of the midshipmen and a party of seamen, commissioned his instruments.

The principal one was what he called a 'patent log', which consisted of a spinner on a long rope, connected to a counting clock secured to the taffrail at the stern of the ship. Captain Ackworth, a genial man, explained the device to the midshipmen, tactfully making sure Snowden and Kennedy were within hearing.

"As the ship goes forward through the sea, she drags the rope and spinner behind. The rush of water turns the spinner and hence twists the rope and driving the counter."

"Yes, Sir."

Said Midshipman Poore, "There's a picture of such a thing in the new book our captain's just received."

Ackworth looked slightly put out, but asked politely, "Which book is that, Lieutenant Snowden?"

"One I have recently received from America, Sir, by a Nathaniel Bowditch. He calls it the *American Practical Navigator*. I have not had leisure to study it closely, but it seems to be a valuable store of information. There is a new method of lunars. The midshipmen and Mr Kennedy have had sight of it."

"I have heard of this Bowditch book, Lieutenant Snowden, but I have not seen it. How did you come to possess a copy?"

"A correspondent of mine in America."

"I would be most interested in reading it. The lunars would be a valuable thing – nearly all merchant ships, and many of our own, are still navigating by latitude."

The marine chronometer had only just been invented. It was still very expensive, and not all naval ships, and almost no merchant vessels, carried them. Without an accurate chronometer, the only practical method for a ship to determine the time, and hence her longitude, was by taking lunar sights, using a sextant to measure the angle between the moon and a celestial body. Although many naval officers and some merchant seamen, 'lunarians' as they were called, were able to use this method, it was a difficult process, and most ships relied only on calculating their latitude, which did not rely on knowing the time.

"Of course, Sir."

"Now, this log of mine has a refinement which I believe is of interest, especially when trying to get the best out of a ship. If you will look here, there is a hand, like that of a watch." He pointed at the top of the log. "This hand will display the speed of the ship at any instant. I recently inspected a steam engine built by Mr Watts, and have expropriated to some extent what he calls his governor, the apparatus that regulates the steam flow to the machine, and adapted the principal so it measures the speed of the log spinner, and hence of the ship towing it. Lieutenant Snowden, we have a fine gale blowing. Please be so good as to get the ship underway and proceed towards the sea while we set the log up."

The anchor was raised and for the rest of the day *Oleander* sailed up and down Sea Reach, as the log was checked against the speed calculated from the time the ship took to transit posts set up on the Essex shore, which were exactly a mile apart. Captain Ackworth was completely absorbed in his work, and the midshipmen followed him around, making notes, sighting along the compass to check the ship's progress against the measured mile markers, and comparing the 'Ackworth', as they had begun to call the patent log, with the traditional ship's log, which consisted of a knotted rope streamed astern, the knots being counted against a sand glass. The ship's carpenter fixed an instrument – a clinometer, Ackworth called it – near the binnacle and this displayed the angle of the ship's heel. Another instrument, an anemometer, was installed on a post on the poop, with which Ackworth intended to measure the pressure of the wind. From time to time they anchored the ship so the rate of the tidal current could be measured, measuring the depth with a Massy sounding machine, which the Navy was proposing to adopt.

As dusk fell and they were making their way back to the Nore anchorage, Snowden and Kennedy were concentrating very hard on conning the ship along the narrow channel, which, despite the late hour, was crowded with shipping entering or leaving London. The ship was moving well, hard on the wind, with the wake hissing, and Snowden was about to take some sail in when there was raucous cheering from the log on the poop and Midshipman Poore appeared beside him.

"Ten knots, Sir, by the Ackworth!"

"Very good, Mr Poore, she is moving well."

"The Deputy thinks she may be the fastest ship in the Navy! What do you think of that, Sir?"

Poore thought better of what he had just said: "Begging your pardon, Sir."

"Pride in one's own ship is a virtue, Mr Poore, but we must not let our enthusiasm run away with us. Mr Kennedy, tops'ls if you please."

CHAPTER 16 – THE SCHEME

Lady Penzance was not quite sure how she had become so interested in Corsica, but she found herself once again in the library, discussing the island with Mrs White.

"It must be very frustrating to the Corsicans, Julia, that they cannot strike a blow against the French."

"It is, Lady Penzance, but we are not organised enough on the Island, and our weapons are inadequate, and many have been confiscated by the French. We can annoy them to some extent, but that is all."

"Is there no latter-day Paoli to lead you?"

"There is not. We have many factions and we fight ourselves as much as the French. We have no organisation. In order to fight the French, we must be organised."

"Could you not fight the French outside of Corsica?"

"How do you mean?"

"Well, the British Army has regiments who are not English. Irish, Scotch, even Indian. Could it not recruit Corsicans and have a Corsican regiment? Your countrymen seem to be brave fighters, and the British Army is, I understand, very well organised."

Julia's face became animated. "There already is a Corsican regiment in the British Army!" She stood up in her excitement "The Corsican Rangers. A small regiment, I think, perhaps a few hundred men. I do not know where it is presently, but it was in Egypt when Napoleon was there. It could be expanded, or a new regiment created. I am sure there would be difficulties, but, as you might say, there is something to build on."

"How many men do you think might volunteer, Julia? Corsicans, I mean. Would they be frightened that the French would punish their families in their absence?"

"I do not know. I should think a large number. Times are hard and the prospect of pay would be attractive. It is not so easy for the French to make reprisals, because they do not have many men on the island and they would rather the country remains calm. If they aroused a new rebellion, much effort would have to be diverted from the war elsewhere to suppress it, even if it eventually failed."

Lady Penzance's eyes were ablaze with excitement. "It seems to me that considerable difficulties would have to be overcome to organise such a thing. Firstly, a credible ambassador would be required to reassure potential recruits. It might be a matter of convincing the women as much as the men. Secondly, there would be the question of transport off the island."

Julia leaned forward. "I think these difficulties could be overcome. I do not know about the ambassador, but I think my husband's ships could assist with transporting the men from the island. Your cousin, Lord Whitworth, might be a useful ally."

"I should think he would be. Perhaps we should go to town."

A few days later, after breakfast, Lady Penzance spoke to her husband.

"Horace, have you made any progress in finding a replacement for Mr Halstock?"

Lord Penzance's face dropped. "I have tried, the position

has been advertised, but the response has been disappointing. In fact, there has been no serious response at all. I am afraid we have frightened men off. My treatment of Mr Halstock will be well known, and perhaps even some rumour of Mr Jenkins' unfortunate behaviour will be abroad. I have been so relying on Mrs White that I have persuaded myself she might stay for a long time. She is a marvel."

"She cannot stay here forever."

"I know, but if she leaves before we have another man in place, there is a good chance we will be in dire straits before long. I just do not have an aptitude for the business. You should have heard her yesterday when we were in town, dealing with the corn merchants. I believe they did not know what had hit them."

"Horace, I hope you will not take exception to this, but I have asked Mr Jenkins …"

"Jenkins, he …"

"Sit down, Horace, and hear me out. I have some sympathy with Mr Jenkins. He and I share a certain weakness. I believe that my own difficulty has been overcome …"

"You mean your money's run out."

"Horace, that was a dreadful thing to say. I have not sat at a table for more than a year now. If I had a mind to, I am sure I would be able to borrow enough to raise a stake of some kind. I do not say that you have stopped drinking because the butler holds the liquor from you."

"I apologise. But Jenkins? He was a capable man in his own way, and I own, for most of the time he was here, he acted honestly. But how will we know that he does not revert to his former ways?"

"I do not believe he will revert. He was here, yesterday, in a very menial capacity, as an assistant to the tranter, who was making a delivery. Julia and I spoke to him and we believe he would jump at the chance to resume his employment here.

It seems to me, Horace, that we do not have much choice. We do not seem to be able to find an alternative, and Julia will not stay here forever. As for the possibility of embezzlement, you will have to audit the accounts. I have discussed this with Julia and she thinks you will have to have a formal meeting every week, at which Mr Jenkins will present the accounts and you will examine them with him."

"You and Julia seem to have things pretty well sorted out."

"Indeed we do, Horace."

Lord Penzance knew when he was beaten. "I suppose I should interview Mr Jenkins."

"You should – he will be here later today." Lady Penzance looked at her husband. "And, Horace, Julia will instruct you in the auditing of the accounts. It is not difficult, for anyone with a clear head, but it will require strict attention to detail."

Penzance sighed. He would miss Julia.

CHAPTER 17 – TRIALS

For the next few days, *Oleander* sailed up and down Sea Reach, and then further into the Estuary, sometimes anchoring while instruments were calibrated or to wait for the tide. Experiment after experiment was conducted. The ship's speed was recorded for every change in wind strength and direction, sails were set, reefed and handed. *Oleander's* trim was adjusted by the crew moving shot fore and aft, and side to side, an experiment so promising that *Oleander* went back to Deptford and took on a quantity of iron bars which were secured low in the hold.

"She'll be stiff as a church with that weight down there," remarked Kennedy to the Deputy, as they took *Oleander* back out into the river.

"I'm sure she will, and really it is cheating, but it will make for some interesting trials."

When they took the ship further out into the Estuary, despite the assistance of the pilot, Snowden found the burden of simultaneously handling the ship in accordance with orders from the experimenters and conning her to avoid other shipping and shoals extremely taxing.

Though the crew was tired, there was no grumbling, even when the ballast had to be shifted about, and Snowden was impressed by the interest the men took in the experiments and their evident pride in the performance of the ship.

One morning, *Oleander* was heading west from the Nore, when the Deputy Master Shipwright came up to Snowden, who was looking intently at the set of the sails.

"A pleasant morning, Lieutenant Snowden."

"Indeed, Sir. How is the work progressing?"

"Very well. In fact, I would say we have gained a good deal of excellent information."

"It is certainly most interesting to see the art of sailing a ship enhanced by the application of science."

"It is, and in this age we must be sure to make use of the latest techniques."

"I have a friend who worked with the American, Mr Fulton, in Portsmouth."

"I have heard a good deal of his work, the torpedo."

"The thing that my friend spoke most of was Mr Fulton's steamboat."

"Mr Fulton has built a steamboat?"

"I believe he has, but I do not know the details. I understand he demonstrated it to Bonaparte, when he was in the French employ."

"Has he? I have some experience of steam engines. Captain Ackworth and I were until recently at Portsmouth, where we are installing a system, driven by a steam engine, which will produce blocks for the Navy. The system was invented by Monsieur Brunel and manufactured here in London by Mr Maudsley. Ackworth and I also visited Mr Watt's Soho Foundry in Birmingham, where we saw a demonstration of his steam engine. All of these men are aware that a steam engine could be used to drive a ship, but they have not put the idea into practice."

"Well, according to my friend, Mr Fulton has demonstrated such a machine on the Seine, at Paris. It was apparently not appreciated by the Corsican, and Mr Fulton repaired to Portsmouth."

"That is well. A ship driven by a steam engine would

have a decided advantage against even a fast sailer such as your *Oleander*, Lieutenant Snowden."

"I know it would. Even *Oleander* cannot sail directly into the wind, or move when there is none."

"I think, Lieutenant Snowden, when today is over we will have gained sufficient confidence in our instruments that we will be able to move to the second part of the trials, which as you know will involve taking the ship to sea and assessing her performance against other vessels."

"Yes, Sir."

They spent a few more days alongside at Deptford, and then sailed in company with several other ships, which had all been recently overhauled in the dockyard, the largest being *Phoebe*, said to be the fastest frigate in the Navy.

For the next two weeks, *Oleander* sailed under the direction of the Deputy Master Shipwright, with Captain Ackworth acting as commodore of what he called the 'experimental squadron'. Though they could see the low coast of Suffolk a few miles away, the squadron kept the sea and did not land. Officers and crew were kept busy working the ship, and the midshipmen taking copious notes. Buoys were laid as marks and the ships were sailed as fast as possible on courses around them determined by the Deputy. It was exciting and *Oleander's* crew entered into the spirit of the work with great enthusiasm.

Nevertheless, by the final day, Snowden felt exhausted with the work and the constant vigilance necessary, and he knew the crew was almost as tired as they had been when they worked the pumps all the way across the Western Ocean.

The Deputy came up to him as he was leaning on the taffrail as the ship made her way homeward along Sea Reach, overtaking the merchant ships making their way into London.

"I expect you are glad our experiments are over, Lieutenant Snowden."

"It has been most interesting and even exhilarating, but I confess very hard work."

"I think you probably have the fastest ship in the Navy, Lieutenant Snowden, and an excellent crew."

"I believe that is so, Mr Briggs, there is certainly nothing in the experimental squadron that can touch her. In a small ship, the men know each other very well, and I believe they are often more cheerful."

"Mr Henslow, Surveyor of the Navy, will be disappointed, I believe."

"Why so?"

"He was the designer of *Phoebe*, specifically intended to be fast."

"He had a hand in *Oleander's* plans as well, did he not?"

"He did, but *Phoebe* is his especial favourite."

"I think, Sir, there probably has never been a ship that has been so worked up for fast sailing. We have had a month doing almost nothing else, and Captain Ackworth's instruments have shown us what adjustments are of service. I never thought I would see a ship go at fourteen and a half knots."

"Briefly, Lieutenant Snowden, only briefly, but nevertheless I concede that the 'Ackworth' did register that speed."

CHAPTER 18 – COASTING

"By sea or by land, Julia?" asked Lady Penzance.

They were again in the library. Mr Jenkins had been employed as factor, and Lord Penzance closely tutored on how he was to supervise the accounts. Mr Jenkins was extremely contrite and grateful beyond measure for the opportunity he had been given, so unexpectedly.

"I would prefer to go by sea to London, Lady Penzance, but perhaps we should reserve our final judgement. We have to go to Plymouth to get the coach in any event, and there will be a choice of shipping there."

"I would also prefer the sea route. I have had some diabolical experiences on the roads to London. I have also had some unfortunate times at sea, but, on the whole, I prefer the latter."

The passage to London in *Kim* was fast, with a brisk south-westerly behind them. They decided not to go ashore at Deal and travel onwards by coach, as some of the passengers did.

"I have done it before, Julia. The luggers that take one ashore are most uncomfortable, and they land on the beach, through the waves, and then the coach journey to London is not trivial."

As they sailed into the Thames, the ship's mate said to the

women, "Look astern now, Ladies. I'll warrant you'll never again see a ship moving like that."

The ship, a low-hulled schooner with tall, tremendously raking masts, heeling to the wind with a huge wave at her bows, and flying a large ensign and a broad commodore's pennant, was catching *Kim* as though she was hove to. Before long, the schooner was abeam, and suddenly Julia grabbed Lady Penzance's arm.

"That's *Oleander*, Percy's ship."

"My word, Julia, I believe you're right." Unthinkingly, Lady Penzance jabbed the mate hard in the ribs. "My son's ship, Mister Mate."

"I heard you, My Lady." He sounded slightly aggrieved.

"And there he is, standing on the deck!"

Kim's Master noticed the excitement and walked over to join them.

"Your son's ship you say, Madam? She's a fine sight."

"That's my son on the deck."

"Let's see if we can attract their attention." He turned to the mate. "Strike the bell, if you please, Mister."

CHAPTER 19 – SEA REACH

"Sir," said Midshipman Poore on *Oleander*'s quarterdeck, "that ship is hailing us."

Kennedy turned and heard the sound of a bell ringing on the small merchantman they were overtaking. There was a knot of people at her taffrail, with two women among them waving vigorously.

"Damned if I know what the commotion is."

"I do," said Poore. "That's the Old Man's mother."

"So it is, Poore." He turned towards Snowden. "Sir! There! Your mother."

Snowden, who was deep in conversation with the Deputy and Captain Ackworth, looked round sharply and followed Kennedy's outstretched arm.

Aboard *Kim*, passengers and crew watched as, with extreme rapidity, the schooner's foresail was dowsed, the topsails backed and her speed matched to that of the coaster. She ranged close alongside and they saw Snowden lean against the taffrail and take a speaking trumpet from a young man.

"Good day. Mother. Where. Are. You. Bound?"

Kim's Master handed Lady Penzance a trumpet and she lifted it hesitantly.

"Hold it to your lips and shout, My Lady. Talk real slow."

She did as instructed, and on *Oleander* her voice could be easily heard. "Percy." Snowden winced as a tide of unsuppressed laughter ran round the ship. "We. Are. Going. To. Mrs Lightfoot's."

"Very. Well. Mother. I. Will. See. You. There." He turned to Kennedy. "Get the topsails on her, if you please."

"Aye aye, Sir."

That evening, Snowden dined with the other officers of the experimental squadron's ships, a rather raucous affair at which Mr Briggs gave a surprisingly amusing speech, and, even more surprisingly, presented Snowden, or rather *Oleander*, with a brass plaque, no doubt manufactured at great speed in the dockyard's foundry.

HMS Oleander

Fastest Ship in the Trials Held off Harwich

Snowden smiled.

CHAPTER 20 – PAOLI

Mrs Lightfoot was a relative of Lord Penzance. The branch of the family from which she came was notoriously impecunious, and it had been well pleased by her marriage to Harry Lightfoot, a prosperous City man. The house gave off an air of understated wealth, the atmosphere was calm and the household operated with unobtrusive efficiency.

Lady Penzance and Julia were sitting with Mrs Lightfoot and her husband after dinner, while their daughter played the piano. Harry Lightfoot looked at Lady Penzance.

"I have not previously given the matter much thought, but after what you have told me, I entirely sympathise with the Corsicans. I am, however, worried about this house becoming a focus for what I might, probably unjustifiably, call 'agitation'. In all my business life, I have endeavoured to keep politically neutral."

"I completely understand, Mr Lightfoot," Lady Penzance replied, knowing very well that Mr Lightfoot did not scruple to court influential people, of any party, in pursuit of his business interests. "And I can assure you we will do nothing to bring disrepute or even controversy to your door."

"I am very glad to hear that, Lady Penzance. However, as I said, I am sympathetic to your cause and, if it becomes necessary, I will be perfectly content to make a financial contribution, so long as it is done with complete confidentiality."

Julia spoke: "Thank you very much, Mr Lightfoot, but at

present there is nothing to fund."

In the morning, after Mr Lightfoot had departed for the City, Julia and Lady Penzance were sitting at a small table in a room at the front of the house, with large windows looking out onto the street, opening their mail.

Julia opened the only letter addressed to her, and gasped.

Lady Penzance looked at her. "My dear, what is it? Not bad news I hope?"

"No, Lady Penzance, it is a reply from Pasquale Paoli, asking me to attend on him this afternoon at South Audley Street. Is that far?"

"Not far, Julia. We can take a cab."

"Will you come with me?"

"Of course I will, my dear."

"Thank you, I will feel much better if I do not have to go alone."

At South Audley Street they were admitted to a room where Paoli sat at a desk. He was an old man, but vigorous, and as soon as Lady Penzance saw him she was struck by his resemblance to Julia, an impression that was strengthened as they conversed and his intelligence and quick wit became obvious. His English was perfect, with almost no hint of an accent. There were two other people in the room, middle aged – James and Sarah Burney, brother and sister. Lady Penzance was speaking of the meeting with *Oleander* in the Thames.

"She was going so fast, much faster than any of the other ships nearby, there was a great wave at her bow. I must confess I felt a stirring of motherly pride when I realised it was Percy's – I mean Lieutenant Snowden's ship. And there he was, on the deck. I saw him speak to Mr Kennedy, the Master, you know, and in an instant, men were running about on her, the sails were taken in and she slowed down and came near our ship."

James Burney seemed to come alive and leaned forward. Talk of a ship, thought Lady Penzance, that's got your attention, and she realised she had been so fixated on Paoli that she had not recognised Burney as a seaman.

"Your son, Lady Penzance, is that the Snowden who burnt the invasion barges in Brittany?"

"Indeed it was, Mr Burney."

"A smart piece of work."

Paoli interjected, "I should have liked to have been a fly on the wall of the room when Buonaparte was informed of it!"

Lady Penzance asked Burney, "I take you for a naval man, Mr Burney."

"Indeed I am, Lady Penzance, or rather was. I have not had a ship in years as I am not always in favour with Their Lordships."

Lady Penzance forbore to ask why, but Paoli interrupted, laughing, "Because Their Lordships have the good sense not to want any republicans commanding their ships."

Lady Penzance found it difficult to contain her surprise. "A republican, Mr Burney?"

"Indeed I am, Lady Penzance, or rather was. The events in France have greatly cooled my ardour in the cause of revolution, but I am an admirer of the American system, and indeed the Corsican system introduced by Signor Paoli."

Paoli looked at Julia. "Your husband, Julia, I have heard he was held in the Château d'If." He grimaced. They both knew of the place's horrible reputation.

"He was, Signore, and I was in Paris, trying to intercede for him, when I was advised to leave and came here. I do not know where he is now."

She spoke now in what Lady Penzance assumed to be the Corsican language. *"Signore, I would like to speak privately with you."*

Paoli looked surprised and, after a short conversation in Corsican, the pair stood and Paoli said, "Mrs White asks that I speak to her in private. Please excuse us."

Lady Penzance saw again the similarity between the pair as they left the room. She also noticed that Burney seemed to understand the conversation.

"You understand Corsican, Mr Burney?"

"I understand Italian, Lady Penzance, which is pretty similar."

"Are you familiar with any other languages?"

"I am. Indeed, I am one of only a few Englishmen who speak Tahitian!"

"Tahitian?"

"Yes, I have travelled to the Pacific, twice in fact."

"Twice to the Pacific? But it seems you are out of favour with the Admiralty?"

"Less so than formerly, Lady Penzance, but I believe I will not have another ship."

"That is a shame, Mr Burney. I know a seaman craves a ship above all else. Percy scarcely has the time or inclination to think of anything else, unless it is playing at cards. I suppose your service was of great interest?"

"Indeed it was, great interest, though I must admit I share Lieutenant Snowden's enthusiasm for cards. I went to the Pacific with Captain Cook."

"Upon my word! With Cook? To the South Seas?"

"I had that honour, twice, and mark my words, it was an honour to be with that great man. The saddest day of my life was when I saw him killed upon the beach."

"You saw him killed? How dreadful. While we await our Corsicans, perhaps you can tell me of your voyages?"

Burney, once warmed to his task, was a good storyteller, and his sister frequently made amusing contributions to the narrative. After a quarter of an hour or so, Lady Penzance asked, "Mr Burney, are you related to our celebrated novelist, Fanny?"

"We are, Lady Penzance, she is our sister."

"They are such wonderful books, so true to life and amusing."

James Burney cleared his throat. "Sarah has also published a novel, and is working on another."

"I have not read your work, Mrs Burney."

"I am somewhat overshadowed by my illustrious sister, Lady Penzance, but pray continue with your account of Captain Cook, James."

They conversed for more than an hour, when Mr Burney said, "I wonder what our two Corsicans are discussing. I hope they are not starting one of their famous vendettas."

At that moment Julia and Paoli re-entered the room. Paoli addressed the Burneys and Lady Penzance: "I apologise for deserting you, but Julia and I found we had much to discuss."

Lady Penzance looked at Julia, who gave her a brief nod.

"Not at all, Signor Paoli. You have some very interesting friends. We have been transported to the South Seas while you were in the next room."

The Burneys left shortly afterwards, and Julia, Lady Penzance and Paoli sat together at a table.

Paoli spoke: "Julia has told me, Lady Penzance, that I am her father."

Lady Penzance could not help herself. "Indeed, I think you

are. If you could see yourselves together, you are alike as two peas in a pod!"

"I too can see the likeness. I held your mother in high esteem, and it was a great sadness to me that our friendship came to an end. It was hard on me at the time, but she was probably right. My life has often been filled with danger and upheaval, and I do not think her spirit was adventurous. I know she fell heavily for Mr Bianco."

He looked down. "He was a good man, but I cannot help thinking of what might have been. Since your mother, I have never considered marrying." He paused. "It grieved me, greatly, to think I had no offspring, but now I find that I have a daughter."

There was another long pause. Lady Penzance could see his eyes were filled with tears. He spoke rapidly to Julia in Corsican, and Julia stood up.

"Lady Penzance, Signor Paoli has asked me to stay here and take dinner with him. I think, if you do not mind, it would be best if I accepted. It will mean you have to travel home alone, but it is not far."

"Of course, my dear. I quite understand you would wish to spend some time with … with Signor Paoli. I will leave now. Shall I send the gig round to collect you? Perhaps ten o'clock would be convenient?"

CHAPTER 21 – PLANNING

The following day, Julia, Lady Penzance and Paoli sat at the small table in Paoli's house in South Audley Street. Though they had decided not to make their relationship public, Julia and Paoli seemed to have grown used to the fact of its existence, and there was now an easy familiarity between them, probably, Lady Penzance realised with a jolt, more intimate and easier than her own relationship with Percy.

"I am still worried about this, Julia. The risks are considerable," said Paoli, "but nevertheless, I admit the scheme has considerable merit, I think even more than you realise. Our men are remarkable fighters, and an additional or enlarged regiment of Corsicans, properly officered and supplied, would be a formidable addition to British forces. In addition, the knowledge that our men were fighting in a single regiment, with recruits from the several areas of Corsica, might serve to unify the country somewhat. I think perhaps you overstate the opposition that might be met from the men's families. Many men already risk their lives by fighting the French irregularly, with no great prospect of success."

He paused. "There are also practical difficulties. The men will have to be recruited and then taken off from the island. I do not know how that is to be arranged, but any large-scale intervention by the French could be disastrous. I believe our next step must be to ascertain whether the British would welcome more Corsicans into the Army."

He looked at Lady Penzance. "I think, Lady Penzance, you should informally introduce the matter to your relation, Whitworth. I can write a letter for you to take to him. As Julia knows at first hand, he is very knowledgeable about the state of affairs in Europe, and, especially after that incident in the Tuileries, has no love for Buonaparte. I think his support, if he gives it, will carry much weight."

Some days later, Snowden visited his mother and Julia. He was in very good spirits and told the two women of the plaque his ship had been awarded.

Lady Penzance interjected, "The Master of the ship we were in said he had never seen a faster ship or one so smartly handled. He said *Oleander* is a credit to you."

"It is very good of him to have said so, but *Oleander* really *is* the fastest ship in the Navy. After all the trials we have done, we know exactly how to get the best out of her in all conditions. I don't believe a ship was ever so worked up before, and the crew is magnificent. The Bermudians were an unknown quantity to me, but they have performed extremely well. We have had very few runners, even though we are close to the attractions of London, and indeed the blandishments of the captains of nearby vessels who are short of prime seamen."

Julia smiled. "My husband, the ship owner, always said that the crews of ships reflected the competence of the Master. A good captain invariably has little trouble with his crew."

Julia's praise made him unreasonably pleased. "Mother, Julia, you are making me blush, but Julia, I take your point. However, our crew has no pressed men, which always makes the ship happier."

"Do you know where you are to go now, Percy?" asked his mother.

"We are in Deptford for a few more weeks and then we are

ordered to the Mediterranean station. I do not yet know exactly where we are to go, but there is much work in blockading the French. As you know, Boney believes he can invade us if his fleet can get out and hold the Channel for a few days. I am sure he is wrong, I think he would have to hold it for months or years, but nevertheless we must keep them bottled up. We will undoubtedly go first to Gibraltar, and I expect we shall be part of a convoy escort on the way."

He looked his mother in the eye. "Mother, I have been wondering why you have accompanied Julia to London. Of course, it was very surprising to see you on the deck of that coaster, but, leaving that aside, you have not in the past been much of an enthusiast for the town."

"Percy, I know what you are worried about, but you may have no fear that I am here to play at cards, and indeed our presence here is occasioned by a much more serious motive. Percy, Julia and I have been having a most interesting time. We are to see Whitworth on the day after tomorrow, you know, our relative …"

"Yes, I met him in Paris."

"We have, I suppose, been dabbling in politics, and we are intending to discuss a scheme we have devised, concerning Corsica."

"Corsica, Mother? I had no idea you were even aware of its existence." Snowden's surprise was evident.

"Don't look so shocked, Percy. I think perhaps, Julia, we should tell Percy something of what we have been doing."

"We should, Lady Penzance, but first I must ask, Percy, that you give us your word that you will keep this completely secret." She smiled at him and he suddenly realised that the phrase 'winning ways' was not an empty one.

"Of course, Julia, you have my word. But secret? What are you up to?"

"You know I am a Corsican, and you know the condition of my country, ruled by the French."

"I do. We rather abandoned the place, but I think we had no choice. I hope you do not mind me saying so, but it seemed rather a savage island to me, though I probably did not see it at its best."

"Well, my countrymen try to fight the French, on the island, but it is very difficult for them. They are not well organised, but the French are, and strong. They confiscate our arms. And now, we have thought, or rather it was your mother's idea, that there is a way of striking at our oppressors." She spoke forcefully, and Snowden could see the passion behind her words.

"We cannot effectively fight the French on the island, but I have no doubt there would be many Corsicans who would seize the chance to fight them elsewhere. There is already a Corsican regiment in the British Army, and our scheme is that a large number of Corsicans could be recruited, and that they could become a useful part of the British Army. We have spoken at length to Signor Paoli about it."

As Snowden listened, he knew he could easily fall under her spell. He turned to his mother. "My word, Mother, did you really think of that? How extraordinary! Well, I know the Corsicans are excellent fighters. I have seen for myself they often want for organisation, but of course the British Army has that in ample supply." He paused, thinking. "Perhaps there is something in what you are suggesting. You say you have spoken to Paoli? He must be very old now."

Lady Penzance replied, "We have, Julia in particular has his ear." I can believe that, thought Snowden.

"It seems to me there would be formidable difficulties ..."

Julia interposed, "We know well there are formidable difficulties, but pray continue, Percy."

"I have not heard before of this Corsican regiment in our

Army. I do not definitely know but I should think the military would welcome more Corsican volunteers. However, to assemble the men and get them off the island would be difficult work. Persuading our government of the merits of the scheme and even bringing it to their attention will also be difficult. How will you do that?"

Julia looked at him. "As your mother said, we are due to interview Whitworth the day after tomorrow, to introduce the scheme to him, to gauge his reaction and to see whether he might be willing to promote it to our statesmen."

Snowden felt as though his world had been turned upside down. He could not recall his mother ever showing any interest in politics, and here she was, plotting with foreigners to raise a regiment. If anybody could make it work, he thought, it was Julia.

CHAPTER 22 – THEIR LORDSHIPS' PLEASURE

Oleander was almost ready for sea when the summons came.

"I am ordered to attend at Their Lordships' pleasure, Mr Kennedy. I should be back tomorrow, or perhaps the day after."

"Very good, Sir."

"As you know, the main priority is those smashers. It has been very good of the Master to let us have them, and we must make sure they're installed to our satisfaction."

"I am still concerned about all that weight so high up in the ship, Sir."

"I know you are, Kennedy, but there is not much point having the fastest ship in the Navy if she has no teeth, and those Carrons are pretty light, and the mounts are works of art, though the yard has agreed to more iron ballast."

"Yes, Sir. If I may make so bold, can you tell me why you are summoned to Whitehall?"

"I would tell you if I knew, Kennedy, but I do not have any idea."

"Aye, Sir, I hope you have a pleasant time of it. The gig is ready and the tide's just on the turn."

The boat wound its way along the crowded river, swept

along by the spring flood. There was, thought Snowden, something particularly pleasant about being rowed up the river in his own gig. The boat was smartly turned out, as were the men, and Midshipman Poore, at the helm, was fairly bursting with pride as he put the boat alongside at Whitehall Stairs. As he stepped out, Snowden said, loudly enough so the men could hear, "Thank you, Midshipman Poore, the boat and crew are a great credit to the ship."

"Er ... thank you very much, Sir."

At the Admiralty, Snowden was ushered into a panelled room with a long table. He sat for several minutes until the door opened and four men walked in, two in uniform and two in civilian clothes. One of these was obviously a clerk, carrying a bundle of papers. Snowden stood and almost involuntarily sat again in astonishment as introductions were made. The men in uniform were Sidney Smith, Hero of Acre, and Captain Wright, Smith's assistant, rumoured in the Navy to be more spymaster than sea officer, and the civilian George Canning, Treasurer of the Navy.

Smith addressed him: "Lieutenant Snowden, I would like you to tell us, briefly, of your service."

Snowden, startled, wondered why the Hero of Acre would be interested in his naval service, and he started, hesitantly. "Well, Sir, I went into *Agamemnon* at twelve years old ..."

He ran through his service in various ships, and noticed the clerk apparently checking what he said against a document.

Smith interrupted, "You are familiar enough with the Mediterranean, I suppose?"

"I believe so, Sir."

"What do you know of Italy?"

"I have spent some time along the coast, and some time in port, mostly Leghorn and Naples. I think I know the coast reasonably well, but of the country inshore I am rather ignorant, as I speak little Italian, and did not stray far from the ship, though I have been inland as far as Florence."

"And Corsica?"

"Corsica, Sir? I was there for several months in *Agamemnon*, a long time ago, Bastia, Calvi, and have touched with it in various ships since."

"Do you know much of the political situation in Italy?"

"Not very much, Sir. I know most of the states are run either by the French or by their puppets. I am not sure the French are always popular, but I do not know definitely."

"Very well, Snowden, would you be so good as to tell us of your recent service in Brittany?"

"You mean the barges, Sir?"

"I do, Snowden."

"Well, Sir, I, I mean rather Mr Stone …"

"Mr Stone, indeed. I think Captain Wright and I share some experiences with that gentleman – we have had the pleasure of being a guest of the French government in the Temple. Please continue, Lieutenant."

"Mr Stone realised that the canal we had seen on our way to Paris …". Snowden related, briefly, the story of the raid on the invasion barges.

When he had finished Smith asked him, "Your ship, *Oleander*, what do you think of her?"

"She's a marvel, Sir, Bermudian built, and with an excellent crew, Bermudians mostly. I believe she's the fastest ship in the Navy, and we know exactly how to get the best out of her. We've established it scientifically."

Canning spoke for the first time. "I admire your enthusiasm for your ship. I have had sight of the reports of the trials, some excellent work has been done there."

"Yes, Sir."

Snowden saw Smith look at Canning and Wright, and they rose, excused themselves and left the room, which became very quiet, except for the scratching of the clerk's pen. Snowden asked him, "Do you know what all this is about?"

"I'm afraid not, Sir. I have only been called in to record the meeting."

"Very well," said Snowden, privately thinking 'lying dog'.

Snowden was left in puzzlement for only a few minutes before the naval officers and Canning re-entered the room. Canning nodded to the clerk, who handed Snowden a document. Snowden took it and suspected he had passed some sort of test. He immediately realised what the document was – his orders.

"I suggest you read your orders, Snowden." Snowden broke the seal, and read:

... proceed with all despatch to the vicinity of Corsica by such ports as are convenient for the replenishment of stores or water. At Corsica you are to render such assistance as may be required to Captain Burney's party ... and then proceed to Malta ...

Snowden thought, Corsica, and then Malta. But what was this party he was to assist?

Smith looked at him and smiled. "Snowden, before we go any further, you must understand that secrecy is of the greatest importance. The situation in the Mediterranean is very fluid and great discretion will be required of you."

"I understand, Sir."

"Fluid elsewhere as well," Canning said.

Smith continued, "Indeed, the general situation is not greatly to our advantage. Nearly everywhere is under French rule, directly or indirectly."

"Yes, Sir."

"Lieutenant Snowden, I suppose you already knew of Signora Bianco's scheme to raise a regiment from the men of Corsica?"

"I did, Sir, but ..."

Smith cut in. "The Corsican Rangers were useful in Egypt, many of them motivated by family feuds against the Buonapartes. You may as well know that I am to command an inshore *fleet* in the Mediterranean, to conduct combined operations against the French." Snowden noticed Smith put particular emphasis on 'fleet' and remembered that his boastfulness was well known in the Navy. "The raising of local troops is to be an integral part of my operations, and I've a mind it will help to do Boney some serious mischief. In short, Signora Bianco's scheme is in line with my own thinking, and I believe it is a thing that should be tried."

Smith continued, "An additional or enlarged Corsican regiment would work very well, especially if we cast the net more widely than the family enemies of the Buonapartes. I intend to recruit from Calabria and Sicily as well. The imposition of foreign rule, even enlightened revolutionary rule, and even if it throws off some despised monarch, is frequently not popular, and we have already had some serious armed resistance to the French. With my inshore fleet, properly organised, the opposition will be most effective."

"I see, Sir."

"Who is to be in Captain Burney's party that I am to convey to Corsica and assist when it is there?"

"Captain Burney himself – he volunteered and speaks Italian and is a friend of the Corsican leader – and Mrs White."

Snowden gripped the arms of his chair – Julia!

"And a Corsican general, Bartoli."

Canning spoke: "To be more specific – we consider the best plan of action is for a covert ambassador, or perhaps more properly a recruiter, to visit the island to gauge the support for such a scheme, and, if there is substantial support, to actually recruit men who can be taken off by our ships. The scheme has the support of our military friends. The preparations necessary for taking the recruits off Corsica will be made in Malta, and there are orders for the Navy there to provide all that is required. Depending on the size of the levy, several ships might be needed."

"Lieutenant Snowden, we have chosen you for this operation for several reasons. Firstly, you have shown yourself to be a competent officer, able to work on your own initiative …"

"Thank you, Sir."

"You have some knowledge of the area, and your ship is efficient and well worked up." He looked into Snowden's eyes. "And, importantly, you have some prior knowledge of the scheme we intend to put in hand."

"I suppose I do, Sir."

CHAPTER 23 – PASSENGERS

Snowden was at breakfast in his cabin when Kennedy knocked on the door.

"Sir, there's a man from the dockyard aboard who says he has orders to convert the cabin into accommodation for passengers, including a lady."

"I know, Kennedy."

"Passengers, Sir, and a lady?"

"Those are our orders, Mr Kennedy."

"And what about you, Sir?"

"I will make do as best I can. I suppose I shall sleep in the gunroom."

"In the gunroom, Sir?" Kennedy sounded horrified.

Snowden smiled. "Hard times are upon us, Mr Kennedy, we must improvise."

The work took two days, and when it was complete, *Oleander* left her berth at Deptford and caught the morning tide to take her to sea. She worked her way round the North Foreland and anchored in the Downs. Kennedy was irritated by the delay.

"Why did our passengers not board at Deptford? We are wasting a good breeze."

"A matter of secrecy, Mr Kennedy. Deptford undoubtedly has its complement of spies. Keep a good eye out for that coaster,

Kim – you remember, the one my mother was aboard of."

"I remember the ship all right, Sir. Do you know when she sails?"

"She sailed this morning. She will anchor at the Nore tonight and should be with us tomorrow, in the forenoon."

"Aye, Sir, I'll make sure a good lookout is kept."

Next day, *Kim* anchored about a mile off, and the gig was sent to collect the passengers.

"Shall I rig the chair, Sir, if a lady is to be coming aboard?"

"Have it ready, Mr Kennedy, but if I am any judge, I expect the lady will climb aboard like the men."

He was right. Julia, who was dressed in red pantaloons, did climb aboard, and it was General Bartoli, a rather stout man, who made use of the chair. Snowden was relieved to see Burney was not wearing a uniform. As he showed the party into their accommodation Burney looked at him.

"Snowden, I won't have this. I'll not turn you out of your own cabin. I'll sling a hammock in the gunroom." Snowden started to protest, but Burney held up his hand. "I'll not hear of it. *Oleander's* your ship and you must have her cabin."

Secretly relieved, Snowden gave way. "Very well, Captain Burney."

The passage down Channel was uneventful, *Oleander* running fast before the northerly wind. Snowden took her well to the west, into the broad Atlantic, before turning south, the instinct to avoid the lee shore of the Bay of Biscay strong within him. They sat at dinner in the cabin, Snowden, Burney and Julia.

"Our General does not seem to like the weather much," said Burney, as he deftly caught a dish which was sliding across the table.

"He does not," said Julia. "I think he had become too

comfortable in London to enjoy the prospect of this adventure very much."

"Paoli chose him, though," said Snowden.

"Yes, he did," said Burney. "Bartoli is younger than Paoli, and I believe Paoli still thinks of him as a vigorous youngster. I am sure you have done the right thing, Snowden, to take her right out here. We'd be feeling the pinch if we were just off Ushant, though she's a fine weatherly ship and I'm sure she'd claw her way off in pretty well anything."

"I think she would, but it is best not to tempt providence for the sake of a day or so. And what of our mission? Are you still confident of its prospects?"

Burney gestured to Julia, who answered, "I am, Percy, I think we stand a chance of recruiting a good number of men, who will be able to damage the enemy."

Snowden began to look forward to the evenings in the cabin, with Julia and Burney. Burney was an astonishingly accomplished man, an excellent seaman (he often took a watch for himself, a much appreciated contribution) and an amusing raconteur. His accounts of his voyages with Cook were spellbinding.

"We'll ruin it, of course," he said, speaking of the South Pacific, "although in my view it is not altogether the paradise it is made out to be. Human sacrifice, that sort of thing. Often the natives are in an almost constant state of war, especially it seemed in New Zealand. A little like the Corsicans," he said, looking at Julia. "An astonishing thing to my mind is that the people of those parts populated the islands, and there are many of them, by sailing to them. Sometimes the boats are quite large, but they are able to navigate from island to island in ways I don't really understand. No chronometers, no quadrants or sextants, no navigation tables. I say, Snowden, you think your ship is fast, but you should see the canoes, double ones they are, in Tahiti. They'd show *Oleander* a clean pair of heels." He took a piece of paper and drew a double canoe with a strange-looking sail.

"That is a remarkable craft," said Snowden. "Perhaps we should build something like it."

"Perhaps you should. Speaking of remarkable craft, in the Sandwich Islands they have flat little boats, almost like wide planks, and they wait just offshore for waves, there's almost always a big ocean swell there, and then they ride down the front of the wave as it breaks, often standing up on the boats. It is a truly astonishing thing to watch. They do it just for pleasure, but a great deal of time is spent on it, by both men and women."

He drew again, and Snowden and Julia looked and listened as he drew and described the various native craft he had seen during his voyages with Cook – kayaks in the far north and junks with high sterns and strange but effective rigs in the east.

At other times, Snowden readily accepted Julia's offer to give him instructions in the Italian language, and these lessons strengthened the bond between them. She concentrated on speaking of the history and geography of Corsica and of her role in fighting the French. Englishmen often disliked the French, but the hatred Julia displayed towards them was of an entirely different order. When he thought of it, it made him shudder, but he realised that if similar feelings were widespread on the island, it would not be just the prospect of regular pay that would recruit men for the British Army.

When General Bartoli recovered, they played at whist after dinner, always speaking Italian, or at least the Corsican version of it. At Snowden's insistence, they played for tokens and no money was pledged. Before long, Snowden came to appreciate that Burney was an exceptional card player, and a friendly rivalry emerged between them. They soon realised Bartoli cheated whenever he had the opportunity.

"Why does he do it?" Snowden asked. They were a hundred miles or so north-west of Cape St Vincent, and Burney was taking the watch.

"I'm damned if I know," replied Burney. "He's not anywhere clever enough to get away with it, but I think stupid enough not to realise it."

"It's not as though there's any material gain."

"I think he just cannot help himself. I have a great admiration for Paoli, but I think in this situation he has made a mistake by choosing him."

He raised his head and shouted, "Mister Poore, that leach is flapping like your mother's washing line, have the men sweat the foresail peak up a little, if you please." He turned to Snowden and said quietly "Excusable in a midshipman, perhaps, but now he's Master's Mate …"

Snowden grinned and went back into his cabin.

CHAPTER 24 – THE RIFLE

Snowden was an enthusiast for drilling the ship's company. The great guns were exercised every day, usually with shot and powder, the operation supervised by Snowden and Trott, the Gunner, with a note kept of the time taken to ready, load, fire and reload. When weather permitted, a barrel or some other target was floated overboard, and when the ship had been turned to run back down on it, men practised aiming and firing the guns with the ship rolling in the seaway.

Snowden racked his brains to think of interesting exercises for the men. Boarders were repelled, other ships were boarded, casualties were taken below, and instruction was given in the use of cutlass and pike. A favourite with the men was practising with small arms, pistols and muskets.

One day, after the main armament had been exercised and the guns secured, the men were drawn up on the maindeck. Snowden, his back pressed against the main shrouds, addressed them.

"As many of you have noticed, Captain Burney here has an interesting new weapon to show you." He turned to Burney, who had a long gun in his hands, which had been the subject of considerable interest while Snowden was speaking. "Captain Burney, please continue. And step forward, Sergeant Riley."

"Thank you, Commander. This is a Baker Rifle," Burney held up the gun, "named after its creator, one Baker. It has a groove inside the barrel which makes the ball spin, and it flies very true. The rifle is much more accurate than a Brown Bess. It is quite slow to load, as the ball with its patch is a tight fit in the barrel."

He handed the rifle to Sergeant Riley. "A heavy piece, Sir."

"It is Riley, but very well thought out. On the butt, there …," he pointed, "you will see a small hatch. Open it, Riley, if you please." Riley examined the gun, found the hatch and opened it. "A cleaning kit is kept in this little compartment." Riley withdrew some small items and held them up. "It is essential to keep the bore clean, or the powder dross will fill the grooves."

"We have been gifted a number of these rifles by a benefactor, and our Commander has agreed that some will be issued to marines and seamen. Sergeant Riley will now load the rifle."

Burney helped Riley to load the gun and turned to Snowden. "Commander, if you would be so good as to have a target released, I will try my poor best to demonstrate the weapon."

Burney took the rifle from Riley and waited in the lee chains as the target floated past, allowing it to get a good distance astern before he fired. Staves flew off the barrel as the rifle ball hit it, and there was a cheer from the men who were crowding along the rail.

Sergeant Riley and ten men, five marines and five sailors, were designated riflemen, and they spent the next few days practising with their new weapons, rapidly gaining efficiency in their handling and in accurately shooting from the decks and from the tops.

CHAPTER 25 – CORSAIRS

Oleander was ten miles from Gibraltar, beating into the Strait against a levanter, when there was a shout from the masthead: "On deck there!" Snowden looked up. There had been frequent sightings of ships as they closed with the Strait. "Frigate two points on the port bow, she's heading towards us I reckon."

A frigate. Very unlikely to be an enemy, but in the fine gale blowing, the distance between the two ships would reduce rapidly and it was best not to take chances. He was just about to send the crew to quarters when there was another hail from the masthead: "British, I reckon."

Snowden turned to Midshipman Pascoe, who had appeared, telescope in hand. "Up you go, Pascoe."

Pascoe hurried to join the lookout in the foretop, and trained his telescope on the ship, the sails of which were now visible from the deck. Snowden saw him talking to the lookout and then shout down to the deck, "British. 34 guns." They saw flags break out on the British frigate. Snowden sensed movement by his side, turned and saw Julia.

"*Pegasus*, she's one of ours. Gibraltar patrol, we'll speak her shortly. I think Clasby has her now."

"You know him?"

"I do, we were in *Agamemnon* together. He was senior midi, had a bit of difficulty getting his ticket, but he's a good practical man. I think you should go below, even in that costume," he gestured to her pantaloons. "He's an eye for the women, and we don't want to advertise we've one aboard."

Oleander reduced sail and the British frigate ranged alongside. Snowden looked at her critically. "Looks like he keeps her up nicely, bit of money to spend, rich family."

He moved to the taffrail, speaking trumpet in hand. After the formalities were complete Snowden shouted, "CLASBY, YOU'VE GROWN."

"SNOWDEN, BY GEORGE THAT'S SOME SHIP YOU HAVE THERE. YANKEE?"

"BERMUDIAN."

"WHERE BOUND?"

"FLEET AT HYÈRES." This was a lie, but it was one his orders expressly told him to tell.

"NOT GIB?"

"DIRECT."

As the ships started to draw apart Clasby shouted, "FRENCH FRIGATES – ACTIVE NEAR TOULON." Snowden waved his hat and *Pegasus* tacked smartly and headed towards the European coast.

The wind dropped in the night, and at dawn, as the eastern sky lightened, the ship was completely becalmed, her yards, despite the sweated up sheets, creaking slightly as she rolled in the swell. As was the invariable practice of all ships at dawn in the Royal Navy, *Oleander* was cleared for action, hammocks lashed along the rail, the decks sanded, with matches smoking beside the guns. So dark was the night that the ship had been cleared mostly by touch, and almost silently. Snowden could not see them, but he could visualise the crew at their quarters, tense because they all knew there had been reports of the noise of unseen ships nearby in the night.

Without warning, several things happened at once. There was a shout from somewhere forward "Starboard Bow", and from that direction came more shouts in what Snowden knew to be Arabic. Suddenly a pair of galleys became visible, silhouetted against the eastern skyline, perhaps two cables length away.

He heard Kennedy shout "Steady, you men" and then he saw and heard the splashing of the galleys' oars as they got underway. Kennedy, his face now visible in the pale light, turned to Snowden: "Corsairs, by God."

The galleys were now gathering way, heading to pass one either side of *Oleander*. Snowden shouted "Guns!" Trott was by his side almost instantly. "Stand by to put shots across their bows. Reload the main armament with canister if you please. Smartly now."

"Aye aye, Sir."

Trott darted off and Snowden heard activity around the ship as his orders were carried out. He noticed Burney on the quarterdeck, rifle slung over his back, sword at his side.

"We have a treaty with them, Snowden, but they don't seem friendly."

Snowden didn't answer, but he agreed, the galleys had seen *Oleander* and were deliberately heading towards her. There could be no innocent explanation.

"Take the trumpet forward, Burney, and tell 'em we're English."

He heard Burney shouting from the bows, but the galleys did not alter course, and their oars did not alter their rhythm. When they were two points off the bows he shouted "Guns, the Carron, across one of their bows."

There was a pause, and then the gun fired, loud in the calm weather. Still the galleys came on. Kennedy, keenly observing the galleys yelled "Down" just before the gun in the bow of one galley fired, followed by its counterpart on the other galley, sending shot whistling over *Oleander's* deck.

Snowden felt the familiar excitement rising. He shouted "Canister, as you bear. Careful now." The only gun that could bear was the port smasher on its swivel mount at the bow. He saw the gunners reload, their movements fast and precise, but unhurried, and Trott patiently sighting along the barrel, his hand on the elevation screw. The smasher fired, sending an enormous swathe of grapeshot into the galley off the port bow, but although the devastation must have been terrible amongst the men on the deck, and some of the galleys' oars paused, they came on, altering course so that they were headed directly towards *Oleander*. Snowden realised what they intended and turned towards Kennedy.

"Kennedy, they're going to try and board us over the bows." He shouted "Stand by to repel boarders, forward." He ran forward, cutlass in his hand and reached the cathead just in time to see a man in a colourful turban, a knife in his teeth, climbing from the galley's bow onto the hook of *Oleander's* port bower anchor, which overhung the ship's side. He pulled out his pistol and shot at the man, who dropped silently into the sea, but others followed him, to be met with a hail of shots from *Oleander's* crew. He saw a man behind the little swivel on the galley's bow swing the gun towards *Oleander* and grabbed the arm of Riley, the marine sergeant who was getting off his knee after reloading his rifle, and pointed. "Get that bastard, Riley."

"Don't mind if I do, Sir."

Riley's rifle fired and the corsair dropped, pulling the gun up as it fired, its shot thudding into *Oleander's* foremast.

"Shot, Riley."

But Riley was already on his knee, patiently reloading. The foredeck Carron fired again, the shot going high but taking down the galley's masts and yards which fell in great confusion amongst her crew. Suddenly, Snowden realised the other galley had backed off and was making its way along *Oleander's* starboard side, the oar blades almost touching the ship's hull. He screamed, "Guns, starboard side."

Oleander's main armament fired, one gun at a time. The broadside may have been puny in comparison with that of larger ships, but it was well aimed and hideously effective. Snowden saw the grapeshot smash into the galley, breaking oars and killing men. He looked upwards and saw Burney with his sharpshooters in the maintop, taking careful aim at the galley with their rifles, and at the rail General Bartoli was firing his pistols, a sword at his side and a long knife tucked into his belt. The galley, her starboard oars disabled or unmanned, drifted into *Oleander's* starboard quarter, and Snowden ran back as he saw corsairs begin to climb aboard the warship. They had no chance against the defending crew, and suddenly the pirates broke, hurling themselves back aboard their galley, which limped slowly off, propelled by only a few oars. Snowden looked forward and saw the other galley, or rather the wreck of it, backing away from the ship, sped on its way by jeers and musketry from *Oleander*.

He turned round and saw Julia in her pantaloons leave the cabin and walk past the men at the wheel. Shocked, he realised her white shirt was patterned with blood and that she carried a cutlass with a stained blade. He grabbed her shoulders, but she shrugged him off, her eyes bright with excitement.

"Julia, what has happened?"

"I've been fighting a Moor, Commandant, like a Corsican."

"A Moor?"

"The one that came in through the cabin window. He is still there, though his roving days are over. And the ship, she is secure?"

"I believe so, Julia. They had no chance really."

Snowden felt a puff of wind, turned and saw Poore nearby, sighting along his pistol at the departing galleys. He shouted, "CEASE FIRE!" And then to Poore, "Put that thing down, Mr Poore."

"Aye, Sir."

"Kennedy, get the rags on her."

Whistles blew and the ship came alive in the freshening breeze. Warrant officers came to report: "No water in the hold."

"Some small shot in the foremast and foretopsail yard, but she'll do for now."

"Foresail and foretopsail will need taking down and patching."

"Second bower cable cut."

And then, the one Snowden was waiting for, the Surgeon's Mate.

"Well, Butterfield?"

Butterfield smiled. "Almost nothin', Yer Honour. Four men with slight injuries, none serious, no dead."

Thank God for that. Kennedy was at his shoulder. "Resume our course, Sir?"

"Yes, Kennedy, if she'll lay it."

"I believe she will, Sir." He nodded towards the galleys, now about half a mile away, raggedly rowing southward, towards the African coast. "Bastards never stood a chance…"

Julia, standing nearby, interjected loudly and with considerable emphasis, "We can catch them, kill them all."

Snowden, startled at being contradicted on his own quarterdeck, was momentarily unable to think of a reply. Despite his instinctive hatred of piracy, he had had enough of massacre and had no intention of risking his ship and men, who he knew would not approve of such a deliberate slaughter, especially as there was no prospect of prize money. However, he did not relish the prospect of arguing the point with a passenger in the hearing of the crew, and he was greatly relieved when Burney arrived, his rifle still on his back. Burney looked at Julia in her bloodstained shirt.

"Julia, they have to work the ship. Let us go to the cabin, out of their way."

Snowden, nonplussed, thought of the cabin's occupant. "Burney, I believe there's a dead corsair in the cabin, so that may not be appropriate."

Julia looked at Snowden and grinned. "I apologise, Commandant. If Captain Burney assists, I will deal with the cabin."

Snowden, relieved, turned to Kennedy, "You have her, Kennedy. I will visit the wounded."

That evening, with the ship making good progress on her east-north-easterly course, Snowden sat at the cabin table with Burney and Julia.

"Why did they do it, Burney," he asked, reflecting on the action at dawn, "attacking a King's ship like that? They must surely have known no good would come of it, from their point of view, that is. Outnumbered, outgunned. It was a stupid, dismal thing."

"I believe they mistook *Oleander* for a Yankee, a merchantman at that. We have a treaty with them, but now the Americans are independent they consider them fair game. But I think I have an explanation as to why they do it in the first place. If you will excuse me briefly, I think I have a book in my cabin with a pertinent section."

He returned moments later and started leafing through the book he had brought.

"Ah, yes, here it is. This is what the Ambassador of Tripoli said to Mr Jefferson, now the American President, when he was asked why the corsairs behaved as they do:

"'The Ambassador answered us that it was founded on the Laws of their Prophet, that it was written in their Koran, that all nations who should not have acknowledged their authority were sinners, that it was their right and duty to make war upon them wherever they could be found, and to make slaves of all they could take as Prisoners, and that every Musselman who should be slain in battle was sure to go to Paradise'."

Snowden shook his head at the stupidity of it. He felt exhausted, drained, even more than he usually did after an action, and he could see Julia felt the same way, but Burney was animated, excited by the prowess of his riflemen. Bartoli was asleep in his chair.

"I wish them the best of luck with the Yankees. I have no doubt the Americans won't put up with any interference in their trade, and I'll warrant we'll be seeing the stars and stripes here before long. Julia, tell us of your own encounter with the corsair."

"There is not much to tell. I was in the cabin, out of the way, as ordered, when a man climbed in through the cabin window. It was dark in there and he did not see me, until my cutlass was in his belly. These Moors are a curse to Corsica and I am sorry we left any alive."

"Julia, I have to obey my orders. Our principal enemy is France and I cannot risk the ship and men by choosing to take action against corsairs. Defending ourselves against them is one thing, actively pursuing them quite another. More of them could have appeared, the wind could have dropped, and it could have ended badly."

"I know you are right, Percy, according to your duty. I am very sorry I remonstrated with you."

Snowden excused himself and went on deck. He walked

forward, praising men who he had seen do well in the action.

"Well done, Riley, a good shot, saved a few men I think."

"Thank you, Sir. That rifle's a wicked thing."

"It is, isn't it? Devilish accurate."

"Sir, is it true what they say about Mrs White?"

"I don't know – what do they say about Mrs White?"

"Killed a pirate, Sir, ran him through with a cutlass."

"That, Riley, is true enough. He climbed off the galley and through the cabin window, so it was his own fault. It was dark and she waited till he was right on her."

"God bless my soul, Sir. I've seen they Corsicans fight, at Bastia, but what a woman!"

Snowden, well aware he was adding to a myth, added, "She wants a rifle and bayonet now, so she doesn't have to get so close to any boarders and risk ruining her clothes."

CHAPTER 26 – LEGHORN

The high mountains of Corsica were in sight as they finished Sunday service. Snowden was about to dismiss the ship's company when Trott raised his hand. "May I speak, Your Honour?"

Snowden feigned surprise, but he knew full well what was going on, as the Gunner had sought his prior approval. "Very well, Mr Trott, what is it?"

"Sir, you know I daub a little." From what he had seen, Snowden knew him to be a talented artist. "Well, Sir, I've painted this, and Chippy's made a frame for her, and if you please, I'd like to present it to Mrs White, with the compliments of the ship's company."

Snowden nodded to Julia. She stepped forward and accepted the painting from Trott, who removed the cloth covering it. Julia looked at the painting and smiled. It was not a conventional portrait, showing as it did, Julia on *Oleander's* deck after the action with the galleys, in her trousers and white shirt, leaning on a cutlass with its point in the deck. She was smiling, with her hair escaping from the bandana in which it was tied.

To an outburst of cheering, she held it aloft so the ship's company could see it.

"Thank you, Oleanders", she exclaimed, "thank you."

In the succeeding days, Snowden kept *Oleander* well off the western coast of Corsica, suspicious of the cloudless, bright blue sky.

"Looks like a Mistral sky to me," he said to Kennedy. "We'll be in for it directly, if I'm any judge."

"Mistral, Sir?"

"Wind that blows down the Rhone, and north-westerly or westerly when it gets here. Often uncommon strong."

"How long do the Mistrals last, Sir?"

"Could be two or three days, Kennedy. We'll keep her well off in case anything breaks. Nasty lee shore, the west coast of Corsica."

The loss of a spar or sails would be dangerous if the ship was close to a lee shore, especially as the shore was Corsica's unforgiving west coast, steep and rock bound, with little shelter. Snowden thought of it with a shudder.

For three days *Oleander* laboured in the Mistral, the bright sunshine and blue water belying the strength of the wind and power of the waves, but it was declining as they approached Leghorn and anchored in company with several merchant ships. There was considerable swell in the anchorage, which seemed to have discouraged the flotilla of bumboats which usually swarmed around men o' war. Snowden was rowed ashore, the men and boat smartly turned out, but since Poore's promotion, the boat was commanded by Midshipman Pascoe.

The boat entered the breakwater and Snowden, accompanied by Burney, made his way to the office the Navy maintained in the town, in the house of the British Consul. It was manned by a Lieutenant, Forbes, who had an air of resignation about him.

"We won't be here long; in fact, I believe, Snowden, that we will be gone next month. No work for me to do, you see.

The Grand Duchy of Tuscany is increasingly under the sway of the French, and you probably noticed there are few British merchantmen alongside."

Burney asked about warships victualling.

"Hardly any, Captain Burney, it's not like it was. Snowden undoubtedly remembers replenishing here when we were involved in Corsica."

"I do", said Snowden, "and great fun it was as well."

Forbes nodded, and exchanged a smile with Snowden before continuing, "But times are so uncertain that *Oleander's* the first man o' war we've seen for three months. The trade of the town is really suffering and there's a lot of discontent. Place has always been heavily dependent on British trade, one way or another."

Burney leaned forward. "Look here, Forbes, we have some really confidential business to conduct."

Forbes nodded. "I thought as much."

"Is your consul reliable?"

"Well, the consul, who had been here for years, has returned to England, and an Italian, Signor Andretti, represents our interests here presently. He appears to be a sound man, but perhaps I would not push his loyalty too far. He must after all be mindful of his business interests."

"Can we meet him?"

"I will enquire whether he is in."

Forbes left the room via a door whose opening gave a brief glimpse into a well-furnished house. Snowden started to speak, but Burney put his finger to his lips, leaned forward and said softly, "Be careful what you say here, Snowden. I am wary of the situation."

Snowden nodded. Minutes later, the door re-opened and admitted Forbes and another man, large and prosperous looking. Introductions were made, and Burney spoke quietly to Andretti, "Signor Andretti, I must ask that everything that passes between us remains confidential."

"You have my word, Sir."

"Is Marco Renzi in the town?"

Andretti's face briefly registered surprise. "I believe he is, Captain Burney, unless he has left since last night. I dined at his house. We Corsicans are a small community here."

"I did not realise you were an islander, Signor Andretti."

"Well, I was born here, but my family is Corsican, and I consider myself to be of that …", he paused and drew himself up, "nationality."

Burney looked at Snowden and gave the slightest of nods. "And the ships Renzi manages?"

"I believe he keeps them in good order, though with the pressure not to trade with the British …"

Burney reached into his coat. "I have a letter here which I ask you to give him. Personally, if you would be so good."

Snowden spoke: "Lieutenant Forbes, I have a list here of stores for *Oleander*, a pretty short list, it must be said, but I would very much like to have it fulfilled. Now, I don't know if you can help me with this, but I'd like to avoid bringing the ship alongside. The men are quite restive, and as we're rather undermanned, I don't want any runners. Would you be able to arrange a lighter or two?"

Forbes looked at him quizzically. Snowden knew what he was thinking. Small ships were generally happier than large ones, and given that an unhappy ship with a desertion problem reflected badly on her captain, Snowden's admission that his small ship was unhappy counted against him, and he saw the distaste in Forbes' glance. Burney, who was the originator of this subterfuge, designed to keep *Oleander's* mission secret, added,

"There are some truly bad apples in the ship's company, I fear. Lieutenant Snowden brooks no dissent, but he has his work cut out to keep them in order."

"I see," said Forbes, scarcely bothering to hide his distaste, but looking at the list. "There is nothing here that should cause difficulty. I think two lighters will suffice, and the swell has almost gone now."

The first lighter arrived alongside *Oleander* at noon on the next day. It would have seemed to the casual observer that the ship was not ready to receive the stores, so that by late afternoon the lighter was only half discharged. Marco Renzi had come aboard *Oleander* as soon as the lighter was made fast, and Snowden showed him to the cabin, where Julia, Burney and Bartoli were waiting.

As soon as Renzi saw Julia he rushed forward and embraced her. They spoke rapidly in Italian, too quickly for Snowden to completely understand, but the general gist of the conversation was that two of Julia's ships were alongside in Leghorn, their cargoes discharged, and nearly ready for sea. The discussions took the remainder of the day, and Renzi, who had impressed Snowden with his energy and ready understanding, left with the second lighter.

Oleander weighed anchor as soon as it was dark and headed south-west, towards Corsica.

CHAPTER 27 – MACINAGHJU

The northern part of the island of Corsica is not far from the Italian coast, and *Oleander* idled away the night and the following day between the islands of Gorgona and Capraia, about twenty miles from Cape Corse, the northernmost point of Corsica. The time was not wasted, however, as there was much work to be done. In the cabin, plans were discussed, revised and finalised, and on deck Snowden and Burney worked with Sergeant Riley, his marines and a group of seamen.

A light wind was blowing from the west in the late afternoon as they got the ship underway, heading south-west. As darkness fell, they saw the land silhouetted against the setting sun. Snowden pointed. "Cape Corse, Mr Kennedy, I recognise it well from my *Agamemnon* days."

"Yes, Sir."

"Unpleasant place in any sort of breeze, as I recall, wind funnels through between the land and the island offshore. There are little round forts on every headland, built by the Genoese. We fired on some of them to chase the French off."

Oleander forged ahead and as they drew closer to the land they used the patent sounding machine, which could measure the sea's depth while the ship was underway. The warm soft breeze drove *Oleander* steadily onwards, silent except for the splash of her wash and the occasional conversation of crewmen, who could be vaguely discerned on the deck in the faint moonlight.

Snowden was leaning over the taffrail in the warm darkness, thinking of the operation to come, when he felt Julia join him. For a moment they were silent, their arms touching as they leant over the rail, looking at the dark line of the land.

"I will miss you, Julia," he said.

"I'll miss you too, Percy. It seems a long time ago that we met at Trevennec."

With a start, Snowden realised he had not thought of home for a long time, so involved had he been with the ship and her business. "Let's hope the estate is running smoothly."

"I'm sure it will be. Your inheritance is safe!"

"But will you be safe, Julia?" He regretted the words as soon as he had uttered them. In Brittany, he had known the loneliness and fear of small-scale operations away from the routine and order of the ship, and Julia had experienced partisan war. She must be fearful of what was to come, but he knew there was no point in trying to persuade her not to land in Corsica.

"I will do my best to avoid harm, Percy, but sometimes things that are worth doing are dangerous."

"I know. Burney is a good man. I think you will be able to rely on him."

Suddenly, she embraced him, holding him tightly, and whispered in his ear. "Thank you, Percy."

There was a footstep nearby, and Julia released Snowden.

"Excuse me, Sir," said Kennedy, clearly determined to ignore the scene he had just witnessed. "Shall I reduce sail?"

"Yes, Mr Kennedy, reduce sail."

Julia squeezed Snowden's hand and went into the cabin.

Oleander slipped in towards the land, her boats towing behind her, the guns run out and the men standing by. Snowden climbed to the foretop, racking his brain for memories of the place. Suddenly he realised that the land they were closing with was an island, an island with a tower on its peak. He climbed down the shrouds and quickly walked back to Kennedy, who was standing with Burney near the wheel.

"We're on course. That island, there, you can just see the Genoese tower on it."

They were using the leadline now, and he was interrupted by the leadsman's chant, "By the mark, ten."

"Slightly the worse for wear after *Agamemnon* gave it the benefit of a few broadsides. There's another one on the headland over there. No need to go too close, bring her round two points to port."

Oleander slid along under mainsail alone, just off the coast, and, at a high headland topped with another tower, turned to starboard, the afterguard listening to the leadsman's muted calls. The land seemed very close and they could hear the soft noise of waves breaking on the beach, dimly visible ahead. On the port bow they could see the faint lights of a village.

"By the deep, five. Sandy."

"Macinaghju, Mr Kennedy, we have arrived. Bring her to and anchor. Keep the mainsail on her, scandalised."

"Aye, Sir."

CHAPTER 28 – LANDING

With Julia at his side, Burney watched as the ship crept under a headland with the round tower at its peak silhouetted against the stars. To port, he could make out dim lights and knew them to be in Macinaghju, a little harbour. After a while, above the slight noise of *Oleander's* passage, he heard the sound of breaking waves and made out the pale gleam of a beach ahead.

On the passage out, he had felt, after so many years of disfavour with the Navy, a sense of belonging, of being a useful part of a ship's company. How he had missed it! And now he had to abandon the ship and her orderly ways and go ashore, to a country he understood only slightly, with a people who had a reputation for savagery and of bearing grudges down the generations. He shivered and checked his weapons, easing his rifle strap against his shoulder. He wore a rudimentary naval uniform which at a casual glance would pass for civilian clothes, but which, if he was captured by the French, would help him justify his actions as those of a naval officer engaged in a legitimate act of war. The alternative, as both Sidney Smith and Snowden's friend Jack had discovered, could land him in the Temple, or worse.

The ship turned into the light wind and anchored. He heard Kennedy say, "Holding, Sir," and Snowden's response, "Very well, Kennedy, embark the shore party." How many times in his youth had Burney thrilled to those words? When he was a young man, with Cook, setting out in the boats had represented the start of new adventures, new sights, smells and experiences. True, there had always been danger, from an unexpected breaker on a beach, a poisonous snake or warlike inhabitants, but this was different. Snap out of it, he thought, as he watched Bartoli and his two servants climb into the boat.

Without any noise, the boat set out for the beach, her passage occasionally betrayed by splashes of phosphorescence from the oar blades as they dipped into the water and then the indistinct outline of the boat on the beach. He saw the boat returning and was gripped with a great feeling of unease.

To Burney's surprise, he heard Snowden say, "Sergeant Riley, stand by."

"Aye, Sir."

There was a muted patter of bare feet on the deck and an occasional clink of weapons as a party of men made its way to the chains. Snowden came over to Burney and Julia.

"I am sorry, but I have been deceiving you."

He saw Julia start. "Deceiving us, how?"

"As you know, I'm a gambling man, much like you, Burney." Burney nodded in the darkness. It was true they were both excellent gamblers, and Burney had even written a short book about it. "I think I have learned to read men to some extent, and I do not trust your General Bartoli."

Julia replied, perhaps rather too quickly, "He is an old comrade of Paoli, my father."

Burney said, thoughtfully, "Go on, Percy."

"It is hard to say what might motivate treachery, and I may be entirely wrong, but as I say, I do not trust the man, and while it is in my power, I intend to take precautions. Bartoli was very insistent we landed at Macinaghju, and I believe that if he were bent on treachery you would be at your most vulnerable when you first landed."

"He cannot be a traitor, he cannot," said Julia.

"Let us hope you are right, but I am going ashore." Snowden turned to Sergeant Riley. "Shore duty, Riley."

"Aye, Sir. Come on you men, you know what to do."

The men moved softly over the deck to the chains, their bayonets glinting in the starlight, and climbed down into the boat. Snowden turned to Kennedy. "You have her, Kennedy."

"Aye, Sir."

"Do not put the ship in any danger. She is your priority, Kennedy."

"She will be, Sir, but best of luck."

CHAPTER 29 – BETRAYAL

As the boat neared the beach in the darkness, Snowden strained his eyes to make out the terrain. Gradually, it began to correspond with his memory of the place, a memory sharpened by the scent of the vegetation on the offshore breeze. There was the high headland, with the tower on top of it, there was the bank of seaweed behind the beach, with a field and a grove of trees behind it.

The boat grounded gently on the beach, and Snowden and the men disembarked, their bare feet almost silent on the sand. The boat backed off and the shore party surmounted the little seaweed cliff, and, with only a whispered command or two, settled into the bushes at the edge of the field, waiting.

More faint lights appeared in the town, giving the impression of activity, and after an hour or so, Snowden was nudged by Riley, who was lying beside him, pointing with his hand. Snowden nodded. Men could be discerned walking along the beach, from the direction of the town, and as he watched he made out the figure of Bartoli.

"A large welcome party, Sir" whispered Riley.

Snowden nodded. "Pass the word, be ready."

He saw Bartoli's men stop and lie down on the sand, their long guns pointed towards the ship. There was the sudden glow of tinder and a flame, and then a dim light could be seen, shining towards the ship and silhouetting the portly figure of Bartoli who was holding it at arm's length.

"Treachery, Riley."

"Aye, Sir."

A lantern flashed in reply from *Oleander* and Snowden heard the sounds of men boarding a boat. He saw the boat push off from the ship and begin to make its way slowly towards the beach.

Snowden felt the familiar excitement rising in him, and nudged Riley. "Shall we, Riley?"

He saw the men stir as word was passed along the line, and then he threw himself down the little cliff, landing awkwardly on the sandy beach, recovered, and then he was running, running towards the men lying on the beach, who, too late, had realised their danger and were beginning to turn towards the noise of the approaching shore party. Snowden kicked at the head of a man climbing to his knees, feeling a sharp pain as his toes bent back with the impact, and then he collided with Bartoli, who was still staring out to sea, with the lamp in his hand.

Snowden grabbed Bartoli's chin and forced it back, his left hand covering the man's mouth. With surprising strength, Bartoli twisted his head round until Snowden saw his eyes, wide with fear and surprise. With his right hand, Snowden pressed the point of his cutlass into Bartoli's side, hard enough so that it penetrated the man's clothing. The man twitched convulsively as he felt the blade on his skin. Steady, boy, he thought, and said conversationally into Bartoli's ear, "Quiet, Bartoli, or die." Bartoli, sensibly, went limp, breathing hard.

Snowden turned and saw that Bartoli's common sense had spread to his men, who were lying on the sand, with the shore party's bayonets pressed into their clothing. He took the lantern from Bartoli's hand, pushed him roughly to the sand, and stood with his foot on the general's neck as he swung the light it in a wide arc. He saw the bow wave of *Oleander's* boat foam white and heard the creaking of oars. Soon sailors were moving on the beach, tying the hands of the captives.

CHAPTER 30 – THE TRAITOR

Burney saw the lantern shine on the beach and shortly afterwards heard the sounds of a struggle, followed by a brisk swinging of the light and then the noise of oars.

He heard the boat bump alongside *Oleander* and Riley appeared on deck, followed by a couple of marines, who stood guard as Bartoli climbed aboard, urged on by the point of Snowden's cutlass. Some dejected-looking Corsicans followed, looking around them with astonishment.

"Get him into the cabin, Sergeant Riley, if you please. Keep a good eye on him."

Snowden came up to Burney and Julia and said in a tone full of regret, "They would have cut you down as you landed, Julia. I am sorry."

They went into the dimly lit cabin. Bartoli was sitting at the table, his head drooping. Julia, her face white with anger, spoke to him in the Corsican version of Italian, too rapidly for Burney to follow, but there was no mistaking the venom in her voice. He tried to reply, but she strode up to him and struck him violently in the face. Snowden stepped forward and grabbed her hand.

"Julia, please, he is our prisoner."

"Prisoner? Hah! He is a traitor. We should ...", she struggled for words, "string him up from the ..."

Despite himself, Burney smiled, though he knew she was in deadly earnest, and from the look on his face, Bartoli clearly did as well.

Snowden suggested, "From the yardarm?"

"Yes, exactly. Why do we delay?"

"If we were to follow the King's regulations, that would not be permitted aboard one of his ships, Julia."

She sneered, "The English Navy, kind to Moors and traitors."

"I said 'if'. However, we are a long way from England, and ..." Snowden looked at Burney, who picked up the cue and turned to Bartoli, speaking in Italian.

"Your fate, Bartoli, rests with me. Snowden here has a reputation for independence, as you know, and violence, and I am sure he would be only too happy to comply with Julia's request."

Snowden, who was following the general direction of the conversation, interjected, his hand on the butt of the pistol in his belt, "Yes, by God, I would, and argue about it later. But Captain Burney is my superior, and if he wishes to spare your worthless life, I must obey him. However, you must answer the questions he will ask you."

Bartoli may have been a traitor, but he was no coward. "I will answer if I wish to do so. Ask, and be damned."

Burney and Julia conferred, and Burney stepped towards Bartoli. "Why did you do this Bartoli?"

Julia interrupted, "He did it because he is a traitor, like all his family."

Bartoli looked at her, and then at Burney. He seemed to be rapidly gaining his composure after the shock of the ambush on the beach. "It is true, English, that I am cousin to Buonaparte, who was wronged by Paoli."

"But you have fought with Paoli, against the French."

"Yes, and I do not regret it. I believed we had a chance of success. But we were beaten, and now the French are here. I believe that under a Corsican, my kinsman, the country will become prosperous. We Corsicans should not fight the French, and we must not", his voice rose, "we must not rely on the English. Paoli in his comfortable house in London with his English friends may believe we should, but I know very well that the English have no interest in us. Why should they? They only see us as a tool to use against the French."

Burney realised that a piece of the puzzle was missing and turned to Snowden. "Can we bring in a couple of the Corsicans who we brought aboard just now?"

Snowden nodded to the marine who was standing by the door. "Fetch those men in, if you please."

The men came in, guarded by seamen with cutlasses in their hands. They stood before Burney, looking disconsolate. Burney asked, in Italian, "Why did you do this?"

The men looked at each other, at Bartoli and at Snowden. One spoke, "Signor Bartoli came to the inn. He told us the Moors were about to land, but that there were not many of them. He gave us money and told us to bring our weapons and ambush them as they came ashore. He said there was no need for a general alarm, and for the town to take to the hills."

"And what did you think of this?"

"Signore, I do not know. It seemed strange the Moors would land unless there were a large number of them, but he said they were landing an important man who had business ashore and had no intention of slaving."

"And the money?"

"Sir, there is that. Times are hard in Corsica, and he offered gold."

"And what do you think now?"

"We do not know what to think. This ship seems English, a naval ship, but there are many ...", he inclined his head towards the two seamen, "men who seem like Moors aboard her."

"They are not Moors, Corsican, but men from the island of Bermuda."

"I have not heard of this Bermuda."

The other man interrupted, "I have heard of Bermuda. I was in a Genoese ship that went to America, to Charlestown, and there was talk of this island. It was said to have reefs and was much feared, but we did not see it, though we kept a good lookout." He looked again at the seamen and realisation dawned on him. "There were many men such as these in Charlestown." And then, as an afterthought, "I wish I had stayed there."

Snowden said to the marine, "Please fetch the Bosun."

The Bosun arrived, and Snowden nodded towards Bartoli. "This gentleman here, Rubert, attempted to kill our landing party earlier."

"So I heard, Sir," said Rubert in his slightly accented voice, and gave Bartoli an unfriendly look. "A traitor."

"I want him locked up secure. Perhaps the sail room would suit. He is to be guarded at all times by two men. Armed men. We must be very careful with him."

"Can't we just ...?"

Snowden held up his hands. "No we can't, Rubert. Just lock the bastard up."

CHAPTER 31 – GIOTTO LUCIANI

Burney sat in the sternsheets of the boat with Julia as it was rowed ashore, thinking that everything was moving far too quickly. Only three hours earlier, Bartoli had been landed on the same beach the boat was heading for, and since then there had been turmoil enough to last a lifetime. He would have liked to have had time to have thought things over.

He felt Julia's hand on his. As though reading his thoughts, she said, "Don't worry, Jimmy, we could not wait. At present they say there are no French in the town, but there will be when news of the events of tonight leak out. Every minute counts."

The boat's keel grated on the sand. Burney jumped from the bow, almost dry-shod, and Snowden carried Julia ashore. The Corsicans who had been captured were sitting on the beach, guarded by armed marines and seamen.

"Stand up," said Snowden, and the Corsicans stood. He turned to the marine corporal, "A light, if you please." The tinder glowed and flamed, and the lantern cast a pale yellowy glow over the group of men as he held it high. In faltering Italian Snowden said, "We are not Moors, but English."

There was a muttering of disbelief from the Corsicans, interrupted by the man who had been to Charleston. "What he says is true. He is the captain of the ship, which is from the English Navy. These men are sailors from the ship, but some of them come from Bermuda. They are certainly not Moors."

The prisoners quietened, and Julia stepped forward, provoking another discussion. She spoke in the Corsican vernacular, one side of her face lit by the lantern, the other half in deep shadow.

"You men came to shoot me down on the beach, because you are brave Corsicans and were told the Moors were landing. But this was a lie. These men are not Moors, but English, and that is an English warship at anchor."

Burney could see the prisoners were paying rapt attention, and even the sailors and marines were captivated by the force of her delivery.

"It is the English who fight the French, the French who bought you from the Genoese, as though Corsica and its people were an olive grove or a vineyard! Yes, the English fight the French, and they will win. You can hear that I am a Corsican, but I will tell you something else. I am the daughter of Pasquale Paoli and he has sent me here to raise men in Corsica to fight the French, in Italy perhaps, as part of the English Army."

There was silence for a moment, and then one of the prisoners asked, "The daughter of Paoli? I did not know he had children."

"Well, he did, one, and I am here."

"The English were our friends before, but they deserted us, leaving us to the mercy of the French. Why would we Corsicans fight for them?"

"For money, of course," said Julia. There was nervous laughter from the prisoners. "Yes, the English pay their soldiers, but you Corsicans will not be fighting for money. You will fight with the English to defeat the French. Already there is a regiment of Corsicans in the English Army, with Corsican officers. Corsica cannot beat the French, but England can, and she will do it quicker with Corsicans fighting with her."

Burney was struck, forcefully, by the power of her speech. He had listened to Pitt in the House of Commons, but this was something different, more akin to stories he had heard of Napoleon's power over his troops, and he realised Julia had some of the same quality. He did not know where she would lead him, but knew very well that wherever it was, he would follow.

Julia continued, "I have been in England and I know her strength, and I have no doubt that she will beat the French." She looked at each of the prisoners in turn. "You may think I am only a woman, but I am the daughter of Pasquale Paoli, and I intend to go inland and raise a regiment. If any of you wish to accompany me, you may do so. You were paid to murder me, but now I offer you the chance to follow me."

There was a tumult of voices, but Julia held up her hand, and as it quietened, she continued, "For any man who joins me now, as my guard, there will be pay, a fine rifle gun, and at the end of my time on the island the English Navy will carry you from Corsica if you wish to leave."

The Corsicans spoke among themselves, and eventually several stepped forward, and after discussions including Burney and Snowden, ten were selected, all young, strong-looking single men, including Giotto Luciani, the sailor who had been to Charlestown. They were each issued with a Baker rifle, with its associated tools, belts, slings and pouches, and loads were distributed amongst them.

For a long time, Snowden stood on the beach, disconsolate and worried, watching as the figures of Julia, Burney and the Corsicans faded into the darkness. The plan had been to recruit men in Macinaghju, but not under circumstances such as these. Bartoli's servants had disappeared, and Julia and Burney were accompanied only by men who, only hours before, had intended to murder them.

Poore and Riley came up to him, and Poore said, "Excuse me, Sir, but sky's starting to lighten. Shall I get the men into the boats?"

Snowden pulled himself together. He had done all he could and his duty was clear.

"Yes, of course, let's get under way. We'll be back here in a month."

CHAPTER 32 – CAPE CORSE

Dawn broke as they trudged along the rough path, led by Giotto Luciani, and over his shoulder Burney saw the rugged outline of the island of Elba, silhouetted against the lightening eastern sky. Soon it was light enough to see the bushes on either side of the path and the occasional tree. The sun rose, welcome on their chilled backs. Giotto led them off the path, to what looked like a shepherd's hut, and they put down their loads and lay on their backs, exhausted. Burney drifted off to sleep, and when he awoke the sun was hot on his face. He sat up and looked around, the rolling maquis-covered hills looking dry and deserted. He gazed out to sea and his heart seemed to miss a beat as he saw *Oleander*, perhaps half way to the horizon, heeled over under the press of sails on her enormous raked masts, making her way south-east, her white wake contrasting with the brilliant blue of the sea.

There's a sight, he thought to himself, with longing, the fastest ship in the Navy, he's got every stitch of canvas on her. For a moment he thought of life on the ship, its ordered environment, dangerous sometimes, perhaps, and rough, but with other people who you understood and trusted, and who shared a common purpose. Some men, he knew, relished independence and were happy to be left to their own devices, but it was more difficult for him to be brave on this Corsican hillside, with barely understood companions who only a few hours ago had tried to kill him, than it was on the deck of a man o' war.

He nudged Julia, who was sleeping on the ground near

him. She raised herself onto her elbows and looked where he was pointing. "There she goes, Julia. Percy's got all her glad rags on her. Isn't she a sight?"

Julia put her hand on his arm and looked at the ship. "She is, Jimmy, and I know you wish you were in her, but we have our work to do here before we can rejoin the Navy."

The Corsicans got up and began to light a fire. Burney realised they had all been asleep at once, and determined that in future a watch would be set. The Corsicans' own guns were beside them on the ground and the rifles were piled together with their butts in the ground. He could see the port of Macinaghju faraway below them, and some other straggling villages on the side of the hill opposite, but the country nearby, for miles he thought, seemed deserted.

Luciani came over, and looked towards the horizon. "A fine ship, Signore."

"She is, Giotto. She is the fastest ship in the English Navy and, I believe, perhaps in the world."

Giotto looked at Burney, taking in his rudimentary uniform. "You are a seaman, Signore?"

"Indeed I am. I am a captain in the English Navy. I have sailed twice round the world, with Captain Cook."

Giotto's eyes widened. "With Cook? I have heard much of his voyages. Signore, Capitaine, I must ask you a question."

"By all means, Giotto."

"I was captain of my father's ship, our own ship, you understand. I took her everywhere in Corsica and often to Italy. I traded with the English in Livorno, but the French have destroyed the trade, and now the ship is in Macinaghju, idle. I am a seaman, I am not meant for a soldier. Is it possible that I might join the English Navy when your ship returns?"

"I am sure you could, Giotto. In fact, I will give you my

word on it. I have no doubt you could join *Oleander*", he pointed to the ship, "if you so wished, under Lieutenant Snowden."

"The *Oleander*, I would very much like to sail in her. She seemed to me to be a happy ship, so clean, with no shouting and the men well dressed. The captain, though, is a frightening man. I would prefer not to fight against him!"

"In battle, yes, he is frightening, but he is a good commander, and the ship *is* happy. There are opportunities in the Navy, Giotto, for good men. Cook himself started as a seaman."

After a rudimentary breakfast, Burney sat with Julia and Giotto and took out his map. He had several maps and charts of Corsica with him, but this one seemed to be the best. It had been published to coincide with Boswell's *Account of Corsica* and showed the principal towns and villages, as well as the mountains of the interior.

Aboard *Oleander*, they had meticulously planned their route on Corsica, but now that Burney had actually seen the island for himself, which seemed to be almost entirely mountainous, with high peaks rising ragged and steep, he tended to think they might have been optimistic in their estimation of the ground that could be covered. It appeared almost impenetrable, Burney thought, as he showed the map to Giotto.

"Pino is our first objective, and then Bastia ..."

Giotto interrupted, "Bastia, no!"

Julia asked, "Why not?"

"It is full of French, full. We will not be able to get near the place, and betrayal will be certain."

Julia looked at Burney. "Perhaps, Jimmy, we should miss Bastia."

Burney heartily agreed, not liking the sound of the place.

"Perhaps, then, we can go from Pino along the coast to Calvi, and then from Calvi to Corti."

Giotto thought. "We have a month, it may be possible. We cannot go into Calvi, it is a fortress, and held by the French."

Julia interrupted, "We shall stay nearby, and persuade people to meet us there."

"Perhaps we can do that. Paoli is very popular in that area."

Burney asked, "Are the men ready to set out for Pino?"

"I believe they are ready, but it would be best to wait until evening, when the sun is lower. In Corsica in summer, it is best to march in the early morning and evening."

Burney thought he could put the wait to good use. "Very well. Would the men like to be instructed in the use of the rifle?"

"I am sure they would like that very well."

There followed an afternoon of rifle exercise, but Burney limited each man to one shot each, for fear of arousing attention. As they were about to set off, they saw a small train of mules walking along the track below them. Burney gave Giotto some money, and half an hour later he returned leading two mules. The mules loaded, the party continued through hilly country, covered by the maquis, with fragrant bushes and occasional groves of trees, along rough, sinuous paths. Progress was slow, and as dusk was falling they came upon a building, abandoned it seemed to Burney, who could not decide whether it was a substantial shepherd's hut or a small chapel. By now the sea on the western side of the Cape Corse peninsular was visible and Burney could see ships and boats making their way along the coast.

CHAPTER 33 – RECRUITING

The night sky was brilliant with stars as Burney, his rifle slung on its strap over his shoulder, stood by the building, keeping watch, thinking of similar nights under the stars in the far-flung places of the world he had visited in his youth under Cook.

Cook, he thought, the finest seaman there ever was or likely to be, the perfect gentleman. Could any other man have done what Cook had? For long years Cook had kept together the little society of his ships' companies, isolated from the rest of the world, beset by unknown and unfamiliar dangers, with hardly a punishment or even words of admonishment. In the last few days, he had steadied himself by thinking – what would Cook do now?

He was startled by a footstep behind him, and turned, shrugging the rifle off his shoulder. "Jimmy, don't look so startled, it's only me."

"I'm sorry, Julia, I was deep in thought."

"You are not much of a sentry, are you?"

"No, I fear I am not."

"What were you thinking of?"

"I was thinking of Captain Cook, and Tahiti."

"And what about them?"

"That I have only just appreciated how hard it must have

been for him. Command is a very lonely thing, Julia, and to be in command for so long, so far from home … It must have been unimaginably hard."

"Did he not have Banks and Solander for company, men who were not directly under his command?"

"He did, but I think that may have made it worse for him. He was the captain of the ship, and in complete command, but Banks was his social superior, and he had to resist pressure from him, sometimes to do frivolous things that might put the ship in peril."

"And now, you think that Cook's position was like your own, perhaps because you are both Jimmies, that I am the Corsican equivalent of Joseph Banks?"

"Good Lord, Julia, I have never thought of Cook as 'Jimmy'. The Old Man, or Captain, but Jimmy, never. And I don't think you are like Banks. He is very talented and has much good in him, but if you don't mind me saying so, you are twice the man he is."

She laughed, "I don't think I mind that at all, Jimmy. But what were you thinking of Tahiti?"

"Well, tonight, standing where we are, you would think Corsica peaceful and beautiful. At first, Tahiti seemed so to me, almost like a paradise. The women, Julia, they were beautiful, and available, and nobody seemed to have to work very hard. But when we had been there for a while, I realised that paradise had some very unpleasant sides to it, bestial. Tribal feuds, like Corsica, but at least you don't have human sacrifice."

"We don't have human sacrifice, but we could probably teach them a thing or two about feuds."

"I am not sure you could, and as for New Zealand, the horror of that place …"

"Jimmy, I think you should rest. Hand me your rifle and I will take a turn."

"Can you …?"

She looked at him, and held out her hand. He handed the rifle to her.

"But it got to him in the end. I was on the beach when he was killed, translating. It was the first error of judgement I ever saw him make, but he lost his temper – he never would have done before."

Before noon, they came to Pino, a straggling village on the side of the hill, with no harbour that Burney could see. He knew this would be the first real test of their mission. It had been planned, in those distant days in *Oleander's* cabin, that Bartoli would make initial contact with the local population. Now they realised Julia's entrance to the village would be by no means unobtrusive, and Burney was an obvious foreigner. The problem had been solved by Giotto, who had volunteered to go himself.

Burney's concern about sending Giotto ahead of them had been countered by Julia. "If he wishes to betray us, he will always have ample opportunity, merely by waiting until we are asleep, and killing or capturing us at his leisure. I am reassured that he has not done so yet."

Burney could not but agree, but wondered at Julia's composure.

Giotto slung his own gun over his shoulder and walked into the village. He returned an hour later. "They will meet us tonight, in the shed of a farmer near the road. I will show you when the time comes."

In the dusk, they walked along the dusty road into the village. Giotto and another Corsican, Fede, led the way, bayonetted rifles at their hips, fifty yards ahead of Julia and Burney, who walked side by side, carrying a lantern. Julia was dressed in pantaloons, with her hair pulled back into a queue, and Burney was in some semblance of naval uniform, epauletted, with his sword at his side and a badged hat on his head. The remaining Corsicans walked behind, rifles ready.

Giotto banged on the door of the barn. The door opened, revealing a dim interior with a small crowd standing around the walls, perhaps twenty men and women. There was an audible gasp as Julia and Burney walked in. Burney held the lantern so it illuminated Julia, and she began, "I am Julia Bianco, and this is Captain Burney of the English Royal Navy. My father, Pasquale Paoli ..."

There was a surprised muttering from the crowd at this. Julia held up her hand and continued, "Yes, Paoli is my father. He has sent us on a mission to the brave people of Corsica. The brave people who chafe under the oppression of the French, the French who speak of liberty and the rights of man, but who bought us from the Genoese, as though we were cattle at a market. We know we are too weak to fight the French, we lack the money and supplies, and we are often divided amongst ourselves, but the English are strong, and they fight Buonaparte and will, I am sure, defeat him."

There was an interjection from the crowd and one man spoke out, "What do the English want from us? We have seen their power, at Bastia and Calvi, but they are not to be relied upon."

"What they want, Signore, are soldiers, brave Corsican soldiers. Not to fight on Corsica, but overseas, in the English Army, in their own regiment, the Corsican Rangers, which is well equipped, and well paid."

There was a murmur of assent, and a young man spoke up, "We know of this regiment, but are they not just Buonaparte's enemies? Buonaparte is after all at least a Corsican."

"Some of them are undoubtedly Buonaparte's enemies, but you volunteers will fight for all Corsicans! Buonaparte is the leader of France, it makes no difference where he was born."

"If we are to join your English Army, how are we to be taken from Corsica, where would we go, and how will we be transported?"

"You will be taken from Corsica by ship. We cannot say where you will be taken, as it is secret, but it will be an English possession. We will send word of the rendezvous well before it is to take place."

The young man conferred with other young men nearby, and then asked, "What is the pay to be ...?"

That night, Julia and Burney sat by the small fire at their camp on a hillside overlooking the sea.

"Well, Julia, how do you think we did in Pino?"

"I think we did well. Giotto spoke to some of the men who were there, and he believes several of them are considering joining us."

"Is the desire to fight the French so strong?"

"It is, they do not like them, but of course times are hard here, and it is always easier to recruit soldiers when there is little work to be had. Many of them go to France, to Marseille, and some Corsicans have done well there, but now, with the English blockades, it is much harder for them to find work."

CHAPTER 34 – CALVI

After ten days of walking, Burney felt tired, very tired. They had generally followed the coast, mostly in darkness. On the map, their progress did not look impressive, but, Burney reflected, there were no straight paths in Corsica, and no level ones.

They had held night-time meetings at several villages. At every gathering, men had pledged themselves to come forward, motivated by, well, he wasn't sure what motivated them, a combination probably of dislike of the French, a thirst for adventure and the prospect of regular pay. They had met no hostility so far, and there had been no attempt at robbery or murder, and, as far as they knew, no betrayal.

And now they were on level land at last, though it was rather marshy and plagued with mosquitos. Across the sandy beach and blue waters of the bay he could see the town of Calvi, with its impregnable-looking citadel on a rocky point of land high above the harbour. Calvi, which the British had taken with such difficulty, now with the tricolour flying above it. He turned to Julia, who was standing beside him at the corner of the farm building in which they were staying, and said thoughtfully, "It must have been very difficult for Nelson to get the guns up there."

After the experience of the last few days, he could appreciate the enormous effort that must have gone into landing guns, each weighing several tons, and manhandling them up cliffs and along rocky paths until they dominated the fortress.

"He had many men, and your Navy and Army are well organised. Nevertheless, it was a magnificent effort. And of course, he had Percy to help him!"

"I think Percy was only about twelve at the time, but,

nevertheless, I'm sure he was a great help to our Admiral."

Except for the sentry, the men were sitting or lying in the shade against the wall of the building. All sober, thought Burney gratefully. In the last few days, some of them had shown a regrettable weakness for wine. He couldn't blame them, they were under great pressure, but it was something more for him to worry about. Without warning, as was his wont, Giotto appeared. "Good evening, Signora Julia, Capitaine."

There was relief in Julia's voice: "Thank goodness you are back, Giotto."

"I am pleased to return myself, Signora. Calvi is full of French and Buonapartists."

"Did you manage to speak to anyone?"

"Yes, Signora, I am friends with a ship chandler", he smiled, "and especially with his daughter."

Julia rolled her eyes. "Giotto, we are all well aware of your attractiveness to members of the opposite sex. You miss no opportunity for reminding us of it."

Giotto smiled, unabashed. "The man found me many cargoes, and I spent much time in his parlour, and money in his store. He and his daughter are both true Corsicans. They will spread the word and you may be sure that people will come here tonight."

As dusk fell, people began to arrive from Calvi. Some walked, a few were on horseback and some came by boat. Before long, there was a considerable crowd, most of whom seemed to have brought food and wine, and, to Burney's alarm, the anticipated secret meeting turned into a social event, with a large fire burning. Julia mingled with the crowd, laughing and talking, apparently in complete unconcern. Burney grabbed her arm and pointed to the fire. "For God's sake, Julia, this must show up like a beacon to the French in the fort."

"There is nothing we can do, Jimmy. I will speak to them now."

From the back of a small cart, illuminated by the fire, Julia addressed the crowd. "People of Calvi! I have been sent by my father, Pasquale Paoli." By now Burney was used to the stir in the crowd that this assertion caused. "Yes, Paoli is my father. And this ...", she pointed to Burney, whose epaulettes glinted in the firelight, "is Captain Burney of the English Navy."

The people turned their attention to Burney, and one man called out, "Were you here, at Calvi, with Lord Nelson?"

"No, I was not. The English Navy has work to do in other parts of the world! I was in the Pacific."

At the end of her speech, which seemed to Burney to be unusually well received, Julia stepped down from the cart to considerable applause. At that moment, there was a whistle from one of the men who had been posted away from the gathering. Burney looked up and then out to sea. Silhouetted against the moon was a small ketch with a large ensign at her mizzen. The flag was indistinct, but Burney had no doubt it would be a tricolour. He watched, horrified, as the ketch headed up into the wind, with the obvious intention of anchoring. He knew a boat would be launched before long. He turned to Julia: "Time for us to go."

CHAPTER 35 – MALTA

Oleander without Burney and Julia seemed empty to Snowden, and progress southward in light winds was frustratingly slow, the aspect of the mountains of Corsica hardly seeming to change. Eventually, Corsican mountains were succeeded by Sardinian ones, and then, for several days the land was out of sight, until, on the morning of the sixth day, Snowden, writing at his table, heard the lookout's shout. He waited, and there was a knock on the door, and the marine sentry admitted a seaman.

"Yes, Pirera?"

"Mr Poore's compliments, Sir, but there's land been sighted."

"Where away?"

"Fine on the starboard bow, Your Honour."

"Thank you, Pirera. Tell Mr Poore I will be up directly."

When he arrived on deck, Kennedy and Poore were peering intently at the patent log.

"Bang on the nose, Sir", said Kennedy, looking up, "a real *Oleander* landfall."

Poore stood up and pointed to a smudge on the horizon. "The island of Marettimo, Sir". And with a hint of pride, "We should see the other Islands and then Sicily."

After two more days of light-weather work, *Oleander* coasted along the north coast of Malta, and then worked into the Grand Harbour of Valletta, past the fortifications of the Knights of

St John, only recently deposed from their centuries-old rule of the island by Napoleon's rude modernity. The Royal Navy, in its inimitable fashion, had, in its short occupation, made Valletta its own, with the beginnings of what Snowden was sure would be a substantial base.

Snowden waited in an anteroom while the Governor's Secretary read his report and made notes. The man looked up with intense interest. "You've James Burney aboard?"

"Yes, Mr … ?"

"Apologies, Commander Snowden." The secretary held out his hand. "Samuel Taylor Coleridge, at your service." Snowden thought the name sounded familiar. "I'm a great admirer of Mr Burney's sister's work."

"Yes, remarkably popular novels I understand, though I admit I have not read them. I have met Burney's other sister. She writes as well, but she's not so successful, at least not yet."

"I have not read anything by the other Burney, but Fanny's novels are wonderful, full of insight, and written with such wit."

Snowden's brain clicked – Coleridge. "I know – Coleridge – the poet. *Ancient Mariner* – was that you? That poem really is something! However did you think of it, the albatross and all that?"

"That is very kind of you, Commander Snowden …"

"Rollicks along, so it does. It's pretty popular in the Navy. I even saw a play based on it at a theatre in Pompey."

"Did you, I never heard of that. I don't really know how I thought of it, these things just come to me."

"Were you at sea, Mr Coleridge?"

"Only as a passenger. Speaking of passengers, I haven't finished your document yet, but is Burney still aboard? I would very much like to meet him."

"He's well worth meeting, a very interesting man, has written a book on bridge, would you believe? He was with Cook, but fell out with Their Lordships and couldn't get a ship. No, he's not aboard, we landed him in Corsica."

"In Corsica! Why?"

Snowden indicated the papers on the desk. "It is in my report, and my orders, and the letter from Their Lordships."

"Sorry, Snowden, I have only just started in on them, but perhaps you could tell me the outline of what they contain."

"Well, we landed Burney on Corsica, with a woman who is Pasquale Paoli's daughter – a Mrs White – and they intend to raise a regiment of Corsicans to fight in our Army. I'm to return there in two weeks, I hope with a man o' war or two, and pick them up with their regiment."

"Paoli's daughter, with Burney, on Corsica. How extraordinary! I'm credited by some with an excess of imagination, but this scheme! Who thought it up?"

"It was my mother, actually."

"Your mother! Is she Corsican?"

"Indeed not, she lives a quiet life at home in Cornwall. Occasionally doing battle with creditors, but otherwise a very peaceable woman. It so happened that Paoli's daughter was staying with her, and she came up with the idea of raising a Corsican regiment. I had no clue at all she had it in her."

"You mentioned men o' war to help you remove this hoped-for regiment from Corsica. I fear you will be disappointed. There is not a serviceable ship here, they have all gone to Toulon. It is thought that the French are disposed to break out …"

"No ships!"

"Not one, Snowden. Even the ones under repair hurried out. I do not know how you will carry your regiment from

Corsica."

"The ships to carry the men are here, Coleridge", he gestured to the window, "you can see them from here, *Rondine* and *Balestruccio* – Leghorn ships, owned by Mrs White's firm. It is not ships to carry the men that I need but men o' war to escort them, and cover the embarkation, in case of interference by the French."

"I see them now, but I must say I hadn't noticed them before. I understand, Snowden, but I don't know what can be done. Excuse me, but I must ask you to sit quiet for a time while I prepare notes for your meeting with Sir Alexander."

Snowden knew that Captain Sir Alexander Ball was effectively the Governor of Malta, though officially he was the British ambassador to the Knights of St John. Snowden sat and looked out of the window at the two little ships alongside in the Grand Harbour, while Coleridge read and made notes. Before long, Coleridge stood.

"An astonishing business, Snowden. I think we can go into Sir Alexander now. You have been in the Med before, haven't you? Do you know him?"

"Not as such, but I believe he has nodded to me on several occasions. He was at the Nile, and his ship once towed ours when we were dismasted. A good bit of work, that was."

Coleridge knocked on the door and they went in. Sir Alexander was sitting at a rather ornate desk. Snowden stood while the Governor read through Coleridge's notes and glanced at the letter from the Admiralty.

"Sit, Snowden, pleased to meet you. I must come down and look at that ship of yours. Extraordinary thing, she looks like she's doing thirteen knots even when she's tied up. Yankee?"

"No, Sir, Bermudian. And she is fast, nothing to touch her. We trialled her in the North Sea, against some very fast ships, and she beat everything."

"I can believe that … but to the matter in hand. According to the notes made by our resident poet", he nodded towards Coleridge, "you are engaged on a scheme to raise men in Corsica. It seems to me that such a thing might be possible, and good fighting men are in short supply, but I wish that you had come here first."

"My orders were explicit, Sir."

"Yes, quite so, Snowden, but we could have been more prepared. As Coleridge has undoubtedly told you, we are quite bereft of ships here. They have all gone to Toulon."

"Mr Coleridge has told me, Sir. I suppose I will have to do the best I can with what I have."

CHAPTER 36 – FEVER

There had been angry shouting, but to Burney's relief no gunfire or battle sounds as they had moved as quickly as they could away from the beach and the French ketch. In the last few days, the party had expanded as men and at least two women from the villages and towns through which they had passed had caught up and attached themselves to the party. The most incongruous were four seamen from San Firenze who were dressed in the style of English sailormen, who said they had acquired their clothes in Leghorn and were set on joining the Royal Navy. More had joined after the meeting at Calvi, and Burney worried that they had become an armed band and that there was a danger of them drifting into probably hopeless guerrilla warfare. Mrs White's Banditos, he thought grimly.

They walked all night. At first the tracks were reasonable, but they became increasingly rough as they started to climb the hills. From time to time a man or mule would slip, with accompanying curses, but by dawn they were well away from the city. As the sky lightened, they came to a building set amongst trees, mostly chestnut, beside a nearly dry river, and Burney called a halt.

He was determined to keep order, and, with the assistance of Giotto and the sailors, they set out picquets and settled down to spend the day in the shade. From time to time there were whistles from the sentries as people straggled into the camp with the intention of joining.

They stayed there all next day, recuperating. Burney was eager to push on, as he thought they were too close to Calvi and its French garrison, but conditions were good, with plentiful chestnuts and wild boars. In the afternoon, Julia began to feel unwell and took to a makeshift bed.

Burney had been hoping for the best, but he had spent years in tropical climates, and when he visited her in the evening and saw she was shivering and hot to the touch, he knew she had contracted the fever that was endemic in the low coastal areas of Corsica.

Julia opened her eyes, shielding them against the dim light. "I ache so, Jimmy, and such dreams! I have the marsh fever, do I not?"

"I believe you do, you must rest." He went to his chest and took out a small bottle. He mixed some of its contents with water in a cup and went back to Julia. "Here, drink this."

"What is it?"

"They call it Jesuit Bark. It comes from a South American plant. It is said to be effective against the marsh fever, though I have not personally used it."

She drank the mixture – "Ugh, that is horrible" – and collapsed back onto the bed.

He handed her some water, and turned to the woman who was acting as nurse, "She must be kept covered up, but please wipe her face with a wet cloth from time to time."

He left the shack, which was little more than a roof on wooden poles, and heard a commotion growing in the band. Giotto came up to him with a man who he had not seen before.

"Capitaine, this man has just arrived from Calvi. He says the French are coming after us."

Burney turned to the man, who was well dressed but carried the ubiquitous gun on his shoulder. "They are coming?"

"Yes, Signore, I believe the French will come. In Calvi they have heard there is a band of banditos and that people have been leaving the towns to join them. They do not have many men in Calvi, but they have sent word to Corti and Bastia."

Burney felt despair wash over him. They had roused the country and there was the danger of war breaking out. He knew that such a war would be hopelessly one sided, and although it might be beneficial to the British cause in the short term, it would be disastrous for the Corsicans, and in the long term bad for the British, as the Corsicans would consider it to be another example of abandonment by the British.

"When do you believe the French will leave Calvi?"

"I think tomorrow morning, Signore."

"Are there people who will betray us?"

"There are some, Signore, we are not united. Some favour the French, but not many. I do not think the French understand what you are doing – they think you are bandits, or at worst intending to raid them."

CHAPTER 37 – MERCHANT SHIPS

"Mr Kennedy, will you walk with me ashore?"

"Ashore, Sir? Yes, of course."

"If you don't mind, I would like us to look as much like seamen as possible."

"Seamen, Sir, I trust we look as though we are of that persuasion already."

"No, Kennedy, I didn't mean to imply that you could be taken for a lubber, I mean as a Bosun's Mate or some such."

"Very well, Sir." Kennedy looked at him. "Will there be fighting, Sir?"

"I sincerely hope not. I intend to inspect the two ships over there without drawing attention to ourselves."

In the hot sunshine, they walked along wharves lined with warehouses until they came to where *Rondine* and *Balestruccio* lay alongside. They were merchant ships, of the type often found in the Mediterranean. Kennedy looked at them appraisingly. "Seem well kept up, Sir."

"They don't look too bad at all. Perhaps not to *Oleander's* standard, but workmanlike." As he spoke, a figure emerged from *Rondine's* companionway. With a start, Snowden recognised Renzi, Julia's man of business from Leghorn. Renzi beckoned to them and they went aboard.

After they were seated round a small table in the ship's small saloon, with glasses of wine in front of them Snowden said, "Renzi, I did not expect you to come personally. Are the ships' Masters not reliable?"

"They are, but they may have limits if they think their ships are in danger. I thought it best to come myself." He leaned forward. "How did it go in Macinaghju?"

Snowden told him about the landing. "It was good that you did not trust Bartoli. Of course, he is related to Buonaparte, and they have a grudge against the Paoli family," he smiled. "I do not know if the grudge is justified or not, but if it was not for the Paolis, Napoleon would probably still be on Corsica, and the world would be a better place. And Bartoli, where is he now?"

"Aboard *Oleander*, in the sail room. I intend to hand him over to the authorities here this morning."

Kennedy interjected, "Why don't we keep the bastard, Sir? You never know when a bargaining chip might be useful."

Snowden said, astonished, "Kennedy, all this time I have mistaken you for a simple seaman! That is a disreputable idea worthy of a politician, or at least a gambler, and I thought I was the gambling man here. I believe by rights we should hand prisoners over to the authorities, but, by God, you have a point."

"Aye, Sir, of course there's no politicking in a man o' war so I'm not much of a hand at it, but a General, and a relation of Boney, must be worth something."

"He is quite right," said Renzi. "Keep him."

"I will," said Snowden. "I hope the subject doesn't come up with their nibs ashore. And now, to the charterparty. I will discuss the matter with Coleridge and arrange to have the documents exchanged as unobtrusively as possible. In the meantime, please have the ships provisioned and watered ..."

Several hours later, as they were walking back to *Oleander*,

Snowden asked Kennedy, "What did you think, Kennedy?"

"The ships seem sound enough, and Renzi and the skippers seem competent. I think they understand what is required of them."

"That was my impression too. I think they are the best we will get, but I am worried about the lack of an escort."

"An escort, Sir?"

"Yes, we were to have a fighting ship to accompany us, at least a frigate, but as you can see there are none here, and we have to be back in Macinaghju directly. The ships have all gone to Toulon."

"So we're on our own, Sir?"

In the afternoon, *Oleander* was visited by Sir Alexander and Coleridge. Snowden thought of how proud he used to be when he showed people round the ship, but he now seemed to be so burdened down with larger worries that he could take no pleasure in it.

Poore, however had no such worries, and proudly demonstrated the log and other instruments. "We know exactly how fast she's going at any time, Sir, much quicker than heaving the log. And we measure the wind, as well, and have a table, here, in this book, which tells us what sails we should set for best speed. Sometimes more is less, Sir – she doesn't like being over on her ear too much, not when she's close hauled."

They looked at the Carronades on the foredeck.

"They look big, Sir, for the size of the ship, but the Master Shipwright at Deptford said they'd do, and he was right."

"Indeed, and have you had occasion to use them?"

The question was directly asked of Snowden, who was lost in thought. "Ah, yes, Sir, we have. We fell in with some corsairs, it's in my papers."

"I have not had a chance to read them thoroughly yet, Snowden."

"I see, Sir. Just past Gib we were becalmed in the fog and two galleys had at us."

"Could they see your colours, Snowden?"

"I couldn't say, Sir, but I believe they may have mistaken *Oleander* for a Yankee."

"Yes, bad business that, it didn't take the Moors long to realise they'd lost our protection."

Coleridge exclaimed, "I daresay the Americans will teach them a lesson in due course. And how did the business go with the corsairs?"

"It was hopeless for them, once we realised what they were about, but they kept at it longer than they should have. These things," he patted the barrel of a Carron, "are frightful, close to like that."

Coleridge asked, "You were on that business in Brittany, were you not, Snowden?"

"I was, Mr Coleridge."

"Blew up Boney's barges, and marched halfway across Brittany, didn't you? Stole a ship to escape?"

"Not exactly. We burnt the barges and chartered the ship. All fair and above board."

"You've a taste for independent operations, then, Snowden."

"I don't know about that, but I seem to be cast in that role from time to time."

Snowden made up his mind, and turned to Sir Alexander. "If you don't mind, Sir, I would like to speak to you in the cabin before you leave."

"Of course, Snowden, but I was intending to ask you for

dinner this evening."

"Thank you, Sir, but I would like an immediate discussion."

"Very well, lead on."

Once they were seated in the cabin with glasses of wine, Snowden addressed the Governor. "Sir, I am very concerned about the party on Corsica. We were to have escorting ships, and now we are left to our own devices."

"I am very sorry about that, Snowden, but when Nelson asks for ships, they are sent."

"I understand. There is no substitute for men o' war, but we may be able to mitigate their absence."

"How so? I will do everything in my power – I recognise the importance of your mission, and indeed the priority that is placed on it by the highest authority. I don't know if you realised that the documents you delivered included a personal letter from Canning."

"I did realise that, Sir, he told me he was sending such a message."

"And another from Sir Sidney?"

"Yes, I knew of that as well."

"You certainly have powerful allies, Snowden, and not just because of that, I am open to any suggestions you may have."

"Sir, I have been thinking of this for some time."

Coleridge looked at him. "You certainly seem preoccupied, Snowden."

"I am concerned about several things, the most worrying is that, if the party returns earlier than expected to Macinaghju, perhaps if they are discovered by the French and pursued, or for some other reason, and have to wait there for several days, they will be cornered, at the mercy almost of the French."

Sir Alexander nodded, "You have a valid point, Snowden. What can we do about it?"

"Sir, I think now we are too late for secrecy, and in the absence of warships we must improvise. I would like to embark a party of soldiers aboard *Oleander* and some ordnance, field pieces, which we could deploy ashore if it is necessary to defend the beachhead."

"That seems reasonable, we have military here kicking their heels at present."

"Thank you, Sir. I would also like to second Mr Kennedy to the two merchant ships, and for him to sail with them. I trust him implicitly and he can organise some guns for the ships. We should also like some men for them. I think we should not commandeer them, as there are probably not sufficient British seamen to man them, but I think we should put a party aboard, if they can be spared. This will take perhaps a couple of days, but I think we should try and get *Oleander* away today – tomorrow morning at the latest."

"My word, Snowden, you are in a rush, but I think you're right. I will ask our military commander to organise assistance. Gentlemen, let us depart."

"Before you go, Sir, I think we should invite Signor Renzi who is supercargo on the two Leghorn vessels."

"Very well. Send someone will you, Coleridge? And let us not forget our Master Shipwright."

By that evening, *Oleander* was abuzz with activity. Normally, this would have been supervised by Kennedy in his calm, competent way, but he had departed to join the two Leghorn ships, showing less reluctance than might have been expected, thought Snowden, as he shouted, "Mind that barrel, there. Mr Poore, please do keep an eye on things."

"Yes, Sir, sorry."

CHAPTER 38 – AMBUSH

It took much longer than it should have to get the band underway. Burney was adamant that it should be done properly, with an advance and rear guards, and, where the terrain allowed, men at the sides of the column. Julia, despite the Jesuit Bark, was still very ill, from time to time delirious, but Burney's suggestion that they should find accommodation for her at some friendly house was rejected firmly.

"I should never be able to escape, Jimmy, I would be here until the French found me, our plan would fail, Corsica would be betrayed again, and I would end up with my husband at the Château d'If."

Her shudder was emphasised by a bout of shivering. They improvised a stretcher for her, and with a man at each corner if the path permitted, or one at each end if it was narrow, they set out.

By now, recruiting did not seem to rely on Julia's presence, and Burney sent men, chosen by Giotto, to spread the word in the area of Corti, Paoli's capital, perched high in the centre of the island. He was desperately worried that they might betray the rendezvous to the French, either voluntarily or under duress, but there was nothing he could do about it.

They moved, as fast as they could, over the summit. The land was rugged beyond belief, with peaks closely jumbled together and the paths hardly discernible. Had Burney not been so concerned with the cares of leadership, he might have appreciated the astonishing views across the sharp summits and steep valleys of Corsica to the blue sea. The sun was hot and there was little shade, but by night it was bitterly cold. Burney tried to ensure, as far as possible, that food was shared so that people did not go completely unfed, but it was a miserable time. They descended into more favourable country, proceeding along a rough and slippery mule track which followed a pine-clad river valley. He was desperately worried about Julia, about the French who they believed were pursuing them, about a possible ambush from the French at Corti, and about what would happen when they got to Macinaghju. How he missed Julia's counsel, but she was bound into her stretcher, often delirious.

The heat was intense, and they had stopped by some tree-shaded pools, which people were drinking from and splashing about in. He was kneeling by Julia's side, while she conversed with people who were not there. Giotto, who had been rear guard, came up beside him and looked at Julia. "She is at the crisis, I think, Capitaine."

"I believe she is, Giotto. The next hour will be critical. We will give her more bark." He called for the nurse, and then turned back to Giotto.

"Capitaine, I have bad news. The French are overhauling us. They are quite close."

Burney had been worried about this since they had left Calvi, and he knew what he was going to do, fight, there was no alternative.

"Giotto, perhaps our crisis has come, as it has for Julia. You must lead the party to the rendezvous while I delay the French. Bring the Rifles over." 'Rifles' was the name Burney had chosen for men from Macinaghju who had been issued with Bakers. They had practised with them and, as Corsicans, accustomed from childhood to handling firearms, had become remarkably proficient. Baker rifles took longer than muskets to reload, but they were deadly things, with much greater range.

The men came over, carrying their rifles and wearing their equipment belts, hung about with a variety of personal weapons, and they started back along the track, to the spot he had selected earlier. He believed it was well chosen, the land too steep to be taken in the flank, but he was not a soldier and he was aware that he might have made some fundamental error.

He lay on the ground in the trees above the bend in the track he had selected for the ambush and looked over his rifle sights, trying to relax and control his breathing. The French party, conspicuous in their blue coats, straggled into sight, leading loaded mules. No scouts, he thought, careless. He counted as the French came into view – twenty nine, thirty, ...

An officer was in the lead. Burney moved his rifle so that the man was in the sights and gently squeezed the trigger. The rifle kicked against his shoulder, he saw the man fall and heard shouts from the other French soldiers, who looked around in surprise. Burney's companion, Georgio, a young Corsican who was the best shot in the band, fired and another Frenchman fell, and then they were firing and reloading as fast as they could. The Frenchmen pointed to where the shots were coming from and, as he believed they would, pressed themselves against the slope of the hill in order to shelter from the fire coming from above them. Some started to load their muskets, but Burney knew the range was too great for effective musket fire. When the French started to fire at them in earnest, Burney blew his whistle, loudly, and the remainder of the Rifles, who had been concealed behind rocks on the other side of the track, opened fire.

The results were devastating. The French were completely enfiladed, without shelter, and they did the only thing they could – throw down their muskets and any other equipment that might slow them down and run for their lives along the slope, above the track, through the trees. The mules bolted, unexpectedly, forward. Burney blew his whistle and the firing stopped. He saw his men below leave their shelter and, not without difficulty, capture the mules. It was over, in a few seconds, it seemed to Burney.

He made no serious attempt to count the French casualties, but it had been a brutal business. The Baker rifles had proved to be formidable weapons. Burney was sure that every shot he had fired had found its mark. He turned to Georgio, "Well done."

Georgio patted his gun. "Well done, Signor Baker. I do not think those Frenchmen will trouble us again."

Burney silently agreed.

That evening, they had rejoined the main party and were still on the path, and when they saw the citadel of Corti, improbably perched on a rocky outcrop, Burney halted the band to await the return of Giotto, who had gone ahead to scout.

Giotto had been right, Julia's crisis had come and gone. Burney knew that the men carrying her had fallen several times and that her stretcher had hit the rocky ground quite hard, but she had survived, though she was weak to the point of complete immobility. He knelt by her.

"I think if we can get past Corti, Julia, we have a good chance of reaching the rendezvous."

Julia blinked her eyes and whispered, "Corti? The last thing I can remember is Calvi."

"Calvi, Julia? You have missed a great deal while being carried along like a dead weight." He suddenly felt tears running down his cheeks, and he took her hand, which was limp and cold. "A weight well worth carrying."

In the event, led by Giotto Luciani, the moonlit traverse of Corti was uneventful, and by dawn the party was well across the plain that surrounded it, sheltered by Corsican pine trees.

The march north would always remain in Burney's memory, a nightmare of exhaustion and fear. Giotto had by now become a very able second in command, and Burney realised that if he ever joined the Royal Navy, he would either be promoted quickly or find some other outlet for his talents. He seemed untiring, marshalling the people, scouting ahead and negotiating for supplies. At Burney's insistence, nothing was taken by force, but paid for, in gold or silver, at probably several times the going rate.

They gave Bastia a wide berth, looking down on it from a distance, the citadel, like Calvi, appearing grim and unassailable, though Burney knew that not many years had elapsed since Nelson had taken it. The problem was now that they were arriving at the Macinaghju rendezvous ten days earlier than they should have, and with such a large company it was difficult to believe they would not come to the attention of the French.

They made their camp at the place above Macinaghju where he had given the rifles to Giotto and his friends, it seemed years ago.

CHAPTER 39 – NORTH

In the grey dawn, *Oleander* worked her way out of Grand Harbour. It felt strange to Snowden that Kennedy was not there, and several times he had started to address his absent shipmate. At first, there was not much wind, but before long *Oleander* was bowling along the coast of Malta in a south-easterly breeze, the sea flat in the lee of the land.

"Twelve knots, Sir," said Midshipman Pascoe, who had been examining the log.

"Think she'll do any more?" said Snowden. "Stuns'ls?"

"I wouldn't, Sir, we wouldn't want to carry anything away, and half a knot won't make much difference to our arrival time. Breaking something, now, that could cost us half a day, if not more."

"You are quite right, Pascoe, we'll leave her as she is for now."

They were joined at the rail by Ensign Watton, the Army officer who was commanding the small detachment of soldiers that had joined *Oleander* at Valletta. "Your ship certainly moves, Commander."

Pascoe exclaimed, "Proven to be the fastest ship in the Navy, by a long way, and perhaps the fastest in the world. Cedar-built she is, very light."

"I don't doubt it, Mr Pascoe. And the crew? I confess I can hardly understand some of them."

"Bermudian, many of them, and a fine body of men too,

but their accent takes some getting used to. They came with the ship when we commissioned her in Bermuda. There's not a pressed man aboard *Oleander*."

The ensign addressed Snowden: "Sir, I'd like to exercise the men on deck. I would very much like to incorporate your marines into my people – your sergeant seems a very capable man."

"Feel free to exercise the men. I am happy for Riley to assist, but I would prefer at least for the time being that he remained under my direct command. The marines in a man o' war have some very specialist duties, as you know." Snowden knew that Watton was somewhat unsure of himself and would welcome Riley as a source of advice, but he was unwilling to give the sergeant and the rifles away to someone who he didn't know.

At that moment, Bartoli, accompanied by two marines, came out on deck for his morning exercise. Watton gestured towards him. "No pressed men aboard your ship, Commander? There seems to be one unwilling mariner."

Snowden smiled, as Pascoe interjected, "General Bartoli. I've no doubt the bastard would like to be elsewhere, but he betrayed us and would have killed our people as they landed if Commander Snowden had not thought ahead and laid a trap for him. Commander Snowden near killed him on the beach. Mrs White was all for stringing him up on the yardarm, there and then."

Snowden moved away. Pascoe leaned forward and said confidentially to Watton, "What do you make of the Old Man?"

"Seems an amiable person, perhaps rather anxious."

"He's a terror, Watton, an absolute terror of a man."

"Really, he seems very, as I said, amiable."

"He is, until he gets into battle. Any sort of a fight and he is in the thick of it, he has no fear whatsoever, and he's so good at it, three steps ahead of the enemy all the time." Watton looked thoughtfully at Snowden, who was talking easily to the Bosun. "Boarded a frigate through the stern windows a couple of years ago, made her strike. And last year he burned Boney's invasion barges, right in the middle of France ..."

"Oh, I remember all that. I won't get into a fight with him."

"You'd better not, Watton, and don't play at cards with him either!"

They ran quickly along the coast of Sicily, and then were left whistling for wind for several hours. The soldiers were exercised using the field pieces that had been brought aboard at Valletta, aided by the ship's gunners.

The wind increased and before long the mountains of Sardinia were in sight, but as soon as Corsica was visible the wind grew light, and Snowden struggled to hide his impatience, though they used the time to practise embarking the soldiers into the ship's boats. They poured over the chart of Corsica and the chart Kennedy had made of Macinaghju, with Snowden thinking intensely how they would respond to threats to Burney's party and how the Corsican recruits could be embarked in an orderly fashion.

Gradually the wind increased, until it was blowing a gale from the west. The ship ran fast with the wind abeam and the seas calmed as she got closer to Corsica, though they stayed well offshore.

CHAPTER 40 – RENDEZVOUS

When the camp near Macinaghju was laid out to his satisfaction and picquets set, Burney called Giotto and together they studied the map, which was by now rather worn looking. Julia lay in an approximation to a bed, against the wall of the hut.

"We have several days here, Giotto. We must decide what we are to do."

"Yes, Capitaine, I agree."

"The first question, and it is perhaps an imponderable one, is how many recruits are going to arrive?"

"I really do not know, but we already have nearly five hundred, and more arrive each day. I think we will have a thousand, perhaps more." He pointed to a band of men entering the camp.

"We must assume that the French will come."

"I agree, Capitaine, they may not know exactly what we plan, but they cannot ignore such a huge gathering. And soon, the French in Bastia will learn of the ambush, if they do not know already, and they will come prepared."

"Giotto, it seems to me that perhaps we must assume we will have fifteen hundred recruits, and that before long the French will arrive as well."

"We have a week before our ships come. Hopefully, there will be men o' war with plentiful boats to take men off the beach, but there may be bad weather, and the beach there", he pointed, "is completely open to the east. I have experience of boat work on open beaches, and embarking fifteen hundred ill-disciplined men is going to be difficult. And, Giotto, it is possible there will be a lack of warships. They are very busy and perhaps they cannot be spared because of some emergency. I think Julia's merchant ships will come …"

Julia made a sound and they turned towards her. She said, weakly, "The merchant ships will come, Renzi will make sure of it. The skippers are steady men."

"Thank you, Julia, but we cannot count on a squadron of warships."

Julia beckoned them to come closer. "I understand what you are saying, Jimmy, and I agree. This camp is all very well for a party of a few dozen …" She stopped and collected herself. "But we have five hundred here already, on this hillside. There is no shelter, no water and little food. We cannot have five hundred, a thousand or more here for a week. The people will become weak, listless, lose morale, there will be fighting, desertion, perhaps sickness," she propped herself up on her elbows, "and as you say, embarkation from the beach will be difficult."

Giotto, who had been listening intently, interjected, "What we are coming round to is that we should go to Macinaghju, to the town."

"Yes", said Burney, "that's about the size of it."

First, Burney realised, they would have to try and get a grip of the recruits. He explained his scheme to Julia and Giotto.

"Giotto will be my aide-de-camp …"

Julia made a choking sound. "Excuse me, Captain Burney RN, I would like to remind you that we are on Corsica, and these people are not …"

Burney blushed and Giotto smiled. "I am sorry. Giotto is to be *your* aide-de-camp and I will be your naval adviser."

"That is an improvement."

"I suggest, Julia, we mark out men with military experience. I think that many of the people are from particular villages. Perhaps we should ask them to form groups of ten and to elect a leader, if possible, someone with military experience. If there is nobody with such experience, we should try and distribute military men so there is one in each group, even if he does not come from that village."

Giotto looked thoughtful. "We should keep the 'Rifles' together, Capitaine, and perhaps we should organise a party of men who have their own weapons and military experience."

"Nearly all of them seem to have weapons, Giotto."

"That is the Corsican way, though the cursed French try to take them from us."

They looked at Julia. "That is a sound plan, Giotto."

Shortly afterwards, Julia, Burney and Giotto, with the Rifles arranged as usual ahead and behind them, went down the hill and along the beach to Macinaghju. The village, which was small and did not give the impression of prosperity, was arranged around a rough wharf, where fishing boats and a merchant ship were moored. There were several men working on fishing gear at the quay, who greeted Giotto and his men cheerfully enough but with a certain wariness. Giotto led them through the village and knocked on the door of a somewhat larger house. He looked back and said, "My house, my parent's house." He pointed to the harbour. "My father owns *Amazzone*, the ship, and is the first man of Macinaghju."

A young woman opened the door, her face bursting with happiness when she saw Giotto. She embraced him and then ran back inside the house, shouting, "Giotto, Giotto, he has returned."

"Your sister?" asked Julia.

"Yes, my sister," Giotto confirmed. "Please come inside."

Giotto led them into a kitchen, where they were immediately joined by Giotto's mother, father and sister. After the greetings and embraces had subsided, Giotto introduced Julia and Burney.

This is going to be hard, thought Burney, *we're going to ask them if we can take over their town, which then might become a battleground. Do your best, Julia.*

"We have a very high appreciation of Giotto, a fine son," began Julia.

Burney nodded in confirmation.

"I am the daughter of Pasquale Paoli."

"Paoli has no daughter that I am aware of," interrupted Giotto's father.

"He *does* have a daughter. I have here a letter written by him, Pasquale Paoli, to me. You can see that it starts 'Dearest Daughter', and orders me to travel to Corsica to raise men for the English Army, to fight away from Corsica against the French."

Giotto's father nodded. "And this gentleman?"

Giotto answered, "He is Capitaine Burney, of the English Navy. He also has orders."

Burney produced his orders and laid the document on the table next to Julia's letter. Giotto's father examined them.

"I saw your English ship, at sea, the one with the enormous masts. And what do you want of us?"

Now for it, thought Burney.

"I want Macinaghju, Signore, for one week only. We wish to embark the recruits in the port, but while we await our ships, we will stay in the town."

"Do we have any choice?"

"No, I fear you do not. I am truly sorry to bring war to

Macinaghju, but I have no alternative."

"And what is to become of us, the inhabitants?"

"I believe it would be better if you left. You may return after we are gone, but there may be danger while we are here. You can take your ship and the fishing boats and go to another port, or you can do as you used to in the time of the slavers and take to the hills."

"We will be ruined."

Julia exclaimed, "Ruined – say you! I am a ship owner myself and I know that ships earn no money tied up in their home ports. Why is *Amazzone* there?"

Giotto's father said vehemently, "You know well why she is tied up. The trade is very bad. We fetch no wine or honey from the Corsican ports to take to Leghorn or Spezia, we bring no cargoes back. There are no English ships in Leghorn any more. The French interfere, they worry that we will smuggle arms to Corsica, and what they call their Continental System, which they say will reduce England, instead reduces us. Sometimes I think I should take my ship off, to Malta perhaps, and charter her to the English Navy. She is a handy ship."

He continued, more reflectively, "I don't think the French will be much of a threat, especially if we leave an interval between leaving Macinaghju and returning. They do not have many troops in Corsica, and they do not want to have to deal with an uprising, which is what they might have if they make reprisals here. I'll call a meeting immediately, perhaps, daughter of Paoli, and Captain Burney, you will be good enough to address it."

As they walked back to the camp, with Julia, still weak, leaning heavily on Burney, they saw that preparations were already underway for the evacuation of Macinaghju. Fishing boats were being readied for sea and baggage of all kinds was piled on the quay.

"*Amazzone*, Giotto, how much do you think she is worth?"

"I will think, Capitaine." He lapsed into silence and then named a figure. Burney thought about his dwindling supply of gold.

"You are joking, Giotto", said Julia, "that's a ridiculous price."

Giotto, as usual, was unembarrassed. "She is the only ship here, and perhaps you have need of one. I do not think, though, that he will sell her. She is his pride and joy."

"A charter, perhaps?"

"Perhaps, but to where?"

"Malta."

Giotto looked at her. "The cargo?"

"Human."

"Ah!"

Julia said, "She is doing no good alongside in Macinaghju and she must be expensive to keep up. You know very well that ships decay through idleness. Your father can sail her to another Corsican port, but she will just lie there instead of here. If you do not wish to work for the English after you have been to Malta, I can get you cargoes in Italy."

Burney thought of the stories Snowden had told him about the business acumen she had displayed when running his father's estate and decided that he had not exaggerated.

Giotto nodded and turned on his heel. "I will speak to him."

The next two days were a ferment of activity for Burney, and indeed for all of the ever-increasing band. Some semblance of order was imposed on the recruits, who had been organised into groups, each with its own leader. There were a number of men with military experience, and these were formed into a company under a grizzled veteran who had served in Egypt with the Corsican Rangers, Sergeant Pietro Girolani. His accounts of his time in the British Army, especially the pay and the division of loot from the defeated French, had swayed the decisions of many potential recruits.

The main route into Macinaghju, the way the French were likely to come, was the coast road from Bastia, about twenty miles to the south. Just before the town, the road ran past a hill, on the summit of which was a Genoese tower, a small round fort with thick walls and small windows, with battlements at the top. It commanded, as it was designed to do, a good view of the sea and of the coast road. Another smaller road wound down from the mountains and this was also guarded by a detachment of recruits emplaced on a low hill. The Genoese fort on the north headland was manned, and a system of runners to carry messages devised.

Sergeant Girolani, relishing the end of his retirement, was a tireless organiser, and it was just as well, for that afternoon there was a commotion of hooves in the street outside the Luciani house.

CHAPTER 41 – THE HILL

The dismounted horseman, accompanied by one of Burney's men from the roadblock, ran into the room where Julia was conversing with Giotto's father.

"Signora, the French are on the road from Bastia."

"The coast road? Did you see them? Where?"

"Yes, the coast road, I saw them myself, at Santa Severa not two hours ago."

"How many?"

"I am not sure, Signora, a great many. Some on horses."

Julia thought, marching men, they will be here tomorrow morning. "Thank you", she said to the horseman, "you have performed a valuable service." She scribbled a note and turned to Burney's man. "Please take this to Capitaine Burney."

Burney was thinking, as he carried another rock to the wall across the road, one of several they had built, that one of the joys of independent command was that you sometimes had to turn your hand to anything, and he was proud of his improvised fortifications. He noticed the messenger run up, and knew, suddenly, what message he would be bearing. He took the message, read it, and walked back along the road to the town. As he turned the corner, he saw *Amazzone* clear the headland and head out to sea.

When he reached the headquarters, to his surprise, he

saw Giotto sitting at the table with Julia, Pietro and three of the other veterans who were viewed as reliable by Pietro and Giotto.

"I just saw *Amazzone* leave, Giotto. I understood you were to go with her."

Giotto smiled, "Let the old man take care of that. He is a good seaman, he doesn't need me. I do not wish to run away from the fight."

Julia and the men at the table smiled at his words and Julia spoke. She was still weak, but her voice had recovered most of its natural strength. "In view of Captain Burney's experience, and my confidence in him, I wish to make it clear that I intend the military operation, which now seems inevitable, to be under his command. Captain, perhaps you could summarise the position."

"Yes, Signora. We have five days until the transport ships are due to arrive. We have prepared as well as we can for the arrival of the French. *Amazzone* has departed for Malta with three hundred people, recruits and civilians, including all the women and children. We now have more than one thousand men in Macinaghju, and others may arrive. Most of them are armed, but there is not much ammunition and we have no heavy weapons. However, our defences are well prepared, we can eke out our food for five days and we have water. I am sure with determination we will be able to hold our positions until the ships arrive."

"It is very likely that the French will arrive by the coast road. It is possible, if they are thwarted there, they will take the high road round the hill, but we should have ample warning of that, if it occurs. However, maximum vigilance must be observed. Antonio, you must ensure there is no disorder in the town."

At Pietro's insistence, the sailors from San Firenze, dressed in their English clothes, had been formed into a police force under the command of Antonio, one of the veterans of the French Army. Burney was determined that there would be no drunkenness or looting, and he mentally thanked the French for providing him with such excellent veterans. He knew that maintaining discipline while embarking a thousand or more men onto ships under fire would be difficult, if it came to that.

As Burney had predicted, the French came by the coast road, in a long straggling line. He watched as they came round the bend and the first men came up to the low wall across the road. No skirmishers, he thought, grimly, the fools. From his vantage point he could see the junction between the coast road and the back road that went behind Macinaghju, but he knew that an alert enemy could send cavalry across country to join the back road somewhere to the west of the town. He beckoned over a messenger. "Go to Giotto. Tell him there are no cavalry. They may come by the back road. Be ready."

"Yes, Sir, there are no cavalry, but they may come to him by the back road."

He patted the messenger on the shoulder and sent him on his way.

The French below him started to clamber over the low wall. It was only two or three feet high and was surrounded by large quantities of loose stones, which Burney hoped would give the impression that construction of the wall had been interrupted and that it was incomplete. He knew experienced troops would recognise it for what it was – a trap – but he hoped that Napoleon had not wasted his best soldiers to garrison Corsica.

The French soldiers stopped and Burney watched as they loaded their muskets and fixed bayonets. He thought their actions did not look like those of a crack regiment, a view confirmed when the men at the front turned and seemed to question their orders, an officer waving them forward. So much for *égalité*, thought Burney – not exactly leading from the front. There were a lot of them, though, perhaps three hundred, and there were two field guns at the rear of the column.

The forward Frenchmen, hesitant, climbed over the wall and advanced round the corner, where they were met by another, slightly higher wall. They began to climb over it and then down the rough slope on its other side, the glacis. When about fifty were picking their way down the slope and onto the rock-strewn road the other side, towards a third wall, Burney tensed, stood up and blew his whistle as loud as he could. There was a moment's silence, the French looking round in dismay, and then the Corsicans concealed behind the third wall fired at the Frenchmen struggling in the rubble. A brave, disciplined force might have been able to use its numbers to get close to the third wall and eventually to overcome it, but these French garrison troops were not of that mettle. They fled as well as they could, but their progress was slowed by the rocks on the road, the rough sloping glacis and the oncoming mass of the rest of the column. Retreating men fell, fought against men still advancing, and sometimes half climbed and half threw themselves over the sloping cliff on the sea side of the road. It was horrible to watch, but before long the column of troops was retreating back along the road, not exactly in a rout but certainly much faster than it had arrived.

Eventually, the French officers managed to get their men under command and halted them on the road, out of musket range, perhaps a quarter of a mile distant. Burney looked at Georgio, one of the Rifles, who was lying on the ground, the muzzle of his weapon resting on a rocky outcrop. "What do you think?"

Georgio looked at him. "I think those officers are as good as dead, Capitaine."

"Well, let me get into position and we will try." Burney sighted at an officer on a horse, controlling his breathing, forcing himself to relax. "When you're ready, Georgio."

The rifles fired almost simultaneously, and two men,

officers probably, dropped from their horses.

"Shot, Georgio."

"Shot, Capitaine."

They reloaded and Burney again sighted at the French, picking out a soldier who he thought might be an officer. A target, he thought, not a man. He fired, missing, but Georgio's shot found its mark.

At first, the firing seemed to be ignored by the mass of men, but shortly Burney could see signs of agitation. An officer drew up a squad of musketeers, pointing towards the riflemen's position, but the distance was hopelessly beyond the range of muskets, and Burney and Georgio shot two of the squad. After that, the retreat of the French continued, a rout now, thought Burney, noticing for the first time the rattle of musketry from the direction of the town. Georgio heard it as well and started to get up.

"The back road. Shall we go there, Capitaine?"

"No, Georgio, the two of us will not make much difference, but if the French retreat, they may come this way."

Before long, they heard the sound of hooves, galloping, and a band of cavalry appeared. Their assault by the back road had clearly not gone well and they were in full retreat. Presumably they intended to rejoin the main body of the French column, and the road was the quickest way there.

They were not easy targets, but Burney and Georgio felled one of them before they reached the safety of the corner of the coast road.

Georgio raised his hat and said ritually, "Thank you, Mr Baker."

CHAPTER 42 – THE WARNING

Later, they sat once more around the table in Giotto Luciani's house. Sergeant Girolani spoke in a calm voice, "They had no chance, Capitaine Burney, they cantered along the road, saw the roadblock and immediately wheeled round. The men got some shots off, but they were gone very quickly. They were right, too, Cavalry's not much use for that sort of thing."

"What do you think they'll do next?"

"It depends. You must never underestimate the determination of the French Army. They've had a mauling today, but if the commander of that column has any guts, they'll be back tomorrow morning."

Burney spoke, "They will have realised we've no heavy weapons. They have probably heard of the Bakers and have figured out we are using them. I think, if I was them, I'd try and get men in place ready to rush the hill, and bring up field pieces to attack the wall on the road. Soon as I'd taken the hill, I'd bring more guns up, and that would make our position in the town quite difficult."

"Our advantage is that we have a lot of men, and the Genoese tower. We must start now to prepare the hill for an attack tomorrow."

Pietro said, "If they were well organised, they would try it at dawn, but from the look of them they won't be able to form up in the dark. It is likely they will wait until daylight, but we must waste no time. We will start now."

At first light, Burney looked over the slope of the hill, amazed at how much could be accomplished in so short a time, if there was plenty of labour available. Men passed rocks along human chains and dug in the unyielding ground with anything they could find.

The French did not attack at first light, but in the afternoon they saw a line of troops advancing along the coast road. Burney had no doubt more would be attempting to flank round Macinaghju and attack from the west, but that was a long diversion across very poor tracks, so they were secure for some time, although he had set a wide circle of picquets to guard against surprise.

As it grew dark, they heard the sounds of digging and of guns being moved, and in the dawn, they saw that the French had constructed earthworks around their field guns, placed to fire up the hill and into the wall on the road. The guns began to fire, but accurate rifle fire from the Corsicans on the hill kept the gunners' heads down, and the shooting was irregular and not well aimed.

About noon, a note from Julia recalled Burney to the town. "How is it going, Jimmy?"

"I think, Julia, the French will need more men and more guns if they are to make progress. Do you have news?"

"This gentleman has just come from Bastia, by a roundabout route."

Burney turned to the man, who was dressed reasonably well but had the ubiquitous gun on his shoulder. It would be strange, thought Burney, to be back in England where men did not habitually carry guns.

"Indeed, pleased to meet you, Sir. You have news for us?"

"Yes. There is a French column approaching along the coast from Bastia. The Chasseurs, who recently arrived in

Corsica, with several guns. I believe that another column has left Corti, with the intention of attacking you from the land."

"You seem remarkably well informed. How is that?"

"Capitaine, I own a house, a public house, in Bastia near the citadel. Sometimes men come to meet women there, you understand. My wife runs that part of the business. The men who visit are mostly Frenchmen, officers, as my house has a good reputation and the girls are pretty. The girls are good Corsicans, most of them, and sometimes the men are indiscreet."

"I see. You have done us a remarkable service, Signor ..."

"I will not tell you my name, Capitaine, but I hope you heed my advice and prepare. The French are very serious and will not give up until you are defeated. I will go now." He stood up and left.

"Well, Julia, what do you make of that?"

"I think we should prepare, and hope that the ships come soon."

CHAPTER 43 – THE SOUND OF GUNS

The wind was still blowing westerly as *Oleander* closed with the coast of Corsica. They were ten miles from the land when there was a hail from the masthead: "On deck there. Gunfire!"

Snowden turned to Poore. "Heave her to, if you please, get her as quiet as possible."

"Aye, Sir."

Snowden ran into his cabin, snatched up his speaking trumpet and rapidly climbed the foremast. "Where was it, Iris?"

"Be dead ahead, Your Honour."

Dead ahead, from Macinaghju. Snowden's heart sank. "We've heaving to, Iris, to get her quiet. Listen carefully." Snowden put the trumpet to his ear and pointed it in the direction the lookout had indicated. He heard it almost immediately, the sound of muskets and a cannon shot. He handed the trumpet to Iris.

"Try it yourself." Iris listened intently for a minute or so. "There be a battle going on, but I don't believe it is ships. On the land, with muskets and small guns."

"I agree, Iris."

"Macinaghju, Sir?"

"I fear it is."

As *Oleander* closed with the land, the noise became more

distinct. Before long there was another hail from the masthead: "On deck, I can see smoke on the land."

Snowden again climbed the foremast, carrying his glass. There was indeed smoke and through the glass he could see it was coming from Macinaghju. He handed the glass to Iris. "Looks to me as though it is coming from the coast road."

"It is, Sir. Are the French attacking?"

"I think they are, Iris." Snowden shook his head. "Dammit, if only we had some men o' war."

"*Oleander* be a man o' war, Skipper."

"So she is, Iris."

As Snowden turned to climb back down the mast, Iris grabbed his arm and pointed to the coast, well south of Macinaghju. "Sorry, Sir, but I just saw a flash of something there, on the road, I reckon. Gimme the glass."

Snowden laughed and said in his best Bermudian, "Gimme de glass, *Sir*." The sarcasm went unnoticed as Iris peered intently through the telescope. *Bermudians*, thought Snowden, *many virtues, but deference is not one of them.*

"Yes, there are many flashes. Sir, Sir, I think there's an army on that road." He handed the glass to Snowden. On the road, perhaps ten miles from Macinaghju, Snowden could just about make out movement. As he concentrated, the movement resolved into what looked like an army, or at least a sizeable column of soldiers.

"I fear you are right, Iris. Thank you for your vigilance."

On deck he closely looked at the compass, and then at Macinaghju, calculating. "Poore, get sail on her, everything you can, and steer north-west. There's an army on that coast road."

"Aye aye, Sir, north-west." Poore gave the necessary orders and turned to Snowden. "An army, Sir, a French army?"

"Yes, and I doubt they're out for a constitutional stroll."

Snowden hurried to the cabin, studied the chart intently, and stood, calculating. *The column, marching, say two knots, Oleander, eight knots.* He went to work with dividers and rule, laid off a course, and went back on deck and spoke to Midshipman Pascoe. "Relieve Mr Poore, Pascoe, if you please, course north-west by west. And get her moving. Strike the ensign. Mr Poore, I want the Gunner, Sergeant Riley, Ensign Watton and yourself in the cabin directly."

"Aye, Sir."

In the cabin, Poore, Trott the Gunner, Riley and Watton stood round the table.

"Sit, please, gentlemen," said Snowden. "Oh, I think we'd better have Bosun as well." He turned to the marine at the door. "Fetch the Bosun, if you please."

Spanish Bob arrived, breathless, and Snowden continued, "It seems to me the French are attacking Macinaghju." He pointed to the chart. "The road from Bastia, where the French have their main garrison, runs along the coast. As you can see, it's about thirty miles long. There are a few small villages along the coast, but the hills are almost uninhabited. Judging by the gunfire, I believe Burney is defending the coast road where it goes round this hill into Macinaghju." He indicated the small sketch of the coastline at the bottom of the chart. "I think and hope that he is holding his ground for now."

Snowden looked round the table and continued, "I think the column I saw from the masthead are reinforcements for the attack on Macinaghju. They're about ten miles short of it now. We must do what we can against them. Now, you can see the coast road is almost at sea level in places, with a steep slope behind it. It seems to me if we got the ship close into the shore, here ..."

CHAPTER 44 – OLEANDER'S RETURN

Burney was just below the summit of the hill, accompanied by Julia, despite her lingering weakness and his protestations. The French were not pressing the attack with great determination, though there was continuous musket fire and an occasional roundshot thudded into the hill. The Corsicans, under Pietro's command, generally held their fire, conserving ammunition, except for the Rifles, who fired every few minutes, sniping at the few Frenchmen foolish enough to show themselves. There had been casualties amongst the Corsicans, but they had prepared the ground well and the wounded were few in number.

"Thank you, Mr Baker," said Julia, ritually, as a rifleman lying behind a low earth bank fired.

"I collected the guns from him personally," said Burney, "in Whitechapel. He showed me how best to use the weapon."

A man ran down from the hilltop fort. "Capitaine, Senora, the ship." He pointed out to sea.

Squinting against the sun Burney saw *Oleander* far away to the south, unmistakable with her huge, raked masts. "By God, he's come back early," he said.

"What is he doing?" asked Julia. "He is heading away from us."

"I think he's seen the French on the coast road. We know they'll send reinforcements, and he's going to give them what for."

"What can he do? There seem to be no other ships."

"I'm not sure, Julia, but if anybody can do anything, it's Percy."

CHAPTER 45 – COAST ROAD

Oleander lay anchored fore and aft behind a low headland, not more than two hundred yards from the rocky shore. The sea was blue, transparent as glass, and the ship seemed to be flying over the bright sand and sea grass of the seabed. They could hear the gentle wash of the waves on the rocks and smell the fragrant bushes ashore.

Snowden, at the foretop, looked down on the coast road, running a few yards back from the shore, and at the French skirmishers moving in a widely spaced line through the maquis on the hill above the road. To Snowden's inexpert eye, the soldiers seemed well disciplined. Though the nearest one was probably only three hundred yards distant, they took no notice of *Oleander*. Snowden supposed that to a landsman, his ship, with covers over the deck guns, and the crew below or behind the bulwarks, looked like a merchantman lying quietly at anchor.

Iris whispered, "Here they come. Cavalry."

Snowden watched as a column of mounted men, three abreast, came round the corner of the road. They wore blue uniforms and their accoutrements glittered in the bright sunshine.

He turned to the midshipman at his elbow, "Compliments to Mr Poore, Pascoe, and ask him to get her underway." Pascoe descended rapidly and Snowden turned to the sharpshooters on the maintop: "Hold your fire until you hear the main armament."

He slid down the rigging and was just in time when he reached the deck to see the buoyed bitter ends of the anchor cables drop over the side. By the time he reached the wheel, the headsails had broken free from their twine lashings, *Oleander's* bow was swinging to port and men were working at the halyards, hoisting the great main and foresail, sheeting them in. The ship came alive.

"For the first buoy, Poore."

"Aye aye."

When they had arrived at the anchorage earlier, they had taken the boats along the coast, and hurriedly sounded and buoyed a safe passage for the ship, as close to the shore as possible. Snowden hoped they had not missed any isolated rocks, but if they had, he thought the lookouts would probably see them through the clear water before it was too late, though the ship was moving quickly now in the onshore sea breeze.

He walked along the deck to the fo'c'stle head, speaking to the men at the starboard broadside guns as he went. At the bow of the ship he spoke to Trott, who was crouched over the starboard Carron. "Ready, Guns?"

Trott did not look up. "I reckon, Sir."

Snowden turned and shouted to Poore near the helm, surprised at the strength of his own voice, "Colours, Mr Poore."

There was a cheer from the men as the battle ensign broke out on the main peak, and a rumble as the guns ran out. The ship was so close to the road that Snowden clearly saw the cavalry officer at the head of the column look up at the sound. He saw *Oleander*, with her huge ensign, guns run out and the black gaping muzzles of the Carrons on her fo'c'stle, and recognised her for what she was, a British man o' war. Perhaps the officer had experience of the Royal Navy's previous actions in Corsica and knew how effective ships could be against unprotected shore targets, but, whatever his experience, he was a quick-witted man and he did something that Snowden had not expected – spurring his horse and galloping forward, his troop following him.

The combined speed of the horsemen and ship meant that the Carrons had no opportunity to fire, and the broadside guns had little effect on the galloping cavalry. The sharpshooters in the tops, however, used their rifles to deadly effect and picked off several horsemen. There was no time to think about the missed opportunity as the infantry column came in sight, still marching despite the sounds of gunfire. The ship came up to them, almost instantaneously, so close to the road that he could clearly make out individual soldiers.

"Let 'em have it, Guns," he said.

The starboard Carron fired, and Poore briefly turned the ship towards the land, allowing the starboard smasher to bear. Snowden thought this was probably the first time that a ship had been got close enough inshore to attack with Carrons, but though the range for the short-barrelled weapons was extreme, the canister shot had a terrible effect on the infantry. Men collapsed, reminding Snowden of wheat cut by the blade of a scythe. The ship raced along the shore, following the line of buoys, smashers and long guns firing as fast as they could be reloaded and aimed. The men ashore had no option. They climbed the low cliff behind the road and took cover as best they could in the bushes on the slope above. Snowden realised these were disciplined, veteran troops, as they took their weapons with them and lay down in the maquis, just above the road, and began to fire their muskets at the ship.

The men towards the rear of the column saw the ship coming and took to the slopes. Gradually the road emptied. Suddenly, Snowden saw what he was looking for and went back to the wheel. "There's their artillery. Heave her to, if you please,

Mr Poore."

"Aye aye, Sir."

Abandoned by their drivers, the gun carriages and baggage wagons stood on the road, the horses drawing them standing still.

"What do you think, Guns?" said Snowden, wincing as a musket ball clanged into the iron chainplate supporting the shrouds on the side of the ship's hull.

"Keep her steady, Sir, and I'll see what I can do."

"You heard the Gunner, Mr Poore."

The ship steadied and Snowden watched as the Gunner carefully sighted along the cannon, nodding to the gun's crew as they made fine adjustments to the pointing until he was satisfied and pulled the lanyard, the cannon recoiling against its ropes. They saw the shot hit the rocks behind the nearest French field gun. The horses shifted uneasily. The second shot hit the gun, the wooden carriage seeming to explode as the ball ploughed into it. The horses had had enough, and they wheeled and galloped headlong away from the ship, back towards Bastia, quickly followed by the other guns and wagons.

"I don't reckon they'll stop for a while," said the Gunner, with evident satisfaction.

Without artillery, there was little that the men ashore could do to retaliate against the ship. *Oleander's* long guns kept up a continuous fire against them and several times they took her in so close that they could fire the smashers, but the French quickly learned their lesson and made no attempt to return fire, and disappeared into the well-wooded countryside. Targets became fewer, the ship's fire desultory, until no Frenchmen were visible and it stopped altogether. As the afternoon drew on, they saw troops emerge from the woods and group together on a section of the road that was high above the sea, a long way to the south. Snowden knew they had stopped the French using the coast road to Macinaghju.

"Boat ahoy."

A fishing boat bumped alongside and an energetic-looking Corsican with a Baker rifle on his shoulder climbed aboard, shouting, "Capitaine Snowden, message for Capitaine Snowden." His way was barred by a party of marines, and from the corner of his eye Snowden saw Pascoe put his hand on the butt of his pistol. The man shouted, "I am Giotto Luciani, I have a message for you from Capitaine Burney and Signora Julia." He waved a letter, which a marine took and handed to Snowden.

Macinaghju

Snowden

This will be handed to you by Giotto Luciani, a most useful person who has been with us since we landed from Oleander.

We have collected upwards of fifteen hundred volunteers. They are mostly armed but have not much ammunition.

We have taken Macinaghju. The civil population has left. There is sixteen feet of water beside the quay. We have fortified the hill to the south of Macinaghju and the way into the town from the west. The French attack us from the foot of the hill, but we can hold out against them indefinitely. The French here are garrison troops and not effective.

A column of chasseurs is to move from Bastia along the coast road. We have heard firing from the south, so you have presumably met them. We hope the encounter went well.

Another column is moving from Corti and will attack Macinaghju from the west.

The situation here is by no means hopeless, but we would very much like to hear that shipping will arrive directly.

Jimmy

Julia

"Fifteen hundred men, Signor Luciani?"

"Giotto, Capitaine. I believe there are fifteen hundred. We sent three hundred away yesterday in my father's ship."

"Your father's ship?"

"Yes, *Amazzone*."

"You were with Burney and Signora Julia the whole time?"

"Yes, Sir. We went to Pino, San Firenze, Calvi. And then the French came after us, so we had to return to Macinaghju."

"Has there been much fighting?"

"Some, Capitaine. Signor Burney ambushed them near Corti. They followed us, but the Bakers stopped them."

"And here?"

"The French attacked us, but we surprised them on the road. Some cavalry went by the back road, but we were ready for them and they ran. They have been attacking the hill since this morning, but our positions are strong, though we have some wounded now and three dead."

"What about water and food?"

"We have water, and food for a few days."

"You are a seaman, Giotto. Can we bring the ships into Macinaghju, to take the men off?"

"If they have less than sixteen feet, it is still possible. Capitaine, if you do not mind me making a suggestion …?"

"Not at all."

"We saw you hit the French gun and their wagons run back along the road."

Snowden nodded.

"It will be very difficult for the French you have just attacked to move through the wood ashore, and they will not have much food or water. The French attacking the hill at Macinaghju can be shot at from the sea. I know because some of them fired muskets at us as we went round the point. It was stupid of me, we were too close, but if you take the ship there, it can fire back at them."

CHAPTER 46 – SURRENDER

It was several hours after Julia and Burney had watched *Oleander* disappear behind the headlands to the south that they heard the sound of gunfire. Julia listened intently. "Was that the Carrons?" she asked.

"Sounded like it to me. They must have the ship very close inshore, and I can hear musketry as well."

Gradually the firing stopped, and they waited anxiously, the men alert at their posts, ready for the French reinforcements. Waited, and waited. Nothing.

"He's stopped them, Jimmy, hasn't he", said Julia "the reinforcements?"

"I think he has, Julia, he must have taken her right inshore. They couldn't get along the road with *Oleander* just off the beach."

The desultory firing from the French at the base of the hill also slowly stopped. Julia gestured downwards. "They saw the ship and heard the gunfire. They have guessed what has happened. They realise there will be no reinforcements."

The sun was low over the island when *Oleander* came into view, sailing slowly with her guns run out, the huge ensign at her main peak, startlingly close, so close that they could recognise Snowden near the wheel, with Giotto at his side, clearly giving directions. The Corsican defenders cheered at the sight of her and redoubled their fire at the French attackers, who started to turn their cannon round to face the sea.

Oleander fired, one gun, and grapeshot whistled over the heads of the French. Burney saw Snowden look through his glass at the shore and then speak to the Gunner. The second shot would not be high, he realised, and so did the French. A pike with a white shirt tied to it appeared above the rampart of the field gun.

"Cease Fire! Cease Fire!" shouted Burney, standing, and the Corsicans complied. He hurriedly took off his shirt, tied it to his rifle and set off down the hill, hoping the white flag had been seen by *Oleander's* crew. A French officer emerged and began to climb the hill, carrying the flag. This was the moment of greatest danger, thought Burney, and found himself shaking. The Corsicans were not the most disciplined of soldiers and it only took one …

Burney could see that the French officer was a short man of about forty, dishevelled looking, his blue and white uniform dirty and torn in several places. They stopped and stood a few feet apart. The Frenchman nodded and Burney returned the gesture.

"*Franççais?*" said the officer.

"*Un peut*," replied Burney. "Captain Burney, Royal Navy."

"Major Neville, *Armée de la République*. It is true then, there is an English Captain in Corsica."

Burney gestured to the ship, now anchored very close to the shore. "We have the advantage, Major. What do you propose?"

Neville nodded, his face grey and drawn. "We will surrender, but my men are frightened of the Corsicans." Rightly so, thought Burney, and then considered his response. He did not want a large number of Frenchmen in Macinaghju. They would have to be fed and guarded, the Corsicans might seek revenge, and there was always the possibility that they could free themselves from whatever captivity might be improvised and attack the Corsicans. He knew what he must do.

"You are to give up your weapons. We will take officers and sergeants prisoner. The rest of the men can walk back to Bastia."

For a long moment the Frenchman looked at him, calculating, defeat and dejection on his face, and then nodded, "*J'accord.*"

Burney, hardly able to conceal his elation, saw boats set off from the ship and row rapidly towards the shore, full of red-coated soldiers, with Snowden seated in the sternsheets of the leading craft. He turned and saw Julia coming down the hill, flanked by two Corsicans supporting her arms. Burney went towards her and told her what had transpired with the French.

"You will have to explain it to the Corsicans, Julia. We cannot take them prisoner, and I will not have any futile fighting."

"You are right, Jimmy, I will explain to them."

"Very well, Julia. Please send twenty men down to help me with the prisoners."

Burney went back to the road, arriving in time to see Snowden, grinning broadly, clamber over the rocks at the summit of the low cliff and onto the road. "Jimmy", he said, taking in Burney's rather bedraggled appearance, "you're looking well, for someone so old. Your rest on Corsica has obviously agreed with you. Is that half a uniform you're wearing?"

"Commander Snowden, allow me to point out that it is half of a *captain's* uniform."

Snowden smiled, "*Touché*, Sir."

"You met the French reinforcements on the coast road?"

"We did, I believe they're making their way back to Bastia, chasing their artillery and commissariat which made a unilateral decision to retreat. Those Carrons, close in ..." He shook his head. "Shall we go over to the 'lobsters' and you can tell us all at the same time what is required."

They walked over to the soldiers and Burney explained the truce he had arranged to Snowden, Watton and Riley.

"We must allow them onto the road, one at a time, as they hand over their weapons. Keep them covered, and when they ..."

Major Neville and three sergeants arrived, guarded by soldiers, but engaged in an animated discussion. Neville looked at Snowden enquiringly: "We have heard you are called Snowden, Monsieur. My sergeant says that it was you who burnt our invasion barges in Brittany. Is that true? It is said that Napoleon turned over his desk in rage when he heard of it."

"It is true, um ... Major." Snowden tried not to show his pleasure at Napoleon's recognition of his exploits, and then, his gambler's instinct urging him to exploit any advantage, he said, "Yes, Major, I am Snowden, and I burnt *Boney's* barges." He used the word as a mark of contempt. "And that is my ship. Please tell your men that I declare the coast road closed", he gestured towards the French soldiers, "please, Major."

Neville went off to speak to his men. Snowden knew that this was self-interest on Neville's part – to be defeated by the apparently famous burner of barges would carry less shame than defeat by an unknown foe, but he also thought it might give the French pause before returning to the attack. He knew that a group of defeated soldiers returning with tales of a legendary foe – himself – would not improve morale in Bastia and might give him a little time.

Snowden walked over to Neville, who was conferring with some of his men. "Neville, you have some wounded men. Do you want to take them with you or leave them here? It looks to me as if there's one or two chaps that ought to be taken off to the ship directly."

"Sir, I cannot leave the wounded here with these people, but please take those two to the ship. I am obliged to you."

It was almost dark when the disarmed French soldiers were gathered on the road and set off, singing, back to Bastia: "*Ça ira, Ça ira, Ça ira ...*"

"The song of the Revolution," murmured Burney, as they turned and walked back to Macinaghju. "Boney wouldn't like that either."

CHAPTER 47 – KENNEDY

Kennedy had known that he was a competent seaman. He had grown up in the merchant service, as an apprentice in one of his uncle's ships, rapidly becoming an Able Bodied Seaman. He had already done one trip to Bombay, and his ship, *Primrose*, was anchored in the Downs, waiting for a West Indies convoy to finish assembling, under the protection of a seventy-four-gun naval ship, *Leviathan*. He thought how imposing the seventy-four looked, her newly painted hull and great yellow masts and yards shining in the sun. He saw a boat put off from the man o' war and make its way towards them.

"Up to no good, them bastards," muttered an elderly AB.

"All of us have tickets," Kennedy replied. "We're all safe."

"Says you," said the AB. "I don't trust 'em. I'm off below."

Kennedy had found himself almost alone on the deck as *Primrose*'s Master went to the chains to meet the naval lieutenant climbing aboard.

"Good morning, Skipper."

After a pause whose length was nicely judged to convey maximum contempt, the skipper answered, "Morning Mr Midshipman."

"If you please, Skipper, have your men assemble on deck."

With great complaint the crew, or at least those members of the crew who had not taken to their carefully arranged hiding places, had gathered on the deck while the lieutenant inspected their papers, grudgingly accepting that they were all in order.

"Thank you, Skipper, that seems to be in order. I am sure you are a law-abiding seaman, so I will not rummage you today." There was an audible exhalation of breath from the crew. "Before I go, are there any here who would wish to enter the King's Service? The pay for prime seamen is reasonable, and the chance of prize money ..." He had clearly made this speech before, presumably to little effect, and his voice trailed off as he turned to go.

Kennedy afterwards could not explain exactly why he had done it, but he was a single man, young, with a thirst for adventure, and he had heard of merchant seamen who had done well in the Navy. He heard himself say, "I'll volunteer, Sir ..."

Now, years later, as he leant on the rail of *Rondine* in the warm night, he thought that he had made the right choice. The Navy, especially for pressed men, and especially landsmen, was desperately hard, but he was a volunteer, a prime seaman, and had done well for himself, accumulating a little prize money, astutely playing the game of shipboard politics, and had eventually become *Oleander's* Master. And now he had an independent command, only of two small merchant ships, but he knew that if this venture went well, he might well be recommended for a commission, and if he was, he had no doubt he would easily pass the examination.

Renzi leant on the rail beside him and spoke, jolting him from his reverie, "How does it go, Kennedy?"

"I believe everything is satisfactory, Signore."

"How do you find our ships?" He gestured to where the outline of *Balestruccio* could be made out against the starry sky.

"They remind me of my time in my uncle's ships."

"Your uncle's ships? What are you doing here?"

"I was young and thought that the Navy would be more

interesting, more exciting."

"And has it been? Would you not have progressed in your uncle's ships?"

"It has been exciting, sometimes too exciting. I expect I would have progressed with my uncle. He is very disappointed that I went off to the Navy. He thinks I will go back to him, though."

"And will you?"

"I will see how it goes in the next couple of years. It is a good time to be in the Navy, it has great need of men, there is prize money."

"And your captain, Snowden, what do you think of him?"

"He is an immensely good officer. The men will do anything for him, especially the Bermudians, and the ship is as happy as a ship can be."

"It seemed so to me."

"I think I am the better seaman, but in a fight ..."

"I have heard."

"He is fearless." Kennedy paused for thought. "No, that's not quite right. He is ... joyous, joyous when he is fighting, something I have not seen before, but there is more than that. He exploits every weakness of an enemy, weaknesses that are hardly there, turns them to his advantage. Ruthless – I think that's the word for it. Ruthless."

CHAPTER 48 – FORTIFICATION

They were in the kitchen of the Luciani house, Corsicans and English, crowded round the table. The Corsicans had left their long guns against the wall at the door, but had retained their pistols and daggers. Burney stood to speak, Giotto translating for the benefit of the Corsicans.

"*Oleander* has been alongside in the port, and the guns and soldiers she brought are ashore. We have used powder from the ship to damage the coast road, and it will be very difficult for the French to bring heavy guns by that route, and *Oleander* will cover the road as well. We will reinforce the hill, but, apart from that, I believe we must defend the town itself, or rather the harbour. We will barricade the streets and place the guns to fire along them. That will be a formidable obstacle to the French. We will have picquets on the coast road and inland to give warning of any French approach."

He paused as Giotto translated. There were murmurs of assent. One man called out, "Barricade the streets, Signore?"

Burney hesitated, knowing what the man was asking. "Yes, we will have to demolish some houses. The English government will compensate their owners."

There was a little cynical laughter from the people in the room, but no dissent. Another man called out, "When will the ships come?"

"In two days." Burney spoke with a certainty he did not

entirely feel. "There will be two merchant ships, *Oleander*, and about twelve hundred men. We may have to embark under fire, and if there is indiscipline or attempts to rush aboard, there will be a disaster. What we will do, in the time remaining to us, is to practise. Sergeant Riley will take charge of drilling the Corsicans. What say you, Riley?"

"Your Honour, British marines will be marshals. The Corsicans will be formed into companies under their captains, and they will march in an orderly fashion to the ships as the previous company is embarked. We will not have a long vulnerable line of men exposed to fire. The men at the rear of each company will be prepared to fire their guns at the enemy if necessary."

More murmurs of approval.

"*Oleander* has taken as much water as she can, as the merchant ships will be very crowded and some men will be on deck in the sun. If necessary, we may be able to transfer water to the merchant ships. *Oleander* will guard the coast road. Julia?"

Julia stood and spoke in Corsican: "We came here with the idea that we could raise a regiment to fight the French. Well, we have raised a regiment, a regiment of Corsican men, and now our only remaining task is to take it off the island. These English know about defending towns and embarking men onto ships. You, some of you, have seen them in action, at Calvi, Bastia, San Firenze." She turned to Snowden. "This man, Capitaine Snowden, burnt the Emperor's barges! In the middle of France! The Emperor was so angry with him that he knocked his desk over when he heard the news!" There was a ripple of laughter. "What I am trying to say is this: I know we are Corsicans, on Corsica, but for this operation to succeed we must obey the orders of the English. They grind slowly, the English, but they grind thoroughly. Thank you, gentlemen."

The next two days were spent in a blur of activity. Snowden was everywhere, inspecting the positioning of the field guns, the barricading of the streets, the drilling of the Corsicans. Often Julia was with him, translating if necessary, giving impromptu speeches – encouraging, cajoling and occasionally angrily remonstrating. As far as Snowden could tell, morale amongst the Corsicans was high.

On the morning of the third day, as he was at breakfast in the Luciani house with Burney and Julia, a messenger arrived with the news they had been dreading. "The French are at Vignale, Signore."

"How many?"

"Just a few, Signore, cavalry. Georgio ambushed them and they turned back. But there are clouds of dust on the road behind them ..."

Snowden turned to Burney, who was looking at the map. "They'll be here by tomorrow morning."

Reports of the French advance became regular occurrences. Sniped at by Corsicans, the French sent skirmishers into the hills in pursuit, and these were in turn ambushed. It was the type of warfare at which the Corsicans excelled. No Frenchman in the approaching army felt safe, and this slowed the French advance. A larger ambush, by a hundred Corsicans, stopped the French in their tracks, while a large contingent of troops attempted to circle round the ambushers, who had long gone by the time they arrived.

In the evening, Snowden heard a cheer from the Corsicans in the town. He sat there, hoping, and a messenger ran into the room. "The ships, Signore, they have arrived."

He climbed the hill, where Burney was standing by the flagpole they'd erected. Julia stood beside him, intently looking out to sea through Burney's telescope. Julia, who had a rifle on her shoulder and pistols in a belt round her waist, turned, her face blazing with excitement. "Percy, they've arrived."

But so, unfortunately, had the French.

CHAPTER 49 – RONDINE

On *Rondine's* deck, Kennedy was also looking through a glass, with Renzi and the ship's Master, Androtti, at his side.

"They've put a flagpole on that hill, Renzi. Could you get that slate from the cabin?"

Renzi returned with the slate. "Write this down ..."

They went into the cabin with the slate and Kennedy decoded the message. In truth, he was adept with flags and hardly needed to consult the book, but he wanted a little time to think.

"We are to go alongside in Macinaghju ..."

"Alongside?" Androtti was incandescent. "My ship, alongside? Macinaghju is shallow. We may go aground, and then the French ..."

They heard it at the same time. The unmistakable boom of artillery.

"Yes, Capitaine," said Kennedy, "Alongside."

Kennedy selected the flags and then hoisted the acknowledgement. More flags broke out on the flagpole ashore. "Pilot will meet us" and then "Channel buoyed." Kennedy acknowledged and then, almost as an afterthought, added another string of flags and saw it acknowledged.

He spoke to Renzi in the cabin. "Can we rely on Androtti?"

"We can, as long as I am here."

"And the other ship?"

"*Balestruccio's* skipper, Disanto, is made of sterner stuff. His brother, you understand, the French ..." He let his voice trail off and Kennedy was not inclined to enquire further, but took *Rondine* close to *Balestruccio* while Renzi relayed his instructions to her skipper.

As the ships closed with the land, they saw *Oleander* to the south, close into the land. In the dusk they saw the flash of her guns and then heard the reports.

"Firing on the coast road", said Kennedy, and then, "here are the boats."

A man came over the rail, followed by several Navy seamen. The man looked at Kennedy. "You are Kennedy?"

"I am."

"I am Giotto Luciani, your pilot. I am a seaman from Macinaghju. We will take this ship in first. The channel is buoyed, but there is only room for one ship alongside. We have several boats ready to tow the ship and men with ropes on the shore."

"How many men will we have to take?"

"Signora Julia was very effective in her recruiting, Signore, and I think five hundred."

"Five hundred. My word. And the French?"

"They have just arrived. We have fortified the town and can hold them off." He pointed south as there was another flash of cannon fire. "*Oleander* is keeping the coast road closed."

As he was speaking, the Bermudian sailors were taking places near the ship's crew, ready to assist in working the ship. Kennedy called Renzi and Androtti over. "Signores, I am ordered to take command of your ship until we are alongside in Macinaghju. I apologise for this, and I hope you will give me your assistance …"

"Assistance?" said Renzi "Of course we will assist you."

"And you, Capitaine?"

"My full cooperation, Signore, but take care of my ship."

"Thank you. I will do what I can. This is what I plan to do…"

The ships grew closer to the port, tacking against the stiff westerly wind.

"Will the wind hold, Giotto?" asked Kennedy.

"I believe it will, Signore, I am not sure, but usually it does."

By now, the gunfire was almost constant, and they could hear the rattle of musketry. The smell of gunpowder overpowered the scent of the bushes on the shore.

There was a shout from forward. "Buoy ahead."

CHAPTER 50 – A NICE BIT OF WORK

From his vantage point on the Genoese tower on the hill, Burney could see the two ships approaching from the sea and the French advance from the interior of the island. The French stopped near the town, and through his glass he could see officers with their telescopes appraising the defences. They were numerous, probably a regiment, perhaps six hundred men, with three guns. Not enough to take the well-defended town, he knew, but certainly enough to besiege it until reinforcements could come from other parts of the island. He also knew, with great clarity, that the hill on which he stood was the key to Macinaghju, and from his vantage point he saw French soldiers break out of the trees and rush towards the slope. Foolish, he thought, as the Corsican defenders, without waiting for orders, opened fire from their prepared positions. The French attack dwindled rapidly, leaving several dead men behind. The Corsicans, under strict orders, did not follow the fleeing French.

He saw boats go out to the two merchant ships, which were beating into the land against a stiff westerly breeze, and called over the English sergeant who was in charge of the captured French guns. "Wilson, three shots at minute intervals, if you please" – the prearranged signal to recall *Oleander*.

"Aye, Sir. Sir, it seems to me we may as well fire towards them Frenchies, rather than just wasting shot and powder."

Burney pointed towards the French Army. "Can you reach

them, Wilson?"

"We can try, Sir. She seems like a good weapon." He patted the muzzle of the cannon.

"Well, go ahead, Sergeant."

The sergeant, who had been laying his guns carefully on the French, said, "Stand clear, Sir" and then fired. On the third shot, a gap appeared in the French ranks, and Burney saw Frenchmen straining against the carriages to turn the guns towards his hill.

"I think we've brought it upon ourselves, Wilson."

"We have, Sir, but we're well dug in and if they fire at us they'll waste their shot. While they're shooting at us, they won't be shooting at the town."

The French cannons fired, but Burney did not see the shot. Eventually one thudded into the hill below them.

"Wasting their time, Sir," said Wilson.

In the town, Snowden and Julia were going around the defences, encouraging the men crouching behind the barricades, heaps of rubble and wood created by demolishing buildings at the edge of the town.

"Do you think the French know we mean to leave by sea?" asked a young recruit.

"We must assume they do, but don't worry, we are well defended. Remember, walk, don't run to the ship."

"Yes, Sir."

"Julia, we should return to the harbour."

At the harbour, Snowden, standing at the end of the quay with a group of men picked for their seagoing experience, watched as the boats that were to stand by to assist the merchant ships left and waited at the end of the entrance channel. *Rondine* came into view, under reduced canvas, following the buoys they had laid. On and on she came, travelling quite quickly, and he heard a shout and the creaking of the spars as the sails were backed. Too soon, he thought, she'll fall off to leeward, but as her bows came level with the quay he realised he was wrong. Kennedy, he thought. Amen.

"Let's have it," he shouted, and a heaving line was thrown from the bow of the ship. One of the men ashore caught it, and men on the quay pulled with a will, bringing the ship's anchor cable dripping onto the wharf.

"Come on," he shouted and, with the men, ran with the heavy cable and dropped the end over a bollard. "She's fast," he yelled, and he saw the ship's helmsman port the helm and the ship's stern began to swing away from the wharf. Water squirted from the rope, which had been led through the ship's port fairlead, as it tightened with the strain of slowing hundreds of tons of ship. He heard the cable creak around the bitts on the ship as the men aboard paid it out slowly to reduce the load in the line.

The ship began to swing her stern away from the quay until she was almost at right angles.

"Sternline," he bellowed, and another heaving line came curving out of the darkness, landing across the quay, where it was picked up by the shore party, who tallied onto it with a will, swinging the ship's stern round until she was parallel to the wharf, the expanse of black water between them steadily narrowing until she bumped roughly alongside, and Snowden leapt aboard, almost colliding with Kennedy.

"Welcome to Macinaghju, Kennedy, and well done."

"Thank you, Sir. Time for a run ashore?"

Snowden laughed "Well, Kennedy, I don't believe the bars are open, and the passengers may become impatient if we don't get a move on."

Sergeant Riley arrived at the quayside. "Are we ready, Sir?"

"We are, Riley, the hatches are already open. You know what to do."

On the hill, in the fading light, Burney saw the ship enter the harbour, swing round and make fast to the wharf. Good work, he thought, as groups of men started to make their way towards the ship from the shadow of the quayside buildings.

The sergeant tugged at his sleeve, pointing to where the French column was halted and where several small bright fires had appeared. "I think they're heating shot, Sir. They mean to fire the town."

Sergeant Girolani arrived. "Capitaine, we can hear the French moving through the bushes below. I believe they may be about to attack."

"Wilson", said Burney, "please put some grape into the bushes where Sergeant Pietro directs."

"Yes, Sir."

The artillerymen pointed the gun under Pietro's direction and it fired, followed by the other gun, sending grapeshot down the hill, scything noisily through the bushes.

Burney called for a messenger. "Tell Capitaine Snowden that the French are heating shot. The buckets will be needed." The messenger repeated the words, twice, and ran towards the town.

Snowden heard the guns on the top of the hill fire, and fire again, and knew that the French were trying to take the hill. If they did, they would overlook the port and the embarkation would become very difficult. The messenger ran up, a young man, panting. "Sir, heated shot, we can see the fires."

"From Capitaine Burney?"

"Yes, Sir, from the Capitaine."

"How are things on the hill?"

"Pietro said the French were about to attack, they are in

the trees. We are firing the guns."

Georgio said, "I will tell the Firemen, Signore."

As he ran off, Julia approached. "What is it, Percy?"

"Heated shot, Julia, but you seem to have prepared for that."

At the suggestion of one of the Corsican French Army veterans, they had dragged boats from the harbour into the streets of the town and had filled them with sea water, ready to be used for firefighting if necessary, surrounded by whatever containers they could find, buckets, barrels, wine jugs ...

The moon was well up in the southern sky now, giving a ghostly light to the scene.

Riley came up. "Sir, the ship's full."

"Thank you."

He turned. "Julia?"

"You know very well, Percy, that I will leave only on the last ship."

It was useless to argue. "Very well." He ran down to the ship, whose decks were close-packed with Corsican recruits. Kennedy was stepping over them, giving orders to the crew. Snowden jumped and stood on the rail, holding onto the mainmast shrouds. "Kennedy, are you ready?"

"Aye, Sir."

He noticed Renzi, standing near the wheel, and called out, "Thank you, Signore, I think you can now be on your way."

They cast the bow line off and a party of men under Snowden's direction took the sternline forward and pulled on it, slipping and cursing as they walked her along the quay. She was a beast to get going, but by the time the stern was level with the end of the wharf she was moving at perhaps a couple of knots and her sails were drawing. The men ashore let go of the sternline, it was pulled aboard, and Snowden watched as the ship moved away down the buoyed channel.

CHAPTER 51 – SIEGE

The weak moonlight illuminated the French as they attacked up the hill – a hopeless frontal charge, which very soon dwindled and retreated in the face of fire from the hill's defenders, followed shortly afterwards by the waving of a white flag and a request for permission to retrieve their wounded.

"They'll need more men than that, Sir," said Wilson. "A lot more, and this fort's a strong place as well."

Burney watched the first ship leave the harbour, the crowd on her decks visible in the moonlight, thread her way along the channel and heave to outside the harbour. After a pause, a boat left her side, heading for the other merchant ship. So far, so good, he thought.

Aboard *Rondine,* Kennedy felt close to collapse. Relief, he supposed. He had got away with it, but now he would have to repeat the exercise. He turned to Giotto. "Ready for the next one?"

The Corsican smiled. "The pilot of Macinaghju is always ready, Signore."

"Boat's alongside, Sir," said a sailor.

Kennedy turned to Renzi and Androtti. "Thank you, gentlemen. You know what to do now."

"Thank you, Signor Kennedy."

His legs felt like rubber as he walked over to the chains, followed by Giotto, and climbed into the boat. Minutes later they were aboard *Balestruccio*.

"Good evening, Capitaine Disanto."

"Signore."

"You saw what we did with *Rondine*? Now we will do the same with *Balestruccio*."

At that moment, an orange flash illuminated the men's faces, swiftly followed by a huge explosion in the town, and then the roar of cannons from the west.

"That's a mortar," said Kennedy. "No time to lose, get the sails on her."

Burney, on the hill, saw the explosion of the mortar shell, followed by the collapse of a house on the edge of the harbour. "That is not good, Sergeant."

"No, Sir. Carrying that thing over those hills must have been a task."

"Is there anything we can do?"

"Probably not, Sir. We could wait until it fires again, and then perhaps we can fire at the flash. Probably hopeless, but we may as well try. I'll get one of the guns moved round again, get some spotters to watch."

The second mortar shell landed in the harbour, sending up a column of white water. On the hill, Sergeant Wilson's spotters stood with their arms outstretched, pointing to where they had seen the mortar's flash. Painstakingly, Wilson looked along each man's arm and then moved to the gun, which he carefully aimed. Eventually, Wilson's gun fired, but they could not see what effect it had had, and the next mortar shell landed in the town. By now, the cannonade from the French guns was almost constant.

Wilson said, "Sir, if we keep a good watch down the hill, in case the French try again, I think we should fire all the guns at the French muzzle flashes. If they attack up the hill, we can turn the guns round again in time. We have plenty of ammunition,

Sir, and firing at the mortar may do no good, but it will at least divert their attention away from the town."

"Very good, Wilson, you seem to be able to re-point the guns pretty quickly."

Kennedy recovered his composure as *Balestruccio* followed the channel into the harbour. The crew shouted in alarm as a mortar shell landed in the harbour, very near the wharf, but berthing was completed without problems, and Corsican recruits immediately began to board, Julia speaking to each group.

Firing was intense, from both French and British guns. Cannons from Burney's battery on the hill kept up a steady fire, and mortar shells exploded, which sometimes led to the loud collapse of walls. Though the French were firing blind, Snowden knew it was only a matter of time before a mortar shell fell on the wharf or, even worse, on the ship. He called over a messenger and gave him a hastily scribbled note. "To Capitaine Burney on the hill, quick."

Wounded men were being carried back to the ship from the fighting on the edge of town, and Snowden realised that the scene on the wharf was now illuminated by red-tinged light.

"Beginning to burn," he said to Riley.

"Yes, Sir, the Frenchies are firing so many of those heated shot that we can't get to all of them before they catch a roof on fire." He paused and gestured to the ship. "I think she's ready to go, Sir."

On the hill, Burney, looking out over the nightmarish scene below him, saw the messenger climbing the slope. He took the man's note, read it and went over to Wilson, who was sighting along a gun. "They're bringing *Oleander* in next. We'll keep the gun crews here, but tell Pietro to take his men down to the harbour."

On the wharf, Snowden spoke to Kennedy, wincing as a

mortar shell landed somewhere behind them. "Take her out, then, Mr Kennedy. I will see you shortly."

"Yes, Sir, and, Sir, best of luck."

Snowden smiled. "And to you, Kennedy!"

They tallied on the sternline, the ship moved, set her sails and was soon in the channel, canvas glowing in the light of the flames in the town. Before long, Kennedy and Giotto were on *Oleander's* deck, where they were greeted by Poore, who seemed exhausted, drained by his spell of independent command. To Kennedy, it felt like coming home.

"Well, Mr Poore, you have seen what the other ships have done, and now we will do the same thing with *Oleander*. Wind's a bit fresher now. Reefed mainsail and staysail only." He turned to Giotto. "Are you ready, Signore?"

"I am, Sir".

After the merchant ships, *Oleander* felt like a thoroughbred horse to Kennedy, forced to walk, but eager to break out into a gallop. Suddenly, Kennedy had an idea and turned to Poore. "Get forward, take Bosun with you. Cut the cable of the best bower so there's ten fathom on the anchor, buoy the end, drop it overside on my whistle. Soon as we're in the harbour, get the cable, and perhaps another one into the longboat and onto the anchor. We may need to warp her off."

Under Giotto's guidance, Kennedy took the ship along the channel. He blew his whistle, and there was a splash from forward as Poore dropped the anchor. *Oleander* sailed into the heart of the inferno that was Macinaghju, men adjusting the mainsheet and peak halyard to slow her down in the breeze, but when the bowline was thrown the ship was just where he wanted her, going at the right speed. The ship turned under the combination of her own momentum against the bowline, the rudder and the pressure of the mainsail – turned, until the sternline was ashore and she was perpendicular to the quay. And then she stopped, her bowsprit overhanging the quay.

"Christ!" said Kennedy.

"Is aground," said Giotto, unnecessarily.

"Bosun", shouted Kennedy, "get more sternlines ashore." He ran to the bow and looked down to see Snowden below him on the quay with Julia beside him. "She's just touching, Sir. I think we should be able to pull her round if we get enough men on the sternlines. I'll back the main."

Snowden looked up at him, his features illuminated by the flickering light of the burning buildings. "I believe she'll come round. Guns ready?"

"Ready, Sir."

"Riley, get men on these ropes. We've got to pull her round."

More lines were passed ashore and groups of men pulled on them, and slowly, very slowly, *Oleander* began to move parallel to the quay. The fires in the town seemed to be getting worse and Snowden thought he could now hear musketry. He shouted across the narrowing gap between ship and wharf to Kennedy and Giotto, "I'm going to look at the defences. If we have to, the rearguard will go to Saint Mary Tower."

Kennedy looked at Giotto, who nodded his understanding and spoke to Kennedy, who shouted, "Saint Mary Tower, Sir!"

Snowden, with Julia at his side, ran into the town, towards the sound of firing.

CHAPTER 52 – AGROUND!

Burney, on the hill, watched in despair as *Oleander* stopped at right angles to the wharf, her bow hanging over the quay, her stern clearly aground. More ropes were led ashore, large numbers of men began to pull on them, and he saw her mainsail hauled to windward to help the process.

"Sir", shouted Wilson, "look! We've hit something." Burney turned and looked where he was pointing. A fire was burning where he thought the mortar was emplaced. The fire grew, and there was an orange flash and the sound of an explosion.

"My God!" said Wilson, "I think we hit the mortar, or its powder. What a bit of luck!"

"Luck or good judgement, Wilson. Well done."

Wilson's guns continued to fire as Burney watched the men pulling on *Oleander's* sternlines, their feet dug into the soil, reminding Burney of village tug o' war competitions. Come on, *Oleander*, he thought, move. She did, agonisingly slowly at first, until the mud released its grip and she came rapidly alongside. Burney went over to Wilson.

"Time for us to be gone, I think."

"Yes, Sir, but one more shot."

The guns fired again into the night and then there was a flurry of activity. Sergeant Wilson drove steel spikes into the touchholes of the guns, before they turned them off their carriages, which were pulled and pushed into the tower amongst the store of powder.

"Three minutes, I reckon," said Wilson as he lit the fuse. "Best be off, Sir."

They threw themselves down the slope and stopped at its base just as the powder store blew up in a huge explosion. Burney shouted into Wilson's ear, "Three minutes?"

"Well, nearly three minutes, Sir."

Burney looked towards the ship, whose decks were already crowded with men. He could see there were not many recruits gathered in front of the quayside buildings.

"Let's fall back."

They moved back towards the ship, alert for any attack from the hill, but none came, though there was clearly intense fighting from the edge of the town towards the west.

Wounded men started to appear from the town, helped or carried by other ragged looking men as they crossed the wharf towards the ship, whose decks were now very crowded.

Sergeant Riley ran up to Burney. "Time to go, Sir. Nearly a full house."

CHAPTER 53 – BARRICADES

Julia, escorted by two Corsicans, followed as fast as she could after Snowden and his party of Corsicans as they ran towards the firing at the end of the street, which seemed to be where the French were concentrating their attack. Snowden had tried to get her to board *Oleander*, but he had given up quickly, realising he had little power over her, apart from the use of force, which she knew would not be well received by the Corsicans.

The end of the street was blocked with rubble. A field gun fired through a gap in the wall, fired as quickly as it could be reloaded and aimed. Men lay concealed in the debris, firing as they saw an opportunity. Ensign Watton ran out of the door of a building and up to Snowden and Julia. "Sir, there's a good view from up there. The enemy is firing from doorways, but the street's curved and they can't bring a gun up."

At that moment, they heard the shrill of whistles from the port.

"*Oleander's* departing, Watton. You're relieved. Please take your men and return to the ship."

"Yes, Sir, but ..."

"I will hold the fort, Watton. Tell Kennedy to get away as quickly as he can. Give me a Baker."

"But, Sir ..."

"Just go!"

"Sir," Watton said firmly, "before I go, I must show you this. Firstly, Sir", he pointed at the cannon, "there's one up the spout. Grape, she's ready to go." He beckoned Snowden into the doorway and pointed into the corner where a match smouldered. "Just touch that ..."

"Thank you, Watton, in the Navy we know how to fire a cannon!" He smiled, "But well done, much obliged to you. Now, get going."

He pushed the young man roughly on the shoulder. Watton moved back a pace and then said, pointing, "One more thing, Sir, this is the fuse for the mine."

"Mine?"

"Yes, there's a mine in the street. It was Pietro's idea. The fuse is about two minutes. You can light it with the ... sorry, Sir."

"Is it a big mine?"

"I'll say, it'll give them a nasty shock, I reckon."

He collected his men and ran with them towards the ship.

Snowden, Julia and the Corsicans had been lying amongst the rubble for perhaps ten minutes when the attack came. Snowden was not sure it was as determined an attack as it might have been, for after all the French must have realised that their enemies were voluntarily leaving, but perhaps forty men came round the corner, yelling, with bayonets fixed. Rifles around him fired, and he pointed his own at a running man and pulled the trigger. The rifle kicked and the man fell. He had seen Burney's demonstrations of reloading the Baker, but he did not attempt it, instead drawing his pistols in anticipation of the assault. The attackers reached the base of the barricade and Snowden stood up, a pistol in each hand, and fired one at the attackers and then another one. He took his rifle off his shoulder, the bayonet glinting in the firelight, and heard himself shout, "Come on then, you bastards!"

The French paused, sensibly thought better of climbing

the rubble wall of the barricade, and ran back, dodging into the doorways of houses. For a wild moment, Snowden thought of jumping down the face of the barricade after them, but a violent tug on his leg unbalanced him and he fell full length onto the rubble.

"Stay down, Percy, that's enough," shouted Julia, almost in his ear. A musket ball smacked into a wooden beam sticking out of the barricade beside them and Julia fired her rifle in reply.

"To the ship!" shouted Snowden. Julia fired again, and then they all slid down the barricade onto the street. Snowden grabbed the match and peered through the gap between the gun and the rubble. There were no obvious targets. He waited until a Frenchman poked his head and musket around a doorway, and touched the match to the hole. The cannon fired with a satisfactory roar, but Snowden did not stop to see its effect. He put the match onto the end of the mine fuse, waited until it was sparkling properly and shouted, "Follow me!"

CHAPTER 54 – DEPARTURE

Sergeant Riley was the last one over the rail, jumping and misjudging his landing so he stumbled into Kennedy. "Sorry, Ken. Time to go."

"The Commander, Riley, he's still ashore. And Mrs White."

"I know, Kennedy, but we have several hundred men on aboard, and if we don't leave now we could lose them and the ship. You know your orders."

"I do, Sergeant, but I command this ship, in the Commander's absence, and we will wait a few more minutes. "Mr Poore!"

"Yes, Sir."

"Please tell Guns to fire the port broadside, roundshot, maximum elevation. We should be able to shoot over the town, and it may do some good."

"Yes, Sir."

Oleander's port broadside fired, together. The balls cleared the town, or at least the buildings near the quay, but they could not tell whether the roundshot had any effect on the French. They watched the street leading onto the quay, but nobody appeared, and, reluctantly, Kennedy did what he had to do.

"Let's get her underway, Poore, as we discussed. Don't send anybody ashore, cut the lines. Foresail only, we don't want her griping up. Heave in quick as you like on the anchor cable."

The great foresail was sweated up. It flapped once and was sheeted in. Axes fell on the mooring lines and men tramped round the capstan. Slowly, *Oleander* drew away from the wharf, gradually gathering speed until there was perhaps a ten-yard gap between the end of the wharf and the ship's stern. And then, she stopped. Giotto, who had been looking astern at the ruin of his town, shouted, "Kennedy, French!", pointing to where a body of men was running across the wharf.

Fools, thought Kennedy, and yelled, "Fire port smasher."

The smasher, which was pointed almost directly astern, fired, grapeshot whizzing close past the men on the port side of the ship, and across the quay. Luckily for the French, the Carron was wooded, obstructed by the ship's mast, and could not quite bear, but the French took the hint and retreated, running ran as fast as they could back to the shelter of the rocks at the base of the hill.

Poore came up. "Sir, she's on the mud. Lot of strain on the capstan. What can we do?"

Kennedy knew that soon the French would bring cannons up, and it would only be a matter of time before *Oleander* was hit and disabled. He spoke to the Midshipman, "Get that Sergeant Pietro here, quickly, and Sergeant Riley. Stay here, Giotto."

Kennedy turned to the little group. "Riley, I want your riflemen in the maintop. Shoot at anything you see ashore …", he thought for a moment, "except our commander and his party, of course."

"Aye, Sir." Riley moved off.

"We've got to get her off before the French bring a gun up. There's very little tide here. We know the ship can be heeled quite easily, and we've got plenty of moveable ballast aboard." He saw puzzled looks on their faces "Our Corsicans. Poore, I want the …" He paused as a volley of musket balls hit the side of the ship. One lucky shot could part a halyard, he thought, as the rifles in the tops returned fire. He shouted, " I want the smasher to hit the end of that street, where it runs onto the quay." He resumed, "Pietro, get the Corsicans moved over to the …" The Carron fired, shot whistling close to their heads and creating a cloud of dust where it slammed into the walls of the buildings at the end of the street. " … to the starboard side, heel her."

Shepherded by Pietro, Corsicans shuffled over to the starboard rail, pressing close together. Pietro then disappeared into the hold, and pushed and shoved the Corsicans below decks to the side of the ship. The Carron fired again and then the broadside guns, but the French fire was increasing.

Poore saw a gun muzzle appear at the corner of an alley leading onto the quay, and ran forward to speak to the Gunner, pointing to the new threat. Before he could speak, the Gunner pulled the lanyard, the gun fired, deafeningly, and Kennedy saw the giant ball crash into the wall near the French cannon, at the same time as a group of men, yelling, wielding swords, attacked the French cannon's crew. He did not see what happened, but was called aft by Kennedy's shout, "Poore, get some men forward with axes, we'll cut the cable soon as we overhaul it."

"Aye, Sir."

The ship was heeling under the weight of the men on the starboard side, and Kennedy shouted, "Lay on that windlass, sheet in the foresail. Over on her ear, that's it."

Suddenly, *Oleander* came free of the mud's embrace and began to move. Kennedy heard the cheer from the men at the capstan as the anchor cable slackened. A ball, a lucky shot, thudded into the foremast. Kennedy looked up and saw the foretopmast wobbling against the dark of the headland.

"Get down from the foretop!" he yelled, and he saw men scrambling down the rigging as the foretopmast crashed down.

"Ease the mainsheet so she don't gripe up. Port your helm. Giotto, how's she doing?"

"A little more to starboard, Sir. As she goes."

A roundshot smashed through the port bulwark, sending splinters whizzing through the air. He heard the cries of wounded men and then the rapid blows of axes as the ship overhauled her anchor and the cable was cut.

And then she was clear of the harbour, and in the channel, heading towards the headland. Giotto shouted a warning and the helm was put over, the great booms gybing across the deck, barely under control, and before long *Oleander* was well offshore, the fires in the town illuminating the men working in the rigging.

"The Skipper!" cried Kennedy, forgetting all protocol. "Did anybody see what happened to the Skipper?"

"It was him that attacked the French cannon", said Giotto, "and then the smasher hit the wall. I didn't see anything after that, I was looking out for the channel."

Kennedy walked forward. "Guns, did you see the Commander ashore?"

"I didn't, Sir, but as I fired the smasher at the French gun, I saw a lot of men attacking it. You know the Old Man, Sir, he'd like as not be leading that."

"Thank you, Mr Trott," said Kennedy and had turned to walk away when the Gunner said, "That wall fell down, Sir, just after the ball hit it. Sort of swayed for a moment or two and then collapsed. I didn't see anyone near it, but the French gun stopped. If the Old Man was under it ..."

CHAPTER 55 – TORRA DI SANTA MARIA

Snowden, Julia and the Corsicans ran along the street, but at its end, where it debouched onto the quay, a building had collapsed, blocking the exit. Snowden turned, and smashed at the door of a house on the north side of the street. They went in, ran through several rooms which seemed to house a chandlery and out the other side into a narrow alley, where, at the seaward end, a French gun was being dragged into position so that its muzzle pointed round the corner of the building. Without pausing or looking behind him to see if anyone was following, Snowden ran at the gun crew, who turned as he neared them, their faces masks of surprise and terror.

"Would you fire at my ship, you bastards?" he heard himself shout, and then he was on them, thrusting with his bayonet, swinging the rifle butt …

Afterwards he remembered a dull blow on his left arm, and then intense pain, and the Frenchman who had inflicted the blow running back up the alley, sabre in hand. He didn't remember, though he was told about it afterwards, anything of the huge roundshot crashing into the wall near him, the choking dust which it generated, and the slow swaying of the wall and its almost gentle collapse.

"Where is he?" screamed Julia at the Corsicans.

"He was wounded by a sword, he is under the wall, Senora," replied Fede. He pointed, "Here." Snowden was barely visible, lying on the ground, covered in rubble, his clothes coated in grey dust.

Julia knelt at his side and put her ear against his face. He was breathing, but shallowly and irregularly. Blood from his wound stained the stones near him, glistening in the light of the fires.

"Fede, help."

The sailors gathered round. Fede knelt beside her and looked intently at Snowden. "He lives, Senora, but he has a cut on his arm, and I think a stone has fallen on his head, and probably, I don't know, perhaps broken ribs."

Julia ripped the sash from her waist and bound it round Snowden's arm as best she could.

"The ship, she has gone, Senora. Where shall we go?"

"To the Torra di Santa Maria, Fede. It is along the coast a little way."

"I know it," said Fede, and turned and spoke rapidly to his companions. Between them they hoisted Snowden onto Fede's back. He staggered at the load, but they set off northwards. They saw no Frenchmen as they took the path behind the beach, on the springy bank of washed-up seaweed. The men, who were wiry and strong, took turns to carry Snowden on their backs. Julia walked behind them, trying as best she could to support Snowden's head. They had been travelling for half an hour or so and were starting to climb up the hill when Fede, who had been scouting ahead, came running back. They hid in bushes as a group of French soldiers walked along the path, Julia with a piece of her shirt in her hand, ready to stifle any moans Snowden might make.

From the top of the cape, in the darkness, they saw *Oleander's* outline, her rigging in disarray but clearly under control as she headed out to sea and then alter course to the north.

Fede looked at the ship. "Are they going to the meeting place, Senora?"

"I believe so, Fede."

"Then we must be on our way."

It was probably only three miles to their destination, but the coast path was steep, rough and winding. They stopped frequently to move Snowden from one man to another, and each time Julia lowered her ear to his face, feeling relieved that he was still breathing. Afterwards, Julia could only half-remember the journey, a nightmarish progression of stumbles and falls. The eastern sky lightened and just offshore they could see the small island of Finocchiarola with a round Genoese tower at its summit, and on the horizon the rugged silhouette of Elba. Below them, at the end of a long sandy bay was their destination, the round tower of Santa Maria, ruined by the guns of Nelson's squadron.

They heard a gun fire and looked round to see a puff of smoke from the tower on Finocchiarola, and then the gun's target, *Oleander*, emerging from behind the cliffs. She was about a mile off, but even from that distance they could see her decks crowded with men. A huge ensign and a hoist of signal flags flew from her main peak.

It was still dark enough for them to see the flashes ripple along her side as *Oleander's* broadside fired slowly and deliberately at the fort. It was impossible to see whether any damage had been done, but the fort's gun did not reply.

"Can you read those flags, Fede?" asked Julia.

"No, Signora, I am a merchant seaman, and those are the signals of the British Navy." He pointed to the ship. "They have been working hard aboard her. She has no foretopmast, but she sails well."

"The Captain, Signora, how is he? This must be very bad

for him."

"I believe he is surviving, Fede. He must live – I know his mother, he is her only child."

Fede smiled in the light of the sunrise as *Oleander* fired again and again at the tower. "I think the French should have left that ship alone, Signora."

As the sun rose, they walked along the beach towards the tower. *Oleander* had ceased firing and was heading towards the beach under reduced canvas.

"We must signal, Fede."

Fede removed his shirt, tied it to the end of his rifle and waved it vigorously. The ship fired a gun and Fede grinned. "They acknowledge us."

They redoubled their efforts, but carrying Snowden along the sandy beach was very hard going. They were a few hundred yards short of the ruined tower when Fede said, "The ship is launching two boats. We may as well stop here and wait for them."

As he spoke, the ship fired two more guns. Julia looked round and saw a party of French soldiers moving rapidly along the path, over the brow of the hill behind them. She grabbed Fede's arm and turned him round, pointing. "That is why they fired the guns, Fede, the French are coming. They will be here before the boats. We must get to the tower, we'll be sheltered there."

Oleander was under way again, working in closer to the beach. Julia could see white water at the bows of the boats as they approached the beach, the rowers pulling hard at their oars.

They staggered along the beach as best they could, and at last they got to the tower, built on a rocky outcrop, which connected it to the land in a sort of natural causeway. The entire seaward side of the cylindrical structure had collapsed under the Royal Navy's bombardment, but the land side was still standing, with the remains of wooden floors inside.

They went in through a low entrance and laid Snowden down. He was still unconscious, but stirring slightly. They clambered up the wreckage inside and looked out of what had been a door opening, about twenty feet above the ground. They could see the French soldiers, now at the end of the beach, and, in the other direction, the approaching British boats. *Oleander* was quite close now, hove to, and the French soldiers hesitated as she fired her broadside at them. As far as they could see, the gunfire had little effect on the French, but they did not advance. One of the boats turned towards the French, but before it fired its swivel, the soldiers took cover behind the rocks at the edge of the beach. They began to shoot with muskets, but the range was extreme.

Julia knelt and laid her rifle on the sill of the door opening, took careful aim and fired. Fede did not see what she hit, or whether she hit anything at all, but it seemed to be the last straw for the French, who retreated inland, chased on their way by another of *Oleander's* broadsides.

And then the boat was just off the beach, behind the tower, and willing hands carried Snowden aboard, laying him along a thwart.

CHAPTER 56 – RESCUE

The sun was well up when Kennedy snapped his telescope shut and turned to Poore, who was standing near him, looking through his own glass. "Poore, the man they're carrying ..."

"It's the Old Man, Sir, I'm sure of it. He didn't look in a good way, Sir, he might even be ..."

"Get the ship turned, Mr Poore, and we'll give them another broadside when the boats are out of the way."

Kennedy watched as the boat with Snowden aboard pushed off from the land and made towards *Oleander*, the men straining at the oars. The boat with the swivel backed off from the land, fired its little gun and turned towards the ship.

Burney, who had also been watching the scene through his glass came up to them. "I think that's Percy, Ken."

"I'm afraid it is, Sir."

"I'll get the hoist rigged." Burney pointed to the forepart of the ship, where men were working on the rigging amongst the crowd of Corsican recruits. "Bosun's a busy man."

Oleander fired her long guns, singly, so that the beach and the land behind it was swept by grapeshot as the boats made their way to the ship. Kennedy did not think the French would expose themselves to that, just to take shots at the boats.

Julia and the Corsicans climbed aboard, looking exhausted. Snowden was hoisted up in the stretcher, steadied by seaman clinging to the side of the ship. As it rose above the rail, the marines lined up on the deck presented arms, the display watched by the crowd of Corsican volunteers. Pipes shrilled, and Julia, with a start, saw Snowden's head move slightly and his mouth form a brief smile.

He was carried into the cabin, where the Surgeon's Mate Butterfield was waiting with a cup of water. Julia raised Snowden's head and the Bermudian put the cup to his lips. He spluttered slightly, but swallowed, and then spoke, but so quietly that they could not hear what he said. Julia moved round the table and put her face near his head.

"The bill, Julia?"

"Not many, Percy." She turned to the Butterfield. "He wants to know the reckoning."

"Twenty wounded, Your Honour, nothing very serious, and none dead from the ship. Some of the Corsicans are wounded bad – I fear for one or two of them."

Snowden nodded and drifted back off to sleep or unconsciousness, Julia did not know which.

Kennedy took *Oleander* well away from the land before turning south. Men worked hastily among the crowd of Corsicans to repair the foretopmast, and in the afternoon it was hoisted up and rigged. Awnings of spare sails were set across the decks to give the volunteers respite from the sun.

At three in the afternoon, they sighted *Rondine* and *Balestruccio,* and *Oleander* reduced sail to match the merchant ships' leisurely pace.

Next afternoon, Julia sat with Snowden in the cabin. The wounds in his arm and head had been dressed and he seemed more comfortable.

Kennedy and Burney entered. "How are you, Skipper?" asked Kennedy.

Snowden's head turned slightly and his lips moved. Julia motioned for them to be quiet and whispered in Snowden's ear. He spoke again. Julia listened and smiled. "He says *'Skipper'*, now, does he? This ship's got very slack in my absence."

Kennedy grinned. "Very sorry, Sir, I am very glad to have you back with us."

Burney interjected, "And that goes for me, too, Commander." He continued, "We've met the two merchant ships and we're proceeding towards Malta. Fine easterly breeze." He turned to Kennedy. "I think we should leave him now."

The trip south in company with the two merchant ships was uneventful, the weather benign and the winds fair. By the time they rounded the western tip of Sicily, Snowden was sitting up, though his left arm hung uselessly in the sling which supported its weight. He looked drawn and pale and his spirit, usually so buoyant, was becoming depressed.

On deck, Burney spoke with Kennedy and Pascoe. "He seems to be getting so down, Sir," said Pascoe. "He is normally such a positive man."

"Complex things, head injuries, in my experience," replied Burney. "We had a man on *Resolution*, fell from a coconut tree and hit his head. He was a good man, always cheerful, but afterwards, for a month or so, he was very subdued. The Commander's brain has been pretty well rattled about and it'll take time to settle down again. He has other injuries as well, and he's used to activity and this forced idleness is difficult for him."

On the morning of the fifth day, the little flotilla was off the north coast of Malta, and by one they were entering Valletta. At Julia's insistence, they had helped Snowden out of the cabin and seated him in a chair on the deck, near the wheel. His colour had improved a little, but he was still weak and rather morose.

The Corsican volunteers cheered as they passed under the

forts and at the sight of the naval vessels, a seventy-four and two frigates, lying alongside the quay, ensigns and pennants flapping in the wind.

"Must have returned from Toulon, Sir," said Pascoe to Kennedy. "A shame they weren't here a couple of weeks ago."

"You say that, Pascoe, but we did very well by ourselves."

CHAPTER 57 – THE POET

Oleander had been in Malta for four days. The Corsican recruits had left the ships and were housed in barracks ashore. Dockyard hands were completing repairs to *Oleander's* rigging, and provisioning was almost complete. Burney came aboard, looking fit and cheerful, and went into the cabin, where Snowden was sitting at the table, which was covered by the chart. Snowden was dictating to Julia. Though he could now walk unassisted, Snowden was not ... Burney thought briefly for the right word ... thriving, that was it, thriving.

"Percy, I hope you won't mind. I've taken a small liberty and asked Mr Coleridge to dine aboard. I hope you and Julia will join us."

Snowden looked puzzled. "Mr Coleridge?"

"The Governor's Secretary, the poet, the *Ancient Mariner*. You met him, remember?"

"Oh, of course. He seemed an efficient man, but I really don't feel ..."

Julie interrupted, "Come on now, Percy. It will do you good to meet someone for a change who isn't a naval officer or some such. You haven't even been ashore since we arrived."

"I agree with Julia", said Burney, "I will make arrangements", and left the cabin.

"Julia, I wish you hadn't ..."

"Don't be ridiculous, Percy, you can't stay isolated for ever."

"Can we get back to that letter, please, Julia?"

"I am not at all sure it is a good thing to do, Percy."

"Let us write it out, and then I can decide whether to send it or not. Where were we?"

"I have been informed on good authority that on the night of 13th inst., when HM ships *Ajax*, *Diomede* and *Adventure* were off the eastern coast of Cape Corse, gunfire was heard from the direction of the coast ..."

"Yes, that's it. To continue: 'including, so I am given to understand, the sound of a Carron. I further understand that the frigate *Diomede*, Commander Jones, immediately hauled her wind, turned towards the sound of the guns, and that she was closely followed by *Adventure* ...'"

"Percy, are you sure you know all this, absolutely?"

"I am, Julia. Jones told me just this morning."

"Very well, then, but you must promise me you'll hold off from sending it until you've thought it over carefully."

"I will, Julia. If I am to send it to Their Lordships, the fastest way to the Admiralty from here is *Oleander*, so I will have the rest of the voyage to consider it. To continue: '... only to be immediately recalled by signals from *Ajax*. Commander Jones repaired aboard *Ajax* and made his concerns plain to Commodore Parkinson ...'"

"I do not think you should name the persons concerned, Percy."

"Why not? I have no doubt that Jones told me the truth."

"I'm sure he did, but you must remember that Parkinson is well connected politically. If this goes to the Admiralty, there could be a tremendous fuss and it could end up – well, you know what can happen. Court martials, civilian courts, vast costs."

"But, Julia, that man Parkinson is a disgrace. He knew very well an English ship was in action just under his lee and he did not help, or even allow his frigates to investigate. 'Not our affair', he said to Jones, 'it is probably the Corsicans fighting amongst themselves'. 'With smashers?' asks Jones. 'I cannot tell what armaments are being used, but I do know that it is not our business. Our orders are to proceed to Malta with all despatch'."

"I know, Percy, but it didn't matter in the end."

"It could have, Julia, that's the point. We were damned lucky. Jones told me he backed his topsails and held back, but Parkinson flagged him twice to form line abreast. Fired a gun on the second occasion."

Snowden stood and rested on the table with his good arm. "Julia, you're right. Let's leave it for now. I've a mind to take a little walk ashore, if you'd accompany me."

"Off the ship, Percy?"

"Yes, just up the quay."

"You must be recovering."

Julia, observing Snowden as the dinner that evening progressed, realised he was improving markedly, though she doubted he would ever regain full use of his arm and he sometimes winced with pain when he moved too awkwardly. In contrast, she thought Coleridge did not look at all well.

"Burney, your sister Fanny certainly sells well", he was saying, "and I believe she is an excellent writer. Wordsworth doesn't approve, but he can be a prig."

"To my shame", replied Snowden, "the only poem of yours I know is the *Ancient Mariner*."

"Wordsworth doesn't like that either."

"It's splendid! I told you I saw a play of it in Pompey."

"A play?" said Burney.

"Yes, indeed, though they used a stuffed parrot instead of an Albert."

"An Albert?" Coleridge looked quizzical.

Burney interrupted, "The birds, Sam. The sailors call them Albert Rosses."

Snowden continued, "Yes, the play was very good. And I do like the poem. Fair rolls along. And that bit about the fresh water in the sea, where did you get that?"

"Well, it was Wordsworth's brother who put me onto it. He's a seaman, you know. He put me onto Cook's voyages. Burney here was with the great circumnavigator, but you probably know that."

"Indeed, we do, Coleridge. And I suppose you have written a good many other poems?"

"Yes, a fair number, and some other things as well."

"Have you written anything recently, Mr Coleridge?" asked Julia.

"Only official documents, I fear. The most famous thing I have written recently concerns the dimensions of cart wheels."

"Cart wheels, Mr Coleridge?"

"Indeed yes, it's a very thorny local subject, subject to much debate."

"And how do the inhabitants take to British rule?"

"Very kindly at present, Mrs White. Captain Ball is almost a hero to them."

"And their attitude to the French?"

"I imagine much like your Corsicans. The French chased

the Knights away, like they did in Corsica with the Genoese, but, as in Corsica, the change of rule did not do the Maltese much good. We will have to work hard to maintain the goodwill of the Maltese people, but, as you know, Malta is a splendid base for our operations. I used to be a supporter of the French Revolution, as was Burney here."

Burney looked uncomfortable. "I think we were too idealistic. We thought there would be a new dawn after the *Ancien Régime* was overthrown, but, well, everybody knows what happened, and now they have Bonaparte instead of Louis and Bonaparte is infinitely more effective and dangerous than any Louis was ever likely to have been."

He turned to Coleridge. "Mr Coleridge, here, is exceptionally keen on climbing up mountains."

"Climbing up mountains?" said Snowden.

"That is not quite true. I am, however, an enthusiastic walker, and sometimes mountains are in the way."

"Where do you walk?"

"My favourite place is near Wordsworth's house in the north, at Grasmere. The country there is high and bleak, but I have a great fondness for it."

"Walking and mountains?" said Burney. "I think Julia and I have had enough of that to last for a considerable time."

Snowden laughed. "Do you think of poetry when you walk, Coleridge?"

"Sometimes I do, but I ... Well, of late I have lost some of my confidence in my own abilities."

"You have lost confidence?" Snowden looked incredulous. "You wrote my favourite poem."

"That may be so, but you are a naval officer, not a fellow poet or a critic."

"But surely, to have written something that an ordinary man like me can appreciate is a great talent."

"That is very kind of you, Sir, but sometimes my poetry is rather unconventional, and some say, improper. And Snowden, I don't think you can describe yourself as an ordinary man!"

"That's very kind of you, Coleridge. Perhaps we should form a mutual appreciation society! Have you nothing to read to us? It would be something to have heard a famous poem declaimed by its author. I would be able to tell my grandchildren."

Julia snorted. "If you go on as you do, Percy, the chances of you surviving long enough to have grandchildren are not very great."

By this time, the wine and brandy had flowed and Coleridge seemed quite affected by Snowden's enthusiasm for his poetry. He stood, slightly unsteadily. "If you like, I do have something I could recite. I wrote it some time ago."

"Go on, Coleridge," said Snowden, "I'm sure it'll be a cracker."

Coleridge straightened his back, cleared his throat and began:

"*In Xanadu did Kubla Khan*

A stately pleasure-dome decree:

Where Alph ...

... he on honey-dew hath fed,

And drank the milk of Paradise."

They applauded, and Snowden said, "My word, Mr Coleridge, I have never heard anything like that, never. It is astonishing that anyone could have thought of that. And so clearly put together. Well, I'm not a literary man, and perhaps I shouldn't comment, but ..."

Burney interrupted, "In my opinion, and I think I may be counted as something of a literary man, or at the very least the brother of literary sisters, it is an astonishing piece of work, Coleridge. Why have you not put it before the public?"

"I don't really know, Burney, I have somehow lost faith in my ability."

Julia thought that almost the last thing she would have expected to have such an energising effect on Snowden was a poetry reading, but it had, and he was animated and happy in a way that he had not been since his injury.

"Could you recite it again?"

CHAPTER 58 – HYÈRES

Their orders had stated ' *... and repair with all despatch to the Nore*', but they had not got away quite so cleanly, and *Oleander* was carrying despatches for the Commander in Chief of the Mediterranean Fleet, Lord Nelson, who was blockading Toulon.

Snowden, though his arm was still almost immobile, was recovering with every passing day, but he had relinquished much of the work of running the ship. Kennedy and Burney took *Oleander* north, and on the afternoon of the fourth day the ship was off Macinaghju. They hove her to, a mile or so off the port, and, through his telescope, Snowden inspected the damage to the town. From that distance, he could make out people by the wharf but could not tell whether they were French soldiers or returned townspeople. The damage did not seem so bad as he had feared, and he could see that the Luciani house was apparently unscathed. They took *Oleander* close into the shore north of Macinaghju, near the round fort on the island which had engaged them, but the tower appeared to be deserted and they went on their way without firing on it.

Oleander rounded Cape Corse as the sun set. The wind freshened overnight, and sunrise silhouetted the mountains of Corsica sixty miles astern, and the brightening sky was clear and a deep cobalt blue.

"Good morning, Kennedy," said Burney as he came on deck and looked around. "A beautiful day."

"Good morning, Sir. That's a Mistral sky I believe, we shall have wind aplenty before long, west or nor' westerly."

"Of course, I remember that blow we had just before we arrived in Corsica. Seems so long ago."

"Aye, Sir, a lot has happened since then. Captain Burney, do you intend to stay in the Navy now you are reinstated?"

"I do not think there is any prospect of Their Lordships ever giving me a ship, Kennedy, and am not sure I would want one. Half pay is all I can expect, and perhaps even a promotion in due course, but I am very glad to have had this opportunity, though at times I cannot say I enjoyed it much."

"No, Sir, it sounded pretty hard. I prefer to do my work at sea."

"I am looking forward to returning to my quiet life in London. But, Kennedy, you do your work very well, exceptionally well."

"Thank you, Sir."

"You're an ambitious man, I think."

"I suppose I am, Sir."

"That is why you left the merchant service, I believe – the prospect of advancement?"

"It was, Sir."

"I had the privilege of serving under Cook, and he had followed the same route as you."

"So I understand, Sir."

"What is your plan, Kennedy?"

"The examination, Sir, and then ..."

"I have no doubt you will succeed." The ship staggered under a gust of wind. "Here comes your Mistral."

Kennedy turned away and spoke to Pascoe. "Let's get the topsails off her, Mr Pascoe."

Oleander, close hauled, sailed between the island of Levant and the French mainland. By the time she sighted the British fleet in the Rade d'Hyères, an anchorage a few miles east of the great French naval base of Toulon, the Mistral was blowing strongly, but the anchorage was well sheltered from the west by the Hyères peninsular and the island of Porquerolles to the south. Snowden saw that Nelson's flagship, *Victory*, and some of the other ships were preparing to get under way. *Oleander's* signal was acknowledged by *Victory* and then Snowden was instructed to repair aboard the flagship.

He climbed painfully up *Victory's* high side. The ship seemed vast and solid to Snowden, used as he now was to *Oleander's* smaller proportions. He was shown into the great cabin, where Nelson sat at a table covered in charts and papers. A secretary took the despatches from Malta, and Nelson motioned for Snowden to sit down. He noticed how much Nelson had aged since he had served under him.

"Good afternoon, Snowden. I haven't seen you since you were a lad in *Agamemnon*. I've heard of your exploits in Brittany of course. A very good job."

"Thank you, My Lord."

"Several of the lads we had aboard *Agamemnon* have done well, but none has burnt any of Boney's barges. And where have you been now? I presume you have written an account. And your arm? The loss of an arm is easier to bear than an eye. I speak from experience."

"Yes, My Lord. I have written an account. I have been to Corsica. We landed a party to raise a regiment of Corsicans for the British Army."

"And did they raise a regiment?"

"Yes, My Lord, fifteen hundred men. They're now in Malta."

"Who did you land?"

"Captain Burney, My Lord, and Mrs White. She's the daughter of Paoli."

"Indeed? I didn't know Paoli had a family. And that ship of yours, *Oleander*. I have read a report of her trials – remarkably fast."

"She is, Sir."

An officer, a large man, put his head round the door. "We are ready for sea, Your Lordship."

"Thank you, Hardy. Hardy, this is Snowden, of that Yankee-looking thing. The one that burnt the barges. He's been in Corsica."

"Pleased to meet you, Snowden."

"Captain Hardy."

Hardy turned to leave, but Nelson motioned for him to stay. "Snowden, your ship's very handy?"

"She is. Quick in stays, turns on a sixpence, nothing to beat her to windward. Or running, come to that."

"Would you mind, Snowden, taking a little diversion with me as a passenger?" Snowden knew, of course, that a question from Nelson was not really a question. "Hardy, as we have such a handy ship among us, I've a mind to take her into Toulon, to have a look round."

"Your Lordship, there is no need for you to go personally. We could send ..."

"You are like an old mother hen from your farm, Hardy!" He turned to Snowden. "Well, Snowden?"

"Of course, Lord Nelson. I will return to my ship."

Snowden climbed as quickly as he could over *Oleander's* rail, oblivious to the pipes and marines. "Kennedy, for Christ's sake, we're to take Lord Nelson, Lord Nelson, on a boating trip into Toulon. In this gale."

"Lord Nelson, Sir?"

"Yes, Nelson! Don't stand there gawping, man, do something."

"Anything particular, Sir?"

There was a shout: "Admiral's barge heading our way!"

Snowden looked up and saw that it was. "Never mind, Kennedy." He hurried into the cabin. "Julia, Jim, Lord Nelson's coming aboard, we're taking him into Toulon to have a look round."

They stared at him in astonishment.

CHAPTER 59 – RADE DE TOULON

Nelson came aboard, accompanied by several officers, some clutching charts and telescopes.

Nelson looked round appraisingly. "I am sorry to spring this on you, Snowden, but you have a fine-looking ship."

Snowden took them to the cabin, where food and drink had been hurriedly laid out, and then went on deck, where he got the ship underway, surrounded by several of Nelson's flag officers. When she was on course and sailing well, he said to Kennedy, softly, so that he couldn't be overheard, "I'm going to the cabin. Be very careful with the ship, keep her well off the land. Don't let these people influence you."

"I won't, Sir, steady does it."

Snowden said loudly, "You have the ship, Mr Kennedy", and went into the cabin, where Nelson, Julia, Burney and two officers were sitting at the table. Burney had his tattered map of Corsica on the table and was pointing to Macinaghju.

"Mr Kennedy brought three ships, one after the other, into the harbour, and took the men off. A smarter operation I've never heard of. *Oleander* went aground on the last trip, but he got her off by moving the Corsicans over to the side and heeling her. She's got a deep keel, you see."

Nelson looked up as Snowden entered and smiled. "And where was *Oleander's* commanding officer when his ship was on the ground?"

"Ashore, Sir. I thought that was where my efforts could be best directed."

"No officer of mine would ever be rebuked by placing himself in the middle of the fight, Snowden. I believe you have the same sickness as me, the longing to be in the action."

Snowden blushed. "I don't know about that, Your Lordship, but the ship was in good hands and it was important to get all the recruits off."

"And how did you get off, Snowden?"

"I don't really know, My Lord. Mrs White here was in charge of that phase of the operation."

Nelson turned to Julia. "Mrs White?"

"We attacked a French gun which was about to fire on the ship."

"*We*, Mrs White?"

"Mr Snowden attacked it, and we, that is myself and four Corsican sailors, followed."

Nelson looked quizzically at her. "And what weapon does a lady such as yourself favour, Mrs White?"

"A rifle, Your Lordship. The Baker is a fine weapon. I find the bayonet too long."

"You have fired a Baker rifle?"

To Nelson's surprise, Julia pulled the neck of her dress to one side, showing her right shoulder, which was adorned with a yellowing bruise.

"It seems you have indeed fired a Baker, Mrs White, and, if I'm any judge, more than once. Please continue."

"Well, My Lord, Snowden was wounded and the smasher knocked a wall down on top of him, but we managed to get him to Saint Mary Tower and hold the French off long enough for *Oleander* to send a boat."

"Saint Mary Tower? Snowden, isn't that the one we knocked about with the *'Eggs and Bacon'*?"

"It was, and I believe Mr Kennedy had a bit of trouble with the one on the island, you remember it no doubt. If you'll excuse me, Your Lordship, I had better just check everything's alright on deck." Snowden went above, reassured himself that the ship was in good order and returned to the cabin. Nelson was now sitting alone with Julia. They looked up as he entered.

"Your Lordship, we are getting quite close to the land."

"I will be on deck directly." Nelson turned to Julia. "Mrs White, I am required on deck. Thank you for your account of your adventures."

Snowden felt a surge of pride as Nelson appeared on *Oleander's* deck and looked around as she passed the headland at the entrance to the Grand Passe of Toulon. Nelson looked at the wake hissing past. "She is certainly fast, Commander."

"She is, Your Lordship, the fastest in the Navy."

"I don't doubt it, Snowden."

A shot boomed out from a fort on the headland. "Let us hope she's too fast for the gunners ashore."

The fore and main tops were crowded with Nelson's officers. One of them stood by the helm with Kennedy, conning the ship with the aid of a large-scale chart of Toulon. As *Oleander* neared the city, the masts and yards of the French fleet in the port became visible and Nelson stared at them intently. More guns began to fire as *Oleander* approached, but the fast-moving ship was at their extreme range.

An officer climbed down from the foretop and made his way back to Nelson. "They are all here, Your Lordship."

Nelson smiled. "Thank goodness for that."

"Some of them have their yards sent down, Your Lordship."

"So I can see. It does not look to me as though they intend to leave directly. We must hope they depart before long, as we cannot destroy them when they are in Toulon."

"No, Your Lordship."

There was a shout from the foremast: "Two frigates making sail!" Just ahead, a roundshot hit the sea, sending up a white spout of water, while Nelson was intent on observing the port and the French fleet in it. They were quite close to the town when Nelson turned to Snowden, "Snowden, I think we have seen all we can without actually going into the port. If you please, turn the ship around and make your way to sea again."

Snowden, who was becoming increasingly anxious, immediately gave the order, and *Oleander* tacked through the wind with a thunder of sails and ran back out to sea, chased by cannon fire. The two French frigates contented themselves with getting underway and sailing after them for a couple of miles, but *Oleander* was faster and had a long head start, and soon they turned back to the city.

Nelson spent the trip back to *Victory* in the cabin with his staff, dictating despatches and orders. "I've given a brief account of your enterprise, Snowden, but I'd be pleased to include your own report with my documents when it is finished. I flatter myself that it will make more impact with Their Lordships in that way."

As Nelson waited on deck for his barge to come alongside, he turned to Snowden, "As you know, Snowden, my view is that the ship and crew reflect the commander, and I am very pleased by your men. In particular, Mr Kennedy is clearly an excellent man."

"He is, Your Lordship ..." Nelson held up his hand.

"And I have mentioned him in my despatch to Their Lordships. You may tell him that."

"I will tell him, Sir."

"And Mrs White. I have never met her like before – 'the Baker is a fine weapon' – that's what she said, and she raised fifteen hundred men. Well ... here is my barge. I wish you a pleasant voyage, Snowden, and hope you make a full recovery from your injuries."

And with that, he was gone.

CHAPTER 60 – THE CHÂTEAU D'IF

When they were well off the coast, Snowden hove the ship to. "We'll keep her like this for the night, Kennedy."

"Aye, Sir. Might I ask, Sir, why we're heaving to rather than making westing?"

"You may ask, Kennedy, but I have had an idea, or rather you had the idea, some time ago, and I am going to see if we can make good on it. I must first discuss it with Mrs White and see what she says."

"My idea, Sir?"

"You remember, when we were in Malta, I wanted to put General Bartoli ashore, and you suggested we keep him, as he might come in handy? I think it may be time for the General to prove his usefulness."

"Yes, Sir. I'll keep her forereaching slowly east by south."

Snowden went into the cabin, where Julia was sitting with Burney. "Julia, Lord Nelson said he hoped you would soon be reunited with your husband."

"Did he? I must say it is very hard for me to be so close to him and yet to be so utterly separated."

"Yes, His Lordship said it as he was waiting for his barge. Do you think your husband might still be at the Château d'If?"

Burney spoke up, "Snowden, the place is a fortress. On its

own island. You can't seriously be thinking that we could attack it …"

"I do not know if he is still there," said Julia. "I expect he is, as I don't see why they would move him elsewhere, but you never know."

"No, Burney, of course I am not thinking of attacking the Château, but perhaps we could try a negotiation."

"A negotiation? What do we have to bargain with?" and then, realisation dawning on his face, "Bartoli, of course."

Snowden turned to Julia. "What do you think? Is he worth your husband to the French?"

"He is a tenth the man my husband is, but he is a general and related to the Buonapartes, so he will count for a good deal. My word, Percy, if you are willing, it would be worth trying."

Snowden slept well that night, the motion of the ship gentle and reassuring. They passed the next day well offshore and saw few other ships, none of which came very close. Charts of Marseille's roadstead were studied and courses plotted.

Bartoli, accompanied by his two guards, was brought into the cabin.

"Please sit, General," said Snowden.

Bartoli looked round suspiciously and then sat at the table. Snowden found that he did not bear the man any dislike, but Julia's hatred was plain. Bartoli glanced at her and then looked away.

"As you know, Bartoli," began Snowden, "we are travelling back to England. When we get there, you will be subject to a trial. I do not know if it will be a court martial or a civilian court."

"On what charges, Snowden?"

"*Commander* Snowden, Bartoli. Treason, perhaps, attempted murder, disobeying orders in the face of the enemy …"

In truth, Snowden did not know if any charges could be brought against Bartoli, and he was about to continue when Julia interrupted.

"I don't know why we don't just ..."

"Thank you, Julia, we know your views. What I am suggesting, Bartoli, is that there may be a way of avoiding a return to England."

"How so, Commander?"

"We are a few miles from France, from Marseille. We can put you ashore."

"Ashore? Why would you do that?"

"Because we can exchange you. Before we can try that, however, I must know that you will cooperate."

Bartoli leaned forward. "I will cooperate. What do you want me to do?"

At first light, flying a huge white flag at the main peak, they worked *Oleander* into the Rade de Marseille. It was anxious work, but the guns ashore remained silent. They anchored *Oleander* just off the north-west corner of the Île d'If, uncomfortably close to the fort's guns. Snowden thought, if they decide to open fire now, we will be lucky to get away, although men stood at the cable, axes in their hands, and others at the halyards, ready to set the sails at the first sign of trouble.

A boat, flying a white flag, came out from the landing stage and headed towards them. Snowden nodded to Pascoe and a long line of flags was hoisted. He hoped this might give the impression that *Oleander* was signalling to a fleet offshore, although if there really was a fleet close enough to see the signal flags, such a fleet would be easily visible from the ramparts of the Château.

The boat came alongside and two French officers boarded,

to the shrill of pipes. The senior officer, who Snowden thought seemed highly competent, saluted and introduced himself as Colonel Lacroix. Snowden took them into the cabin, where Burney was waiting.

Snowden declared, "This is Colonel Lacroix, Burney. Colonel, you have some Corsican prisoners in the Château."

"We may have. Why do you ask?"

"Because, Colonel, we would like to propose an exchange."

"And who do you have?"

"We have a general, a Corsican."

"What is his name?"

"Bartoli."

"I have heard of Bartoli. He fought against us."

"Never mind that. He is related to Napoleon, a cousin." Snowden, the gambler, noticed a slight narrowing of Lacroix's eyes.

"To Napoleon?"

"Yes, he is. How many Corsicans do you have?"

"Presently, we have three. Only high-ranking persons are kept here. The others, they are not worth imprisoning, we let them go and they live in Marseille or return to the island. Most of them stay, I believe."

"The names of your prisoners?"

Lacroix looked at his companion, a lieutenant. "Torre, Grimaldi and Bianco," the man said. Bianco! Julia's husband. Snowden and Burney, gamblers both, inwardly rejoiced but betrayed no emotion.

"Very well, we will exchange our general for your three prisoners."

"I must ask for directions from my superior in Marseille."

"*Colonel* Lacroix", he emphasised the word 'Colonel', "I am sure you have authority to authorise the exchange, and I must have your consent now".

"May I see your prisoner?"

Snowden turned to the marine at the door. "Bring him in, if you please."

Bartoli, flanked by his guards entered the cabin, resplendent in full uniform. Snowden was not sure what uniform it was, but it was certainly impressive. The French Colonel looked at him. "You are General Bartoli, Monsieur?"

"I am." Bartoli thrust some papers forward. "Here is my commission."

Lacroix looked at it briefly. "From the Corsican Republic. How did you come to be a prisoner of these English?"

"I tried to fight them in Corsica, when they landed, but they captured me."

"Why did you fight them?"

"I believe Corsica is better under the French. I am a relative of your Consul, Buonaparte."

"He is our Emperor now, Mon Général."

Bartoli smiled. "Emperor – I did not know that."

At that moment, Kennedy entered the cabin, carrying a note. "Signal, Sir." Snowden read it briefly, scribbled something on the paper and handed it back to Kennedy, who rushed out. He looked at Lacroix. "Colonel, I cannot stay here any longer. I must have your answer – will you exchange the prisoners?"

Lacroix smiled. "Very well, I will have the men brought to the landing stage. When you see them there, bring your General ashore and we will exchange." Snowden nodded. "A question, Monsieur. You said your name was Snowden?"

"I did, Colonel."

"Were you in Brittany, Snowden? Was it you who burnt the barges?"

"It was, Colonel. How do you know of that?"

"Your name is known in France, and besides, I was with Napoleon when the English attacked St Malo. A diversion, as we know now, to allow you to do your incendiary work."

They'll have a price on my head soon, thought Snowden, but he held out his hand and said, "Thank you, Colonel."

The Frenchmen turned to leave.

The hour that followed was tense in the extreme. Snowden was desperately worried for his ship, anchored below the guns of a powerful fortress, but he realised it must be worse for Julia, who was somewhere below decks. He had not been able to bring himself to speak to her, but he presumed that Burney had. He turned to Poore. "Mr Poore, please find Mrs White and ask her to come on deck directly."

Julia appeared, looking pale and drawn. She did not speak, but leaned on the rail, gazing towards the fortress. The lookout in the maintop, whose elevation gave him a good view of the entrance to the fort, shouted down, "Party coming down to the jetty!"

Snowden snapped his telescope open. Colonel Lacroix, at the head of a party of soldiers, stepped onto the wharf. In the midst of the soldiers were three men who were clearly prisoners. "Stand by, Burney," he said, and then turned to Julia, handing her the telescope without speaking. Julia steadied the glass, focused it and Snowden heard a sharp intake of breath.

"He's there, Percy, thank God."

"Off you go then, Burney."

Bartoli was hoisted into the boat, which was flying a large white flag, and Snowden watched as it was rowed towards the landing stage, Burney sitting in the stern with Poore at the helm. The boat went alongside and Burney climbed onto the jetty. Snowden watched as Burney went up to Lacroix, shook hands and gestured to the boat. Bartoli was helped ashore, and the prisoners walked across the jetty and climbed down into the boat. Burney again shook hands with Lacroix, sat himself in the sternsheets, and the boat, its white flag still flying, was rowed rapidly back to the ship.

"Let's get her underway, Kennedy, quick as you like."

"Aye, Sir, I am very keen to be gone", he glanced at the fort's cannons, "it only takes one mistake, one idiot, and the whole lot of them will be firing on us."

Snowden too was so anxious to leave the guns of the fort and so absorbed in the task of getting the ship underway that he did not see the reunion of Julia and her husband. It was several hours before he was satisfied the ship was safe and well on her course and returned to the cabin, where Julia, radiant, was sitting next to what Snowden thought was a rather ordinary-looking man. The man rose.

"Percy, this is my husband, Roberto."

CHAPTER 61 – GIBRALTAR

Two days later, Snowden was leaning on the rail, watching the coast of Ibiza slide past as *Oleander* ghosted along before a light northerly breeze.

Julia came up beside him. "I will miss your ship, Percy."

"Your husband owns several ships, Julia."

"He does, but nothing like *Oleander*."

"There truly is nothing like *Oleander*, Julia."

"Do you know what Lord Nelson told me?"

"I shudder to think."

"Percy, he behaved perfectly well!"

"There is a first time for everything!"

"He said 'It's not the ships, it's the men in them'."

"That is not quite original, Julia, but it is true, to a certain extent."

"And you, Percy, you've made *Oleander* what she is now, all these different men working together, English, Bermudians, Corsicans. I will miss you all."

"Well, don't be premature, we've a few weeks before we reach the Nore."

"That is what I came to speak to you about, Percy. My husband and I, and I believe the other prisoners, will leave the ship at Gibraltar. Roberto and I will go back to Malta and the others will try for Corsica."

Snowden was gripped with a sudden, overwhelming sadness, as though his whole world had been taken from him. He did not realise, until then, how much he cared for Julia. "I had thought ..." What he had thought, he realised, was that Julia would be a presence in England whenever he was there, something for him to look forward to when he was away. With a flash of insight, he saw that Julia had her own life to lead and she belonged here, in the Mediterranean. She had a husband, ships, a business to run. He had been selfish to imagine her in England.

Julia saw the pain in his eyes and reached out and took his hand.

"Julia, of course, I am sure you are doing the right thing, your life is in the Mediterranean, not England. It is just, I suppose, that I have only just realised what you mean to me."

"And you to me, Percy. As you say, my life is here, but there is more to it than that. We have raised fifteen hundred men to fight the French, and I believe we may be able to raise even more. After all, there are supposed to be two hundred thousand people on the island. If we return to Malta, we can work with the British and make a contribution to the defeat of the French."

In Gibraltar, *Oleander* anchored briefly while despatches were delivered and collected, and then Burney and Snowden watched as Julia and the Corsicans were rowed towards the shore, each lost in his own thoughts.

Eventually, Burney spoke, a catch in his voice, "I will certainly miss her, Snowden."

EPILOGUE

Snowden leaned over the rail of the merchant ship *Kim* as she threaded her way down the busy Thames, watching lighters, barges and colliers jostle for space, and thinking of the events of the last few days. He had delivered the despatches *Oleander* had carried back from Gibraltar and the Mediterranean, and his own and Burney's reports. Snowden was not a vain man, but he was ambitious, fully aware of his own value, and he had been gratified by the attention that had been paid to his operations by the Admiralty.

Even the First Lord, Earl St Vincent, had complimented him on his actions against the French soldiers. "I must say, Snowden, that I would never have thought it was possible for a ship to engage infantry in that way, and with smashers. Remarkable." Snowden had replied that the geography lent itself to such operations, but St Vincent had waved away his modesty and broadly hinted that promotion would not be long coming.

There was one disagreeable note, although that did not directly involve Snowden. The behaviour of Commodore Parkinson, who had ignored the sound of battle from Macinaghju, had become widely known, even though Snowden had refrained from sending his own angry complaint, and there was talk of a court martial, though Snowden thought that Parkinson's connections in the establishment could protect him.

As they passed Deptford, he saw *Oleander* lying to a mooring, awaiting her turn for careening. *Kim's* skipper came to stand beside him. "Famous, that one – there's an account of her in the Mediterranean been published today, written by one of the crew. Very remarkable, engaged the French Army so it seems."

Snowden laughed, wondering which crew member had sold the story. Someone who could write and had a bit of initiative. He could think of a few suspects.

"A fast ship too, she overtook us in the river a couple of months back. Never seen a faster one. You should see her go."

Snowden turned, smiling. "Indeed you should, Skipper."

HISTORICAL AND GEOGRAPHICAL NOTES

While most of the events in this book are fictitious, I have tried to make them as historically plausible as possible. There was a Corsican regiment in the British Army, but I believe they mostly made their own way to join the British at the Maddalena islands in northern Sardinia. The Corsican Rangers were commanded by Hudson Lowe, who, as Governor of St Helena when Napoleon was held there, was criticised for his harsh treatment of Bonaparte. I wonder if his Corsicans' dislike of the Emperor had rubbed off on him.

I hope that the geography described in the book is reasonably accurate. I have been lucky enough to have sailed in most of the locations described. Corsica is beautiful in a slightly savage way, Macinaghju is an attractive port, and the battered Torra di Santa Maria perches on its rocky islet.

The Mistral still blows from a cobalt-blue sky; and the Château d'If stands grimly in the Rade de Marseille. Follow this link for photographs of some of the places featured in the book:

Cape Corse

The title of the book is 'Cape Corse', as this is how it was known by the Royal Navy at the time, rather than 'Cap Corse' (French) or 'Capicorsu' (Corsican). I have used the Corsican spelling for the port of Macinaghju, which is often called Macinaggio. A glossary of terms used in the book can be found here:

GLOSSARY

74 - two decked warship, larger than a frigate, nominally armed with 74 guns.

AB - Able Bodied seaman.

ancien regime - the former Royalist regime of France overthrown by the Revolution.

Armée d'Angleterre - the army assembled by Napoleon at Boulogne for the purpose of invading Britain.

Barbarossa – most famous of the Moorish corsairs.

Billy Ruffian – *'Bellerophon'*, famous British warship.

blockade – during the French Revolutionary Wars the Royal Navy closely blockaded the entire French coast for many years, winter and summer – an outstanding display of seamanship and determination which had the side effect of making the Navy extremely efficient, in contrast to its French counterpart which was bottled up in port.

Board of Trade – department of the British Government which became responsible for enforcing the Merchant Shipping Act later in the nineteenth century.

bomb, bomb vessel - a small ship built for the bombardment of shore targets, armed with a mortar and rockets. The most famous bombs were Erebus and Terror.

bosun (boatswain) – senior seaman.

braces – ropes to control the yards which support square sails; hence 'lee braces' are braces on the side of the ship away from the wind.

Brittany Canal - canal which links the Channel and Biscay coasts.

Bumboat – small boat selling goods to the crews of ships.

capstan – winch with vertical axis, on sailing ships driven by men pushing wooden bars as they walked around it.

Cordouan lighthouse - a huge lighthouse which marks the entrance of the Gironde.

careen – to haul a grounded ship down so that her masts are nearly horizontal.

Carron (carronade) – a gun manufactured by the Carron Ironworks of Scotland. The company was founded in 1789, and now manufactures domestic sinks.

Carteret – port on the western side of the Cotentin Peninsular noted for its exceptional tides and vast sandy beaches.

chasse-marée – literally 'tide chaser', a heavily canvassed French vessel used for smuggling and similar activities.

Chesil Beach – a long shingle spit which joins Portland to the mainland. With the wind from the west or south west it forms a lee shore, especially for vessels proceeding up the English Channel. The beach is very steep, and the undertow from the surf in rough conditions makes escaping from the sea very difficult.

Chouan - name given to the Bretons who violently opposed the Revolution

ci-devants - "former people" such as aristocrats from the Royalist regime

coasting – trading along the coast rather than 'deep sea'. In British ships coasting is traditionally limited to the area between Brest and the Elbe.

cockpit sole – the 'floor' of the cockpit.

Congreve rocket - a rocket with an explosive warhead, similar to the familiar firework rocket but much larger.

Downs, The – anchorage off the east coast of Kent.

Eggs and Bacon – familiar name used by sailors for *HMS Agamemnon*. Several ships were given such names, including *Bellerophon* -"*Billy Ruffian*", and *Temeraire*, Turners "*Fighting Temeraire*", *Saucy*.

fall – rope system supporting a ship's boat.

famous victory - a reference to Southey's famous anti-war poem, "After Blenheim".

fo'c'stle – (abbreviation of 'forecastle') accommodation at the fore part of the ship where the crew lived 'before the mast', as opposed to the officers living in the aft end of the ship

fother, fothering – to stem a leak below the waterline by stretching a sail over the hole.

Fortuneswell – a village near on the north west part of Portland.

Fouché - minister of police, responsible for massacres during the Revolution.

jib boom - spar extending from the bowsprit.

Gironde - the estuary of the Garonne and Dordogne rivers, connecting Bordeaux with the Bay of Biscay.

Genoese tower – round forts built by the Genoese, very common around the coast of Corsica. The one at Myrtle Point was the prototype for the British Martello Tower

Hard Times of Old England – English folksong.

Hawke's squadron - in November 1759, in a rising gale, a British squadron under Admiral Hawke chased a French fleet into Quiberon Bay and won a famous victory.

Heart of Oak – official march of the Royal Navy, composed by William Boyce in 1759 with lyrics by David Garrick.

heaving line – thin rope used for throwing from one vessel to another.

helm down – turning the ship's head into the wind.

helm up – turning the ship's head away from the wind.

high water at Dover - tides are governed by the phases of the moon. The time of tides in the Channel are often referenced to the time of high water at Dover.

hove to - a sailing ship is sometimes stopped in heavy weather by backing one or more sails, and keeping the ship close to the wind by putting the helm down

in irons – ship stationary and pointing directly into the wind with the sails flapping.

Iroise – Royal Navy frigate which had been captured from the French. French ships captured by the Royal Navy generally continued to use their original names.

ketch - a small vessel with two masts, the after mast shorter than the forward one

King – In Weymouth Bound, Not by Sea, and Cape Corse, the king referred to is George III, 'Farmer George'. George was very fond of Weymouth and spent long periods there. As described in Weymouth Bound, he was renowned as an early riser.

landing – smuggling contraband ashore.

Le Petit Neptune Français - an eighteenth century pilot book describing the coasts and ports of France.

leach, or leech – the aft side of a fore and aft sail, or the lee side of a square sail

Leave Her Johnny – chanty with improvised derogatory words about the ship and officers traditionally sung when the crew is about to pay off at the end of a voyage. Perhaps the most authentic version was recorded by Bob Roberts.

Leghorn – Livorno, a major port on the coast of Italy near Pisa

Levanter – easterly wind in the Mediterranean

Lilli Bulero – satirical ballad about Ireland. Signature tune of the BBC World Service.

lugger – a vessel, generally a small one, propelled by a lugsail, rather than a gaff mainsail.

luff – to turn the ship into the wind so that the 'luff' or fore part of the sail flaps

main topsail – upper sail on the main mast.

maintop, foretop - platform for a lookout at the top of

the mast.

Marins - marines of the Imperial Guard.

Midi Canal, Royal Canal - a remarkable summit level canal, completed in 1681, which connects the Garonne at Toulouse with the Mediterranean at Sete.

midshipman – trainee officer in the Royal Navy.

Mistral – wind which blows down the Rhone and into the Mediterranean.

mizzen – aftermost mast of a ship.

painter - a rope attached to the bow of a small boat used for towing etc.

pawl – ratchet.

Pool of London – part of the River Thames below London Bridge where ships worked their cargo.

Popham – Royal Navy signal code devised by Admiral Sir Home Riggs Popham KCB, a naval officer who led a varied and interesting life.

port (starboard) tack – ship sailing so that the wind is coming from the port (starboard) side.

port wheel - when ships were steered by tiller, "port helm" meant moving the tiller to port, steering the ship to starboard. When wheel steering became widespread, this lead to considerable confusion.

privateer – a privately owned ship with a 'letter of marque' from its government permitting it to attack and capture ships belonging to enemy nations

prize money – when an enemy ship was captured the value of the ship was assessed by a prize court and the proceeds shared between the officers and crew of the capturing ship.

Quiberon - peninsular in Brittany.

queue - ponytail

race (tide race) – an area of confused breaking seas caused by the tidal stream running strongly over obstructions. Two races feature in the book: the Portland Race, an area of confused breaking seas off the tip of the Isle of Portland, and the Race of Alderney, between Alderney and the adjacent coast of France. Both are extremely dangerous in some states of wind and tide. In the Race of Alderney, off La Foraine beacon, the tide can run at up to nine knots.

Rance - river, now dammed by a hydrogeneration scheme, which enters the sea at St Malo.

revenue cutter – small ship used to supress smuggling.

scandalised mainsail – reducing the power of the mainsail by lowering the peak of the gaff.

scarfed - a joint between two pieces of wood, with the ends chamfered so that they fit snugly together.

schooner - usually small ship which has two or more masts.

sextant – instrument for measuring angles, most commonly between a celestial body and the horizon.

sheer - the curve of the deckline of a ship or boat, so that the bow is high and able to ride above waves.

St Peters - or St Pierre, the main town of the island of Guernsey.

staysail – a sail set on the forestay of the mast.

steep to – a coast is said to be 'steep to' when the sea bed rises quickly near the land

swivel – gun supported on a mount which allows it to be aimed easily.

tack – turn the ship through the wind.

Talleyrand - cardinal and foreign minister of France.

Temple – a prison in Paris used for housing political prisoners, including the royal family. One of Napoleon's last acts was to order its destruction. As a superstitious Corsican, he was unnerved by a letter Sidney Smith had displayed in the window of his cell there, prophesying that Smith would end up in the Elysee, and Bonaparte in the Temple.

thwart - a seat running "athwartships" or across a boat.

tiller – lever attached to the rudder which is used to steer the craft.

trenail – a wooden dowel driven into a hole bored through two pieces of timber to fasten them together.

Ushant – a large island surrounded by smaller islands and rocks on the north western extremity of Brittany. Tidal streams run fiercely through the channels.

Vilaine - Breton river which flows into the Bay of Biscay. It is now dammed by the barrage at Arzal, and is navigable as far as Redon.

William – third son of George III. He spent a considerable time in the Royal Navy, and was a friend of Nelson. The Duke of Clarence, he later became William lV, nicknamed 'the Sailor King'.

ABOUT THE AUTHOR

Paul Weston

Paul's writing is informed by his career as a merchant seaman, on tankers, offshore, and on ferries, as well as his experience in business and engineering. A prolific inventor, he has several patents to his name. He has been sailing since childhood, initially on his family's converted fishing boat 'True Vine', and in his teens, crossed the Atlantic in a home designed and built 26 footer, and in his twenties raced to the Azores in another 26 foot boat. In 2021, with his wife Sally, he completed an intermittent four year voyage to the Mediterranean and back by sea, river and canal in 'Mitch', a 31 foot Mitchell Sea Angler. They have now reverted to sail, and own 'Kadash', a 40 foot aluminium lift keeler in which they have cruised in the Mediterranean between Elba and Almeria.

BOOKS IN THIS SERIES

*Paul Weston Historical
Maritime and Naval Fiction*

Books in this series have plausible and fast moving plots, are historically and technically accurate and informed by Paul Weston's knowledge of the sea and ships.

Weymouth Bound

The merchant ship Cicely is captured by the ruthless Captain Morlaix of the French Navy. Apprentice Jack Stone's life is changed forever, and he determines to do what he can to survive and to frustrate a French plot which will strike at the heart of the British establishment

Not By Sea

Napoléon knows that if he is to win the war, he must invade England, but the Armée d'Angleterre is blockaded in Boulogne by the Royal Navy. Napoléon entrusts an alternative scheme to the brilliant Captain Morlaix which if successful, could lead to the subjugation of Britain.

Printed in Great Britain
by Amazon